Picturing Perfect

PICTURING PERFECT

Melissa Brown

Montlake
Romance

The characters and events portrayed in this book are fictitious. Any similarity to real persons, living or dead, is coincidental and not intended by the author.

Text copyright © 2013 Melissa Brown
All rights reserved.

Printed in the United States of America.

No part of this book may be reproduced, or stored in a retrieval system, or transmitted in any form or by any means, electronic, mechanical, photocopying, recording, or otherwise, without express written permission of the publisher.

Published by Montlake Romance, Seattle
www.apub.com

ISBN-13: 9781477849910
ISBN-10: 1477849912

Library of Congress Control Number: 2013913625

*For my parents, Bob and Deb Bresloff,
for giving me the most incredible example of true
and unconditional love. I am proud to be
your daughter. Every single day.*

PROLOGUE

I had a plan.
I knew exactly how my future would be. I wanted to marry my boyfriend Tucker, to have a nice long engagement as we planned the perfect wedding ceremony. My father would walk me down the aisle as my white dress dragged gently against the tile of our church floor, knocking the pews like a silent bell as I strolled down the aisle. I wanted to work as a teacher until I achieved tenure. Then, after all of those things had taken place, we would make the decision to start a family. We'd have two little girls who each had my blond hair and blue eyes. They'd be two years apart and the best of friends. And as for me...I would be prepared, stable, focused and ready. And happy...I would be happy.

I would not be twenty-two years old, terribly *un*happy, *un*settled, *un*married. And I certainly would not be standing in the bathroom of my employer (which, by the way, was not even a school), peeing on a stick in front of my co-worker.

"It's going to be okay, Hadley," Ellie said as we stood near the sink waiting for the three minutes to go by. Three minutes of watching my plans bounce around the walls, threatening to leap out the window. Three minutes of feeling my heart pound furiously in my chest, dreading the outcome of the test.

"What if it's not?" I asked her, my eyes red and puffy. Ellie scrunched up her lips. That's what she did when she was hesitant. She had no idea what to say to me.

I've always been really observant and perceptive when it comes to people's body language. They barely needed to say anything for me to know exactly what they were thinking. I was dreading Tucker's reaction to learning he'd be a father in nine short months, rather than the five to eight years we had discussed. He wasn't ready for this. I wasn't either. And we...well, we were barely hanging on as it was.

"It's been three minutes," Ellie said, with hesitation in her voice. "Do you want me to look?"

I didn't answer her right away. My pulse raced. Sweat poured out and my hands shook as I gripped the sides of the pedestal sink.

"Hadley," Ellie whispered as she stroked my shoulder with her fingertips.

"Yes, please," I said, taking a deep breath in and out. "I can't look."

I closed my eyes, waiting to hear the news. I heard Ellie pick up the small plastic stick from the ledge below the mirror. She sighed loudly before speaking, and just with that sigh, I knew my world had changed. Completely.

CHAPTER ONE

Six months earlier

Auden and I were floating in a gondola, soaking in the last few moments of our vacation. Auden was flirting with the gondola driver as he toured us through the channels. Champagne tickled my taste buds before gliding down my throat. The smell of linen drifted in the air as we passed in between the buildings lined with hanging laundry. A woman with long brown curls peeked out from behind a brittle gray shutter. For some reason, I knew I'd seen her before. She winked at me and butterflies stirred in my stomach. Something felt off about that wink; it was eerie, creepy and ominous. I looked to Auden for reassurance, but she was gone. And suddenly, I knew this was not my first time in the fragile boat.

"Hadley," a distant voice said to me. I turned to see the gondola driver looking down, peering into my eyes. "Wake up," he said.

The room eventually came into focus as I was pulled from my dream. No longer sitting in a gondola, my still body was on a bed in a beige, sterile room. Tubes were attached to my right hand and my other hand was squeezed tightly by the grip of another person. My head was elevated, and thick plastic tubing rested inside my nose. I blinked my eyes again and again as I attempted to get a clearer view of my surroundings.

"Why is she so hazy?" Despite my fuzzy brain, I knew that voice. At least, I thought I did. It wasn't the voice of a stranger. It was Tucker. My Tucker.

"It's the medication," the doctor responded. "She's going to be in and out of consciousness for the next few hours."

"She's going to be okay, though," Tucker said, and I felt him squeeze my hand again with his own.

"Well, as I told her mother earlier, her pneumonia is severe. She should have gone to a hospital in Europe—"

"She's too stubborn," Tucker interrupted, the irritation in his voice hovering above me.

Tucker constantly reminded me of my stubborn streak, my determination to follow my plans through to the very end. And if that meant ignoring the harsh pain in my chest so I could finish my once-in-a-lifetime trip with my best friend, then so be it.

"The nurses will be administering the antibiotic every few hours and the breathing treatments will help her. But she's going to be here for several more days until I'm comfortable that the infection is under control."

"Tuck," I managed to whisper. The pain in my chest stopped me from saying anything more. It felt like someone was reaching into my lungs and squeezing them with all their might. A groan escaped me and Tuck squeezed my hand harder in response.

"Shh," Tucker said, placing his finger to his mouth before turning his attention back to the tall, balding doctor with deep-set wrinkles in his face. "But she'll be okay, right?"

"Young man, she's going to be fine with the proper treatment and care. Let's just get through the next few days before you demand any promises from me, all right?" The doctor shook his head before placing my chart at the foot of my bed and walking out of the room.

Tucker was micro-managing him. Even in my haze, I could see that. Tucker was a lot to take sometimes. His strong personality could be overpowering and was often resented by those older than us. When he left, the quiet of the room was deafening. The tension was palpable. And I was terrified to make eye contact with my boyfriend.

Tucker was seething. Even in my partially conscious state I could feel the pressure coming from his hand. I could hear his long, drawn-out breaths as he inhaled and exhaled in a steady but harsh rhythm.

"I'm sorry," I whispered. A lone tear ran down my cheek. I stared at the beige walls, hoping they would somehow comfort me. But they couldn't offer me anything but silence.

"Don't, Had. Don't do it. I'm too pissed right now, especially at Auden. She should have taken you to the hospital weeks ago." He huffed, pushing himself up from his chair and walking to the other side of the room. He was right and I knew it.

Backpacking through Europe had been Auden's and my very last adventure before starting our new lives. We had graduated from Bradley University in May and by the end of June, we were on a plane headed to London. For one entire month, we bounced from country to country, city to city—dancing to accordion music in Munich, touring the Louvre in Paris and riding in gondolas through the channels of Venice. It was one of the most exciting times of my life.

Two weeks into the trip, though, my chest started to feel tight, and walking long distances became difficult. Something was wrong. My twenty-two-year-old body wasn't cooperating, and our adventures became more and more difficult by the day. Auden suggested stopping in to see a doctor, and so we'd visited a small public health clinic in Switzerland. A very kind clinician gave me a prescription for a weak antibiotic. Every morning, I washed that small red pill down with water, and every evening I was in more pain than the day before. I was getting worse instead of getting better.

Finally, our trip came to a halt when Auden's nerves got the better of her one morning after I had struggled to wake up, take a shower and get dressed. In tears, she begged me to go home, and I found myself on an eight-hour flight back to Chicago, only to be taken directly to the nearest hospital. I couldn't breathe and started to panic as we stood at baggage claim.

Auden looked me in the eye and said, "That's it, Had. It's time."

Tears streamed down my face as I nodded and followed her to the nearest waiting taxi. My mother met us at the hospital. After waiting hours in the emergency room, I was given a chest x-ray that determined I had a severe case of pneumonia as well as pleurisy, which was causing the intense, shooting pains in my chest as the swollen membranes around my lungs began to rub together awkwardly inside my body. My oxygen levels were dangerously low and I was admitted right away.

Throughout the evening, they administered antibiotics through my IV, as well as nebulizer breathing treatments every hour on the hour. But still the pain in my chest was as strong as it had been when I was struggling to walk down the cobblestone streets of Venice. I was scared of what I had done to myself by putting this off for such a long time.

"Hadley," Tucker's harsh tone snapped me out of my daydream. "The doctor said the amoxicillin they gave you in Lucerne made your infection worse. It wasn't strong enough to get the job done, so it aggravated it instead of helping. You're on the most intense antibiotics they have now, so you'll be okay. But you're going to be here for a while." His voice was softer than it had been just moments before, but I could still sense his anger and disappointment.

I nodded and felt the plastic tubing brush against the inside of my nostril. It was terribly uncomfortable and I wanted nothing more than to yank it out. But I couldn't. I needed it. The cold oxygen forced its way into my resistant body. My arms, my legs, everything was sore, as if I'd just run a marathon.

I wanted to go home. I wanted to escape the prison that was my hospital bed. I wished it were all just a terrible dream. I drifted back to sleep, wishing I could change things. As my eyelids grew heavy, I was already dreading what the next few days, weeks, months would bring...knowing that nothing would go as originally planned.

CHAPTER TWO

"I still don't understand why you applied for this job," Tucker said as we sat in a crowded Italian restaurant. His chocolate brown hair had just been cut. His cologne was heavy as he glowered at me with his hazel eyes. Tucker had only an hour for lunch before he needed to get back. I would've been happy to meet anywhere, but he insisted on fancy places like this...even when we were just getting a quick bite. It was just part of his upbringing.

I wasn't exactly from the "wrong side of the tracks." I had been raised, just like Tucker, in Wilmette, one of the wealthiest suburbs in Illinois. I had grown up in a very comfortable household. My father was an orthopedic surgeon and made a great living, allowing my mother to stay home with me. As an only child, I didn't want for anything. But Tucker...Tucker was from the wealthiest area of our city. His family was part of what people called "old money." They had a private chef, housekeepers and gardeners for the grounds of their estate.

Tucker was jaded because of his indulgent upbringing. But it didn't intimidate me. I didn't care about his money. Huge estates with mile-long driveways were never my thing. I'd always been fine with the idea of earning a teacher's salary and living in a modest home. Tucker...well, I wasn't so sure we shared the same vision of the future. He was an investment banker and a brilliant one at that.

The job I had applied for didn't pay well. I'd made the mistake of telling Tucker what I would be earning if I was offered the position. I swear I could see the disapproval in his eyes then, just as I could now.

"I've told you this already, Tuck. I had to cancel my teaching contract because I won't be able to start the school year. I'm still in bed most of the morning, and school begins in two days." I said, twirling the pasta on my plate.

"But you're doing a lot better. I'm sure the school would've worked it out with you. They hired you back in May, for God's sake." He wiped his chin with a napkin, before tossing it carelessly onto the table. Pushing his plate away, he shook his head while taking two large gulps of water. His elbows crashed down onto the tabletop as he perched his chin on his hands, waiting for an explanation.

I loved Tucker, but I would never have described him as even-keeled. He wore his emotions on his sleeve and wasn't afraid to let people know when he was pissed off. Entitled? Yes. Spoiled? Probably.

Me? I was naturally a more reserved person when it came to my emotions, but I'd adjusted to talking things through with Tuck since that was what he insisted upon. I'd gotten better at it and could hold my own during conversations like this one. Six years ago, watching him toss that napkin would've bothered me, but now it didn't even faze me. It was just Tuck being...well, Tuck.

"I spoke with the principal and we both agreed that it was in the best interest of the students for me to re-apply in the spring," I said calmly. Tucker nodded, but he didn't look at all convinced. His lips were pressed into a thin line, and he paused and narrowed his eyes before speaking.

"That's fine. But why developmentally disabled adults? It just seems like a total 180-degree shift."

"It's not, though," I attempted to explain. "I'll be teaching them life skills. I'll be teaching, just in a different way. In a non-traditional way."

"You said this was a work facility...for adults." He still looked puzzled.

"It is, but many of these adults are still learning their basic skills. I get to help them learn how to cook, how to tell time and count money. I'll *still* be a teacher."

"I guess so," he said, pushing the chicken breast around his plate.

"Why is this bothering you so much?"

"I just know how much money your parents spent on your education. You worked to earn your teacher's certificate. I'd like to see you use it. And eventually get your Master's." He shrugged as he glared into my eyes.

"I know, and I will...eventually. But right now I need to earn a paycheck and this seems interesting. Plus, they don't need me for four more weeks. I have time to get better."

Getting over pneumonia had been challenging. I was in the hospital for an entire week, as it took a long time for my medication to break up the infection. It was mid-August and I still took an albuterol puffer wherever I went. Most days, just going to the grocery store was enough to knock me down for a few hours. My body had been through a lot and I needed to listen to what it was telling me. I wasn't ready to work. Turning down that job had made my heart ache, but it was the right thing to do.

Auden was the one who'd found the job listing for Sunnyside Association. She knew I wouldn't be ready for the school year and had searched job websites for me whenever she had spare time, which was often. Auden was a free spirit who hadn't quite committed to a career path. She loved people and travel and she hated the idea of a mundane desk job, so she was putting it off for as long as possible. She had dual degrees in chemistry and business, and had been leaning towards pharmaceutical sales. But somehow, I didn't see her sticking with that in the long term.

"What time is your interview?" Tucker asked as he stabbed a piece of his chicken with his fork.

"Two o'clock," I replied.

"Well, good luck." Tucker gave me a half-smile. I knew he was doing his best to be supportive. I just wished I knew what it would take for him to actually feel happy for me.

~

After lunch, Auden called my cell.

"Hey, there," she said. "Are you ready for your interview?"

"I think so," I replied, biting the side of my lip.

"You'll impress them, don't worry," she reassured me. "What does Tucker think? Is he excited for you?"

My silence answered her question.

"Please tell me Tucker's not being a royal pain in the ass about this."

"He just thinks I gave up too quickly with the high school position."

"You're not ready to be on your feet for seven hours a day. And I know you; you would push yourself too hard and end up back in the hospital."

"I know," I said.

"What does your mom think?" Auden asked. I could hear the slight hesitation in her voice.

"You know my mom. *Whatever makes me happy makes her happy.* It's impossible to get her to have an opinion about anything," I replied. And it was the truth.

"Okay, forget about Tucker and your mom for a minute. You're going to ace this interview and have a new job. It's very exciting." Her voice was soothing on the other end of the line and I realized she was right. I was excited about the interview and I couldn't let Tucker's bad attitude affect me.

"You're right," I sighed into the phone.

"Jason said hi, by the way," she said, her voice teasing me.

"Geez, give it a rest. I'm not thirteen anymore," I said, rolling my eyes.

"I'm serious. Ever since you got sick, he asks about you all the time. He wants to make sure you're all right. It's sweet."

My stomach flipped slightly in my belly. Despite him being Auden's older brother, I hadn't thought of Jason in quite a while. It wasn't so long ago that thoughts of Jason had consumed my adolescent brain. But since I had fallen for Tucker and become part of a couple, that part of my brain had been quiet.

"Okay, sorry." She laughed quietly into the phone. "I really do wish you lots of luck today."

"I'm heading to the interview now. I'll let you know how it goes."

"Great. I'll talk to you later," Auden said.

After hanging up the phone, I went home to change into my best interview suit. I'd lost quite a bit of weight since May when I'd interviewed with several schools. But luckily, with a black patent leather belt, I managed to make the pants fit around my drastically smaller waist.

With one last puff from my inhaler, I grabbed my portfolio from the kitchen counter and walked out the door, hoping for the best.

~

The doors of Sunnyside Association were heavy and clunky as I opened them. A loud squeak followed as they closed and I looked around the industrial building. I could hear the sound of conveyor belts and other machines. At first, I wondered if I was in the wrong building, but then I remembered the nature of the place. This was a work facility. They were most likely assembling items for companies. The woman behind the window looked tired but friendly. Her blond hair was pinned up in a bun and she had a warmth to her that made me feel comfortable. She smiled at me, raising her eyebrows.

"May I help you?" she asked as I read her nametag.

"Yes. Hi, Natasha," I said, my voice cracking a little. My nerves were getting the best of me. "I have an interview with Pamela Rodriguez. My name is Hadley Foster."

"Ahh, Hadley," a voice said from down the hall. A petite woman with jet-black hair and dimples walked quickly to where I was standing.

"I'm Pamela. It's a pleasure to meet you. Come with me," she said, leading me down a long hallway with several glass doors. She opened one of them and gestured for me to walk into her office.

Taking a seat in a simple navy blue chair, I placed my portfolio on her desk. Pamela slid into her leather chair and linked her hands together, with a large smile on her face.

"I'm very excited to meet you, Hadley. Your application was impressive."

"Thank you." I nodded nervously.

Pamela looked down at my résumé.

"I see you have your teaching certificate. May I ask why you're not pursuing a job with the school system?"

"Sure. Well, I came down with pneumonia and I'm not quite ready to start a school year, but I want to use my skills. When I saw your ad, I thought it was a great opportunity."

"Oh," she paused, "as you can imagine, it takes a special person to work with this community. I hope that you aren't looking at this as a temporary position until the semester ends."

"No, I'm not."

She didn't look convinced. "Let me tell you about the position," she said.

"Great," I replied.

"You will be pulling clients throughout the day from their work areas to teach them life skills: telling time, counting money, exercise, cooking. You'll also take groups on field trips to the library, coffee shops, out for ice cream." She looked at me expectantly.

"That sounds wonderful," I replied.

"How do you feel about music?"

"It's one of my passions."

"Oh good, because part of the job is to spearhead the big musical performance our clients perform every year. It's a huge fundraiser for the facility. Basically, it's a lot of skits, plus lip-synching to their favorite songs. We perform it here in the gymnasium and we pack the house."

"Wow, that sounds exciting," I said, marveling at how much fun this job seemed to be.

"Well, Rhonda, the woman who held this position before you, wasn't nearly as enthusiastic as we would've liked. The show was basically the same thing every year. We'd like to have this year's performance stand out. Something new, something exciting to get our clients enthused again. Does that make sense?"

"Absolutely." I nodded.

"Great. Now, before I get to know you better, let's take a tour, and you can see what we're all about." We walked out of the office, turning once again down the long hallway. It led to three large work areas. Groups of adults sat in clusters, busy working on individual projects.

"We have three areas: A, B and C. They're easy to remember." She chuckles. "As you can see, we have many clients at Sunnyside. We have about eighty-six clients who currently attend every day. You'll be able to interact with most of them."

Pamela led me to the area marked "B." Two small conveyor belts stretched across the middle of the room. Several clients sat to the side of each belt, assembling small pieces of cardboard. Pamela introduced me to the older woman seated at a desk, overseeing all of the work.

"This is Sharon. Sharon is in charge of Area B. Our clients in Area B are our highest functioning clients, and they are able to handle the most complicated of tasks. Here, they're assembling cardboard cutouts for a local hardware store's packaging."

"Do you have a lot of contracts from local businesses?" I asked, genuinely curious.

"Yes, we do. There are days where we run out of jobs for them, but that gives us an excuse to have an impromptu party or movie." Sharon gave me a small wave as I followed Pamela through areas A and C. These rooms were similar to Area B. More conveyors, more Sunnyside employees assisting clients with their projects. There were quite a bit of smiles and laughter. It really seemed like a welcoming place.

Pamela and I returned to her office once we'd toured the entire building. She waited until we were seated once again before continuing, "As I'm sure you were able to see, we have a variety of different clients who come to us each day. Some are in their twenties and live with their parents. Some are older and live in group facilities. They come here to earn a paycheck, but they also need to build their skills in other areas, and that's where you'd come in."

"I understand." I nodded.

"Now, Hadley, why don't you tell me more about yourself, and we can get this ball rolling," Pamela said with a big smile. I took a deep breath, relaxed and sold myself as best I could.

CHAPTER THREE

Sunnyside Association was just that—sunny. It was sunny and friendly and full of smiles. I'd surprised even myself with how much I looked forward to coming to work every weekday. I loved my job. I freaking *loved* my job. Each morning, my co-worker Ellie and I waited outside the building, clipboards in hand, marking attendance as our clients arrived. Some were escorted by their parents; others arrived with their roommates, or a worker from their group home drove them in a bus or mini-van.

A large blue and white bus arrived bright and early on a cool October morning. The first off the bus was Bryce. Not a big surprise. He hated buses and cars and practically bounced out of his seat when they arrived each morning. Bryce usually had his iPod clipped to his t-shirt, the cords of his earbuds dangling from his ears. He's a music junkie—one of my favorite things about him. The music was something his group home had encouraged to distract him from the ride. Pretty soon Bryce had memorized an entire catalog of Cat Stevens songs, his very first obsession, and was making his way through the rest of the 1970s. I kept hoping he'd reach the '80s, my very favorite decade for music...and movies...and pretty much everything in pop culture. I'm kind of an '80s junkie.

"Who are we listening to this morning?" I asked as Bryce pulled one earbud from his pink ear.

"ABBA," he smiled wide, knowing I despised ABBA. Little stinker. Bryce knew how to make me laugh and did it frequently. He had cerebral palsy and it affected his speech and facial gestures. He had decreased muscle tone and needed, many times, to use a walker when he was having a difficult day. He was a hard worker, though, and sometimes a bit of a busybody. He liked to spread the gossip like crazy and always had crushes on girls. I adored him.

"I'm telling you, I'm going to burn an '80s disc on iTunes for you and you'll be hooked." I said this to him practically every morning. But he just shook his head, holding his hand up in front of his face as if begging me to stop. I still hadn't made that mix for him. His birthday was coming up in a few short weeks and I'd be able to surprise him then.

As always, Ellie and I pretended to fight over Warren, our favorite client (even though we weren't supposed to have favorites—or at least not advertise them). Warren had Down syndrome, like a lot of our other clients. He was twenty-four and lived at home with his mom. He had bright blue eyes and golden blond hair, just like me. And he had to be the biggest flirt on the planet. Each morning, he planted kisses on my cheek as well as Ellie's, just to hear us laugh and to spur the argument over which one of us Warren adored the most. His smile was bright and wide each and every day. Some mornings, I lived for that smile.

"Morning, beautiful," Warren said, greeting me with my morning peck.

"Thanks, handsome," I replied, rubbing his elbow gently as he walked towards Ellie, his lips already puckered. Ellie laughed and joked with him as I helped another client. Shirley's walker was stuck on several rocks on the sidewalk and she was starting to get angry.

The last few clients trickled off the bus as Ellie and I greeted them, checking them off on our attendance sheets.

"Did you watch Grey's last night?" Ellie asked, running her fingers through her hair.

"You know I never miss that show. I love me some McDreamy." I laughed, fanning myself.

"You're only in love with him because he was in that '80s movie. I swear you're obsessed with that decade!" She laughed. She was right, though. *Can't Buy Me Love* was one of my favorite movies. And I've had a soft spot for Patrick Dempsey ever since he rode away with Cindy Mancini on his lawn mower.

"How can you not be obsessed with that decade? It was totally awesome to the max," I said in my best Valley Girl voice, flipping my hair behind me. Ellie rolled her eyes and shook her head.

"Ells." I heard a deep voice coming from inside the building.

"Yeah, babe," Ellie said, whipping her head around to face her husband and co-worker, Nick.

"You're needed in Area B. Mindy is asking for you."

"Ah," Ellie said with an understanding nod.

"I got this. Go check on her," I reassured her as she hurried towards Nick. Mindy had been struggling lately and her attachment to Ellie became extreme when she was upset. Some days she'd go hours without a problem, but today didn't seem to be one of those days. In the six weeks I'd worked there, I'd witnessed Ellie in action and was impressed at her selflessness and easygoing personality. She was doing the work she was born to do.

Unlike me, she didn't have a different plan. Ellie Miller had always wanted to work with those with special needs. When school districts in the area didn't have the need for more special ed. teachers, Ellie had pursued working with adults. She and her husband, Nick, had fallen in love instantly the day Ellie started working at Sunnyside. They'd married one year later. Both of the Millers had taken me under their wing, giving me guidance with the clients and encouraging me in all aspects of my job. I felt lucky to have them as my co-workers.

"Hadley, did you sign out Bus Number Three for this afternoon?" Nick asked, walking outside.

"Yeah, I'm taking a few clients to Starbucks for a coffee break. It's field trip day."

"Crap. I was going to take a group to Target for shopping and Carl said Bus Number Two is in the shop. I guess I'll reschedule."

"Don't be silly. Isn't there a small café in the same strip mall as Target?"

Nick looked a little confused, but nodded. "So?"

"So, instead of Starbucks, I'll take my clients there. We can share the bus. When you finish shopping with your group, we'll meet back up at the bus."

"Wow, awesome. Thanks. Rose really needs to get out of this place, even if only for an hour," Nick said, shaking his head slightly as his eyes widened.

Nick was right about Rose. Rose was profoundly autistic and was overwhelmed easily. We'd all noticed her anxiety had been at an all-time high as of late. The workload in Area C had been slow and it was making her really uneasy. She liked noise and craved a little bit of chaos at all times. Target was one of her favorite places in the world. When she was in a loud, busy environment, she lit up.

"All right, I'll grab the keys for the bus around two o'clock and we'll head over to the mall."

"Awesome, thanks so much." Nick gave me a brief nod before walking back into the building.

Quickly, I checked my watch to see how much time I had before my money class began. Ten minutes. Perfect. I had plenty of time to drop by my office and gather my teaching materials before collecting my clients from their work areas. Every week, I met with three clients and we practiced counting coins. It was my job to review the coins with them, helping them to count basic change independently. The goal was for them to pay for snacks from the snack cart or purchase something from the vending machines on their own.

Ten minutes later, Lucy was studying the quarters and nickels in front of her. Her brow was furrowed as she twisted her jet-black hair in between her fingers and I knew she was about to break down. Whenever her fingers moved towards her curly hair, I did my best to keep her from losing it because when she got frustrated, I lost her for the rest of the lesson. She would tune me out and many times asked to return to her work area.

But I was determined to help Lucy. I was determined to watch her buy a can of Coke all by herself. I knew she'd be proud. I knew she'd probably jump up and down, hugging the person standing closest to her. I wanted that so bad for her; I could feel it in my bones.

"Take a deep breath, Luce," I said, the rise and fall of my chest deep and controlled, hoping she'd follow my lead. She did.

"That's good," I continued. "Now, let's take a look at these two coins. Which one is bigger?"

"I don't know," Lucy said, staring at the wall.

"Lucy," I said. She ignored me.

I took another deep breath. "I love Lucy? Look at me, please" I said, my voice gentle. She giggled. She loved that nickname, even though she liked to pretend she despised it. Lucy loved attention.

"Don't call me that," she said, prolonging the game.

"Fine, I won't." I shrugged. "Please look at the coins."

Lucy let out an enormous sigh, before leaning her chin on her open hand and staring down at the coins in front of her.

"It's too hard," she whined.

"You can do this. Show me which one is bigger."

Lucy bit her lip and moved her finger to the quarter.

"That's right. Now, try to remember what we talked about. We're looking at a nickel and a quarter. Are nickels bigger than quarters?"

"I don't remember." She shook her head violently.

"Shh, Luce, I know you can do this." I reassured her, patting her gently on the hand.

"Quarter is bigger?" she asked. Her eyes were glassy and pleading.

"That's right." I smiled wide, clasping my hands together with pride. "So, we know quarters are bigger. Now, which one is the quarter?"

A satisfied look crossed Lucy's face as she picked up the quarter and placed it into my open palm.

"You got it," I said, patting her on the back. She smiled with a sigh.

"You take a little break. Take these two quarters," I said, emphasizing the words as I placed two quarters in her hand, "and get yourself a can of Coke."

"Really?" she asked. This was a first. I'd never treated her to a soda before.

"You earned it," I replied. Lucy jumped out of her chair and ran to the cafeteria. Her laughter filled the hallway as she ran.

"No running in the hallways, Luce," Pamela yelled.

I worked with my other two clients as Lucy happily slurped her can of Coke. Before we knew it, the clock struck 9:30 and it was time for them to get back to their work. Money class had ended.

∼

Several hours later, Nick and the clients climbed on the bus for the field trip. After a confident breath and a glance in my rearview mirror, I put the bus into reverse and pulled out of the parking spot. I had learned how to drive the buses my first week on the job. Since I took clients to the library on a weekly basis, and on weekly field trips on Fridays, it was an important part of my job. It was intimidating at first, but I got pretty comfortable with it.

"I'll let you drive back," I said to Nick, raising an eyebrow.

"Gee, thanks." His words dripped with sarcasm. Nick hated driving the bus...with a passion.

"Don't worry, Princess," I teased him. "I'll drive."

"Nice," he said with a chuckle. "Wake me when we get there."

~

The smell of roasting coffee filled the air in the small café named Beans. Classical music played softly in the background. A handful of patrons sat at small wooden tables, many typing on their laptops.

"Come on, everyone. Let's go look at the menu."

"Hadley," Riley said, pushing a mass of curls from her eyes, "I don't like coffee."

"You don't have to drink coffee. They have tea and hot chocolate. Probably apple cider, too."

"Mmmmm," said Violet, a towheaded sweetheart who loved junk food more than anyone I'd ever encountered. "Hot chocolate!"

Chuckling, I led Violet to the counter and helped her as she ordered her drink. One by one, each client made their way to the counter, ordered and paid. It took quite a bit of time and I was grateful that the people behind us seemed to be patient. That didn't always happen. When I'd first begun my job, I'd offer to let others go ahead of us. But I'd stopped doing that after a few short weeks. We may have taken a little longer at the register, but we were polite patrons who waited our turn and treated the employees with respect. There was no reason why we should take a step back so that impatient customers could get their mocha latte just a few minutes earlier.

"I would love a medium chai tea, please," I said to the redheaded barista with tiny freckles on her cheeks. She smiled and entered my order into the computer. When I handed her my money, though, she just shook her head.

"I don't understand," I said, puzzled.

"It's on us," she said with warm eyes.

"Um, thank you," I replied.

"You're doing important work. And you're so patient. It's my pleasure." My heart swelled as she said those words. I'd never thought of my work as important. I'd only thought of how happy it made me.

I joined the others at a large table in the corner. Just as I was pulling my chair out, I heard a familiar voice say a name I hadn't heard in years.

"Haddie?" *He* called me Haddie. *He* was the only person I'd ever allowed to call me by that nickname. And there was a very special reason for that. *He* was my world, my obsession, my everything. The boy who had captured my heart when I was only eight years old.

Jason Kelly. My very first crush and my best friend's older brother. The boy who made my pulse race so incredibly fast, it was sometimes hard to breathe around him. I felt my palms sweating as I turned to him.

He looked just as I remembered. Sandy brown hair, a little spiky in the front. Hipster glasses sat on the bridge of his nose and tiny dimples indented his pale cheeks. His eyes were wide as he approached.

"I thought that was you," he said.

"Jason...wow, hi." I replied, clearing my throat to help the words along. He wrapped me into a tight hug and I smelled the familiar scent of *Jason*.

"How are you feeling?" he asked, looking concerned as his fingers grazed my arm. My skin tingled with that simple touch.

"Much better now." I smiled, softly gesturing towards the group, "You guys, this is an old friend of mine. His name is Jason."

"Hi Jason," Violet said with a chocolate mustache above her lip. "You're handsome."

"Well, thanks," Jason said with ease.

He was always good at taking compliments. Humble and friendly, smart and witty. The list went on and on—with so many positive qualities it was impossible to name them all. I took in the sight of him. I had to chuckle when my eyes were greeted by the gray t-shirt underneath his plaid flannel button-down.

"867-5309?" I asked with a laugh. Jason had been wearing crazy t-shirts for years. And he was just about as obsessed with the '80s as I was. I wondered if he knew that we still shared an affinity for that decade. I wondered if he remembered much about me at all.

"Jenny, Jenny." He nodded. "It's a classic. Unfortunately, sometimes girls think I'm trying to pick them up with it."

"Those girls need to listen to better music."

Jason threw his head back with a hearty laugh.

"I agree," he said.

"Would you like to join us? We can pull up a chair."

"Sure, I can do that for a few minutes. I'm writing, but I could use a break."

He quickly grabbed a wooden chair from a neighboring table, flipping it around effortlessly so that he straddled the back of his chair. His knee bumped my thigh and goose bumps ran down my arms. I was desperately trying to get my heart rate under control, but I felt like I was on autopilot. *Tucker. Tucker. Tucker.* I said to myself. Nope, didn't help. Even Tucker couldn't push the redness from my cheeks. Even Tucker couldn't stop the adrenaline pulsing through my veins. *Tucker? Tucker who?*

"So, how's everyone doing this morning?" Jason asked. His knee brushed mine again. This time it was a slower movement, more deliberate. I felt a chill run down my spine. The most delicious chill I'd ever felt. *What is happening to me?*

Riley wrapped one of her silky curls around her fingers as she stared at our new companion. Riley was boy-crazy and not afraid to show it. She took a sip of her drink, never breaking eye contact. I glanced at Jason, wondering if her forward behavior was making him uncomfortable. But if it was, you'd never know it. He was calm and collected, flashing a grin at her pale face.

"Congrats on the new job," he said to me before glancing around the table. "Do you all work together?"

"No, silly," Riley said in her high-pitched voice, "Hadley works *for* us."

Brian cackled, slapping his knee as he threw his head back in laughter. Riley loved making others laugh, so she began to chuckle loudly to spur Brian on further. It worked. The table was in hysterics.

"Not exactly," I said, smirking. "But she's kind of right. These are my clients. This is Riley, Brian, Violet, Tina and Sam."

"Well, it's great to meet Hadley's bosses," Jason said with a grin. Riley chuckled again.

"I like you," she said, her smile wide.

"Well, thank you. I like all of you, too."

Jason turned his attention back to me. I could feel his gaze burning my cheeks. I attempted to keep my breath steady as I turned my attention his way.

"How's the writing?" I asked, scratching the back of my neck.

Jason cracked his knuckles before he spoke. He always did that when he was uncomfortable. I was surprised to see he was still doing it. I guess some things never change.

"I'm in kind of a slump," he said, shrugging.

"Writer's block?" I asked, taking a sip of my tea. Jason nodded as he ran his fingers through his hair.

"Auden said your books have really taken off. You even made it to the top 100 on Amazon?" I asked, trying to sound casual. What Jason didn't know was that all three of his books were on my Kindle. I'd read them all and loved them. Usually I was a contemporary romance reader, but his words sucked me in and I got all wrapped up in the suspense of his stories. He was so talented.

"Yeah. I got lucky, I guess."

"I'm sure it's not luck. You're just being modest."

"Maybe, yeah." He tilted his head to the side and grinned. His dimples reappeared and I practically choked on my tea. *Get a hold of yourself, Hadley.*

"So, how's Tucker?" he asked, hesitating at his name. That simple question jerked me back to reality and the fact that I'd had the same boyfriend for *six years*. The boyfriend

I assumed I would marry. The boyfriend who had been my world for so long.

"Oh, he... he's fine." I smiled politely, not offering any other information. The table was quiet as we sipped our drinks.

"Well, I should get back to my writing," Jason said, standing.

"Of course." I smile.

"It was wonderful to meet all of you," he said as he shook each of my clients' hands one by one. He was always so friendly and warm. It killed me in the best possible way.

"Hope to see you around, Haddie." He smiled, patting me lightly on my shoulder before placing his chair back where it came from and walking back to his waiting table.

Glancing at my watch, I saw it was time to meet Nick and the other clients. *Thank God.* I needed to get my head on straight, and there was no way that would happen with Jason Kelly sitting just five feet away from me. I gave him a quick wave as we walked out of Beans. Back to Sunnyside. Back to a place where I could think, where I could focus, where I could remember what it had been like before Jason Kelly walked back into my world.

CHAPTER FOUR

Jason

Madeline Kramer was a royal pain in my ass. No one else's. Just mine.

She wouldn't cooperate. She wouldn't do the things I wanted her to do or say the things I wanted her to say. And she was driving me *insane*. She was a product of my imagination, and yet I couldn't control her.

I'd been stuck on Chapter 18 of this book for two weeks and it was driving me nuts. Madeline had been the *one* character I could count on with my writing. The *one* character who led the way and spoke to me, the one who guided my books towards a suspenseful plot and a satisfying ending. She was the one who made people want to read my work. In the three books I'd written, she'd never let me down.

Until now.

It was the "Book Four Curse" my buddy and fellow writer, Cameron, had warned me about. I'd allowed him to psych me out. That little shit.

I'd been staring at my Mac screen for what felt like an hour, ever since saying goodbye to Hadley and her Sunnyside clients. The blinking cursor taunted me from the empty page. Glancing at my watch, I was shocked to see that only a few minutes had passed. Damn.

Maybe I needed to stretch my legs. Just as I was standing up, my cell rang. Usually I put it on vibrate when I work. Must have forgotten this morning.

It was my sister, Auden. Expert timing, as usual.

"Hey, sis," I answered.

"Afternoon. How are ya?" I could tell she was smiling through the phone. The ever-so-chipper Auden. She could be a tour guide with her constantly sunny, yet difficult, personality. Although sometimes, I had to admit, we were actually a lot alike.

Stretching my neck, I replied, "You know...better than some, not as good as others."

"You always say that. How's the writing?"

"Madeline won't cooperate," I huffed.

"She's such a pain in the ass." She laughed.

"Tell me about it. How are you today?"

I had to wonder if she'd spoken to Haddie. I couldn't imagine Haddie had called her after our chance meeting, but you never know.

"It's a slow day. I met with a few doctors this morning, but none of them were really biting."

Auden had just started her job in pharmaceutical sales and it was pretty cutthroat. With her personality, I knew she could pull it off. But she didn't seem that into it.

"That sucks."

"Oh well, that's life. And you? Just writing all day?"

"Actually, I just saw Hadley. She was here with some of her clients."

"Seriously? Oh, yeah, it's field trip day. Cool."

"Yeah, it was good to see her." I replied, trying to brush off my lingering thoughts of the gorgeous blonde who still smelled like strawberries.

"I know you've always had a soft spot for *Haddie*," she said. I could hear her smirking through the phone as she enunciated the nickname. Brat.

"She's a nice girl," I said, a little too defensively.

"*Woman*," my sister corrected me. My brain knew that Hadley was grown up. But to me she would always be my little sister's best friend who had a pretty obvious crush on me.

She was the eight-year-old who used to blush when I entered the room. I hadn't noticed, being only eleven myself, but my older sister, Maya, always had. Hadley was the thirteen-year-old who made me mix tapes with her parents' old stereo unit when I bought my first car. At first, I had been bummed that I couldn't afford to replace the old cassette unit with a CD player, but I listened to those tapes every single day. When my dad offered to install a CD player for my birthday that year, I turned him down. That was my only tape player and I couldn't stop listening to her tapes. "Soft spot" didn't even begin to tell the story of my feelings for Hadley. She always got under my skin in a way that I never really understood as a teenager. Now, I got it. But I still had no idea what to do about it. She had a boyfriend, and from what Auden told me, they were pretty serious.

In many ways, I'd been waiting six years for that relationship to end. But it still hadn't. I wasn't *really* waiting around for Hadley. I dated. I dated a lot, actually. And I'd had a few serious girlfriends. But for some reason, things always came back to Hadley... my Haddie.

"Yes, woman," I said, rolling my eyes and shaking my head at my sister as if she could actually see me through my cell.

"Whatever, Jase. Listen, I'll let you get back to Madeline. Will I see you this weekend at Mom and Dad's?"

"Yep, Sunday dinner. Wouldn't miss it."

"See you then," she said before hanging up her phone.

I pressed End on my phone and opened my awaiting laptop.

Damn you, Auden. For making me ponder things that I really didn't want to think about. Things I've been happy to keep tucked away in my brain.

Somehow, two cappuccinos later, I was able to finish Chapter 18. Glancing at my watch, I realized I needed to head into the city for dinner with my friends. I'd have to continue writing later.

I was kind of pissed at myself, though. I had to retype the name Madeline several times as my brain replaced it with Haddie. Why did I torture myself like that? She'd been with Tucker for six years and a chance encounter in a coffee shop wasn't going to change that. I needed to get a grip.

~

"What's up with you?" my friend Evan asked as he poured me a beer. I ran my fingers through my hair, placing my glasses on his counter and pinching the bridge of my nose. Hoping for clarity, hoping to make sense of my afternoon.

"Have you ever run into someone from your past? Someone you couldn't get out of your head?"

Evan chuckled and cocked an eyebrow, "You're kidding, right? Have you met my wife?"

"Oh damn."

Stupid question. Of course Evan understood. He and his wife Kate were two of my closest friends. I'd met Kate during their breakup. Trust issues and misunderstandings had torn them apart, but they'd realized they couldn't be without each other. They'd been back together for about two years now. They were married, they were happy, they were settled. They were everything that I wanted to be. But all of a sudden, my vision of settled and happy was including someone who wasn't mine, who couldn't be mine.

"I ran into someone from a long time ago. Someone who used to mean a lot to me. Seeing her again, it's messing with my head. I can't stop thinking about her."

"Ex-girlfriend?"

I shook my head. "Nope. My little sister's best friend."

"Ahhh. She grew up nicely, eh?" he teased.

"She's always been beautiful," I said, "But when we were kids it was just...I don't know, it never made sense to date her. She was off limits because of Auden."

"I see. Well, is she still off limits?"

"Yeah, but for a different reason. She's been dating this guy since high school. They've been together for years. And Auden thinks they're on their way to being engaged."

"Shit, that sucks."

"I know," I said, cracking my knuckles before leaning my head in my hands.

"When will you see her again?"

"My parents are planning a birthday dinner for Auden in January. I'm sure she'll be invited."

"And her boyfriend?"

"Yeah, he might be invited, too. This is messed up, isn't it?"

Evan put his hands up in mock surrender and took a step back. "I'm not gonna judge, man. All I know is that I couldn't get Kate out of my head and eventually everything worked out."

"But she felt the same about you," I said, tilting my head and glaring at him from above the rim of my glasses.

"I'm guessing this Hadley feels it, too. Just give it time."

Just then, Kate entered the kitchen, tying her hair up in a bun. She rested her hand on my shoulder and leaned in to give me a welcoming hug. I knew by her hug that she'd heard most, if not all, of the conversation.

"Jase, we've talked about this," she said.

"What's that?" I played dumb.

"You're very good at reading people. You read me right away when we first met. You sensed how conflicted and unhappy I was."

"That was different," I said, taking a swig of my beer.

"Nope, it's the same. What does your gut say about her? How does she feel about you?"

"My gut tells me she's into me. But she was always into me when we were kids. So, that could be all it is. Memories. And, it seems pretty arrogant of me to assume those feelings are still there."

"I disagree. Some feelings get stronger over time," she said, her eyes softening as she looked at Evan.

He grabbed her hand and pulled her in for a peck on the lips. Her fingers brushed the lip gloss off of his bottom lip before turning her attention back to me.

"So, what do you think I should do?" I asked.

"Spend time with her. Make up a reason to see her," Kate said.

"Sounds kinda stalkerish," I said, waiting for Kate to smack me in the arm. Which she did.

"It's not stalkerish if she *likes* you. It's romantic. It's sweet."

"And if she's not into me?"

"Then, you'll be able to tell and you can walk away," Kate said.

"And then you'll know, dude," Evan adds.

"Okay." I drained the rest of my beer and gave them both a relaxed smile. "Let's talk about something else."

"Like what?"

"How are book sales?" Kate asked.

"Decent. They've actually picked up a lot."

"That's awesome," Evan said.

"So, what's on the horizon for Whitman Kelly?" Kate asked with a wink.

She knew I hated when she referred to me by my real first name. I'd adopted it as a pen name, but it still felt foreign to me when my friends used it.

"Book four has been rough. It's just not flowing out of me like it usually does."

"You're distracted," Kate said as she narrowed her eyes. She'd always seen through me. Part of the reason we became friends so easily after we attempted to date.

Kate squeezed my hand before pulling a frying pan from the cabinet. Without a word, Evan followed her lead and gathered onions and peppers from their refrigerator.

"Can I help with that?" I asked.

"Nope," Kate said, pouring olive oil into the pan.

"Okay...well, my agent's pissed. She's trying to get a publishing deal for the Kramer series, but none of the publishers will bite until the series is finished."

"Better finish it, then," Evan teased as he chopped the onion.

"Shit, I know." I nodded. "Only forty thousand words to go."

"No problem," Kate said, waving her hand in front of her face as she stirred the sizzling vegetables.

"Riiiiight," I replied, shaking my head. Forty thousand words was no picnic. It would take time. Weeks, if not months. And with thoughts of Haddie filling my brain, I worried it could take an entire year to get the right amount of focus necessary to write the rest of the book.

"You'll figure it out, man." Evan patted me on the back. He drained his beer and leaned against the kitchen counter. I hoped he was right. If not, it was going to be a long year.

CHAPTER FIVE

Hadley

When I returned home from work on a bitterly cold December afternoon, the lights inside the condo warned me that my mom was home from work. Usually I arrived before her and was able to relax by myself for a while before putting on a brave face and making supper. A ripple of unease drifted through my limbs as I parked my car. *Deep breaths, Hadley. She's still the same woman she's always been.* Only she wasn't and I knew it.

The smell of garlic hovered in the air and I heard the sound of oil sizzling in a pan. *At least she's cooking.*

I placed my purse near the door, taking a puff from my inhaler as I walked into the kitchen. The stone face of my mother greeted me.

"Hello, honey." The words fell from her mouth with a half smile. The half smile that I had seen for about two years, ever since she became heavily medicated so as not to be a danger to herself any more. The medication was effective, but the result was a woman drained of almost all emotion. No opinions, no tears, no anger. Nothing. I'd learned to let it roll off my shoulders as best I could. But most days I felt like an orphan. The woman who had raised me, who had supported me the first nineteen years of my life, had vanished.

I tried to see her as a roommate rather than a mother. And sometimes that helped. But most of the time I found myself yearning for the mom who used to sit at the edge of my bed and talk to me for hours about boys, friends and movies. I missed the mom who had called me every week my first semester at college and sent care packages every chance she got. But that was before our world was turned on its side. Before my dad's diagnosis. Before everything in our lives seemed to change for the worse.

"Hi, Mom. How was your day?"

"Same," she replied, shrugging her shoulders. My mom worked for a local library. It seemed to be the perfect job for her since losing him. Every day she worked in the quiet. It was peaceful and placid. It helped calm the destructive voices that used to loom in her brain.

"I got my ninety-day review at work today," I offered, knowing she wouldn't take the initiative to ask anything about my day. She stirred the onions and garlic in the saucepan. I saw a slight nod and realized that was all the recognition I would get. Shaking my head, I took a deep breath and walked towards her, rubbing my hand on her back lightly. She turned to me with another small smile.

Her doctor once told me that despite her lack of emotion on the outside, I needed to give her time. That she'd eventually adjust to her medication and be the Allison Foster that I grew up with. So I wouldn't give up on her. I still showed her kindness and affection in the hopes that one of these days, she'd place her hand on mine and give me the warm smile I had missed for so, so long.

I waited another minute, even though I knew she wasn't going to congratulate me. With a sigh, I shook it off and took two plates from the cabinet, carrying them with me to the table.

"What's for dinner?" I asked, trying to hide the disappointment in my voice.

"Taco salads," my mom replied as she added flank steak to the sizzling pan.

"Sounds great," I replied, placing assorted fresh vegetables on the granite countertop. This place was relatively new. The doctors had suggested we move out of our old house. Too many memories. For my mom, it was too much, too much of him. Too much loss. But for me, this place was sterile, foreign and not my home. It only made me miss him more.

∼

The only sounds to be heard were the clinking of forks against the ceramic plates as my mom and I picked at our salads.

"Tell me about your review," Mom said in between bites.

Doing my best to hide the shock from my face, I answered, "Pamela, my supervisor, is really happy with my work so far. She said the clients have grown attached to me. She wants to review me again after the huge musical performance in a few months, but overall I was given an excellent rating."

"Congratulations."

"She wants me to get started on planning the show later this week. I need to come up with a theme, but that shouldn't be too hard. Plus, we have a spring dance and I'm in charge of that."

"Sounds like you'll be busy," she said.

"Yeah, sounds like it," I said, pushing the taco meat around my plate.

"I'm happy for you." My mom's half smile was strained.

"Thanks," I said, unable to look up from my plate, afraid my sadness would show.

"I'm...I'm trying, Hadley. I know things aren't the same. But I'm trying."

Mom ran her fingers through her hair as I looked up into her eyes. This was the first time she had ever said anything at all about what we used to be, what we used to have. It had always been left unsaid, packed into a little box that neither of us was comfortable opening. But she'd lifted the lid and I was grateful.

I nodded, smiling softly and wishing I could jump up from my seat and hug her. But this was a big step for my mother and I didn't want to scare her.

So desperately, though, I wished the old Allison were sitting in front of me. I needed to talk to *that* Allison about the thoughts running through my head since I'd seen Jason at Beans coffee shop. I couldn't get him out of my head. I needed my mom to reassure me that it was nothing. That I was just being transported back to a time of innocence, when Jason was my infatuation. She'd remind me that I'd been with Tucker for years because he was a good match for me. We had similar ambitions and determined personalities. She'd remind me of how much Tucker had been there for me when Dad received his diagnosis. But this Allison didn't do that. This Allison just wanted to get through the day. I had lost my dad and my mother was unrecognizable to me. But as she tilted her head and looked me in the eyes,

I saw a small glimmer of the Allison Foster I used to know and it gave me hope, the tiniest bit of hope. And that was enough for now.

∽

Later, when Tucker called, I felt hopeful. We'd been drifting apart and I wasn't sure how to feel about it. Part of me was clinging to the boyfriend I'd had for six years. The boy who held my hand as they buried my father. The boy who held my hair when I was so suffocated by my grief that vomiting was the only way I could express my sadness. But that boy had changed. He was focused on his career now and was not as patient as he used to be. As a result, we were disconnected. Part of me knew that he no longer saw me as a part of his future. And I couldn't help feeling like I was hanging on to something that might no longer exist.

"Any New Year's plans yet?" Tucker sounded upbeat.

"You know I wouldn't plan anything without you."

"Well, I have something planned."

"*Excuse me?*" It was impossible for me to hide the irritation in my voice. Was he planning to spend New Year's without me? Maybe this *was* the beginning of our end. Just as I was about to speak my mind, he interrupted.

"I was thinking we could stay at a bed and breakfast in Lake Geneva. We could stay for two nights and celebrate New Year's at one of the restaurants near the marina."

"Oh." I paused. "That sounds nice."

I was placated, feeling grateful for his thoughtfulness and hopeful that maybe a weekend away was all we needed to be the former versions of ourselves again. The ones who had fallen hopelessly in love.

Confusion spread through me though, as I had to be honest with myself. I was thinking about a certain best friend's brother and I was terrified of what Auden would think. Not that I thought she'd disapprove of my having feelings for her brother again. But I worried she'd think I was just being silly—that I was using this rough patch with Tucker as an excuse to escape to something simpler, to someone who reminded me of childhood. A time when everything made more sense.

"You sure?" Tucker asked after a long pause. Guilt consumed me when I thought of letting him down. I had to give us a chance. I had to know for sure what fate had in store.

"Of course I'm sure. It sounds perfect," I replied gently. He sighed into the phone. I'd calmed his nerves and I was hoping our New Year's escape would bring us back to who we used to be.

CHAPTER SIX

Hadley

"Tucker, this is amazing," I said, looking around the cozy yet modern room of the bed and breakfast. It was New Year's Eve and we'd arrived for our time alone together. Our drive up had been pleasant, listening to music and laughing as we reminisced. Memory after memory made us laugh and smile and the thought of that tugged at my heart. I missed who we had been and I hoped we could get back there again. I felt like we'd found ourselves in a gray area of disconnect, both wanting to savor what we once had, but both afraid it was no longer possible. If we weren't talking about the past, we didn't talk at all. Thank God for the distraction of smart phones.

"You like it?" he asked casually as he placed our bags next to the king-sized bed covered in gorgeous gray and turquoise linens. A fireplace in the corner of the room had been lit for us. The room glowed from the soft flicker of burning flames and I felt myself being swept up in the romance of it all.

"Like it? I love it," I said, running my hands down the soft cotton of the pillowcase.

"Good," Tucker whispered into my ear as he wrapped his arms around my waist. His nose pressed against the skin behind my ear and he moved it back and forth, nuzzling the sensitive part near my earlobe. He knew the most ticklish spots of my body. *He knows me so well.*

Placing my hands on top of his, I turned to face him, pressing my lips to his and looking him in the eye. My breath hitched.

Why am I so nervous?

Tucker and I weren't virgins. We'd done this many times. But it'd been quite a while, and this occasion held tension and pressure that I was desperate to remove from our strained relationship.

Tucker took a deep breath before kissing me lightly on the tip of my nose.

"Our dinner reservation is in about thirty minutes. Probably better to wait until later for this," he said, turning away and walking into the bathroom. Pulling nervously on my sweater, I waited for him to finish. I'd like to say that I was disappointed he'd stopped things from getting more intense, but relieved was probably a better word. Dinner sounded like a great icebreaker and, if I was being honest with myself, I desperately needed a cocktail to loosen up. Make that two.

~

Several hours and many cocktails later, Tucker and I stumbled from our cab outside the bed and breakfast. Tucker paid the driver and led me to our room. Dinner had been awkward at first, but with each empty glass the conversation grew easier. Before long, Tucker had managed to draw me into him like he had years ago. Lightly caressing my arm with his fingers, whispering into my ear at midnight, telling me how much he loved me. Like most couples who have been together for awhile, we said the "L" word all the time. So much that it had become routine. We said it before saying goodbye and when we were ready to hang up the phone. But nothing was routine about *these* "I love you"s. I was craving Tucker and the physical compatibility we'd shared for years. Before we started to move in different directions.

"C'mon, baby, let's get you upstairs," he said, taking my hand and leading me to our room.

Once inside, I removed my coat and scarf, feeling really tipsy and warm. Glancing in the mirror, I saw the effect of the alcohol on my now scarlet skin. Every bit of me tingled and I felt amorous. So amorous. No matter how many issues Tucker and I may have had, I wanted him.

"Tuck," I said, pulling my hair out of its bun.

"Yes, baby," he said, walking to me, his hands reaching out to touch my arms. He stroked the skin until goose bumps rose up to meet his fingers. I shivered and Tucker chuckled, loving the reactions he got from me. Our bodies started to fall into the routine we'd set a very long time ago.

He kissed my neck, creating a light trail marked by his lips. I gasped and shivered as chills ran down my spine. Running my fingers through his black hair, I pulled him up to me, pressing my lips to his. Gentle at first, he bit my lower lip, increasing the intensity and making me squirm as his teeth threatened to pierce my skin. He laughed as he crushed his lips back onto mine, easing his tongue into my mouth. Together our tongues stroked each other in a comfortable rhythm. I heard the familiar sound of my zipper as Tucker removed my little black dress. He'd always been smooth with that. There were times in college that I hadn't even realized I was half naked. I'd be standing there, kissing him, so into it and clueless that my top was off as well as my skirt. Tucker had skills.

As I stepped out of the dress, I leaned against the bed and removed my bra. Tucker looked me up and down like a predator. I felt hunted. Desired. Ready.

Tucker guided me down onto the bed, removing his shirt and pants as we kissed, stroked and nuzzled on top of the down comforter.

"I want you," Tucker said, easing my panties down my legs. When I said nothing in return, he asked, "Do you want me, Hadley?"

Although I had no idea why, this tiny voice in me said no. I ignored it, though, allowing my hormones and lust to take over completely. *I want this. I do, I do.*

"Yes...yes, I want you."

"Good, that's what I thought," he said, plunging his tongue into my mouth once again, this time not nearly as gentle. He wasn't holding back. He was taking what he felt was already his.

Within seconds, Tucker was inside me. I gritted my teeth as my muscles struggled to relax. Normally, Tucker would sense my discomfort and slow down, knowing it'd been a while. But not tonight. Tonight he was urgent and determined. Tonight his thrusts were harsh and fast and I found myself holding on to his shoulders, just trying to keep up with him.

Just as a familiar pressure was building inside of me, Tucker cried out and sank into my arms. Sighing, I lay there, staring up at the spinning ceiling.

What the hell was that?

"Fuck." He ran his fingers through his dark hair and leaned back. "Sorry, that didn't last so long."

"It's all right," I said casually, attempting to blow it off as the room spun in circles. But I couldn't help it. My body was disappointed. As much as I'd hoped he'd give me the release I was seeking, I knew it wasn't going to happen.

"That's what happens when we go so long without having sex," he said, pulling out of me and walking to the bathroom. For a moment, I lay stunned, my stomach flipping uncomfortably. It was true. It had been a long time since we'd had sex. But even though he was right, his words stung. His tone was harsh and detached.

Hoping to calm the twisting and turning of the room, I kicked my leg over the side of the bed and planted it on the floor. *Do not throw up, do not throw up.*

In between being coherent and completely asleep when Tucker came back to bed, I turned my body toward him, hoping for some resolution, some comfort, *something*. But within moments, he was snoring and I lay there, unable to drift to sleep, wondering what had happened to the man next to me. He was no longer the boy I once loved.

∼

I woke up shivering, teeth chattering, skin covered in goose bumps. Even though Tucker had gotten himself underneath the covers, he'd left me on top of the comforter without a stitch of clothing on my body.

Damn him. I deserve better than this.

Tucker was a selfish man. Why had it taken me so long to really *see* him? Had he always been like this? Or had something changed in him? Was this why I'd avoided being intimate with him the last few months? Because I knew he didn't deserve me?

Pain pounded in my forehead as I stumbled to the bathroom. A white terrycloth robe hung from the door. I put it on and felt slightly better, but still shivered from the cold. I was chilled to the bone, but mad as hell. I wanted to wake Tucker and demand answers. Demand to know why I was being treated this way. But I knew where that would lead...and I didn't want to have that conversation in the middle of the night, only to wake up next to him in the morning. It would have to wait. But something in the pit of my stomach told me this was the beginning of the end. We weren't going to make it. I felt it in my gut.

Climbing back into bed, I eventually stopped shivering as I listened to Tucker snoring next to me. As I lay there, though, a memory crept into my brain. I must've buried it, but all of a sudden, it felt fresh, as if it'd just happened. As if I was trapped inside of it.

"Where is he?" Auden snipped. "He was supposed to be here an hour ago. Try his cell again."

"He's not picking up," I said with a shrug.

"Then let's go without him."

"No...I mean, not yet. Give him a minute."

"He does this all the time, Had. He expects you to wait on him. Aren't you sick of it?"

"He's not always like this. Sometimes he's sweet."

"He was in high school, but not anymore."

She was right. Since our first semester of college had begun, Tucker was different. He'd pledged a fraternity, one of the most elite on his campus in Champaign. Auden and I were "GDIs" (Goddamn Independents) according to him. He seemed disappointed in both of us for not going Greek. What he didn't get was that Auden and I didn't want that. We'd made several friends on campus and didn't feel the need to join. The Greek system wasn't popular at our tiny college in Peoria. We were content; we didn't need or want it. But for Tucker, it was his world. And the more he was wrapped up in that world, the more we drifted apart.

My cell remained silent as Auden tapped her foot on the hardwood floor.

"Shit. C'mon, Had. We only have another week left of break."

"And?"

"And I don't want to spend all that time waiting around for him."

Sending a final text to Tucker, I resigned myself to not seeing him for New Year's Eve. Oh well. Two minutes went by before my phone rang. I pressed the speakerphone button. Auden would get pissed if she didn't get to say her piece.

"Now you call me," I said, the sarcasm dripping from my words.

"Hey, baby," he slurred into the phone.

"We've been waiting for you for over an hour. Where are you?"

"Dave's place."

"Oh," I said, my heart plummeting into my belly. Dave was a friend of Tucker's who had pledged with the same fraternity. They'd become inseparable and Dave was always making sarcastic jokes around me. He thought it was ridiculous that Tucker and I stayed together long distance. But we were less than an hour away. We saw each other a lot (at least we did before his frat had constant parties during the fall months) and Tucker had a car, so we didn't really view it as long distance.

Dave was definitely not a fan of mine. He wanted to pick up girls with Tuck by his side. And he wasn't afraid to refer to me as "The Cock Block." Nice. Tucker acted like it was no big deal, so I tried not to make it one.

"You knew we were waiting on you and you went to Dave's? What for?" Auden asked, her words snide.

"Calm the fuck down, Auden. It was just a couple beers." Exasperation poured from the phone. Even through his slur, we could hear his irritation. He was never able to hide that easily.

"Hey, don't talk to her like that," I said, feeling myself being pushed to my limit. I didn't raise my voice often. But no one talked that way to my best friend and got away with it.

"Fine, whatever. Sorry," he said, his voice lowered slightly. This wasn't the first time they'd been pissed at each other. We'd played this routine out many, many times before. But I still held out hope they'd get along again eventually, like they had in high school.

"Everyone's waiting at Joe's," I reminded him.

"Do you have a curfew?" Tucker asked. Auden fumed.

"It's New Year's and I have cool parents. So, no," I said, grabbing my backpack from the floor.

"Are you sure you wanna go to Joe's? Dave said there's a kickass party downtown. We could get a hotel room."

"We told him we'd be there," Auden snapped. Joe and Auden had engaged in a flirtation for months over email. She was eager to see him. "If you want to go downtown, go with your precious Dave. Hadley and I are going to Joe's."

"Fine, maybe I will. Better than going to some lame ass 'sleepover' at Joe's," Tuck said.

"What? Tucker!" I said with wide eyes. "It's New Year's Eve. I want to spend it with you. Can't you see Dave back at school?"

I didn't even attempt to mask my disappointment. We'd been dating for two years and this was to be our third New Year's Eve together. The thought of being ditched pissed me off, but even more than that, it hurt. A lot.

"I guess I can catch a cab. Gimme an hour, though."

"Don't do us any favors," I said.

"Look, sorry. I'm having fun. What do you want from me?"

"Forget it. Happy New Year, Tuck." I slammed the phone shut and pursed my lips into a thin line.

"I'm sorry," Auden said.

"Let's not let him ruin our night. Let's go."

Joe's was fine. Nothing exciting, but a bunch of friends ringing in the new year with drinking games, more shots than I cared to remember and guitar jam sessions. Every so often, I'd glance at the door, hoping Tucker would show up. But that didn't happen.

The next morning, when Auden dropped me off at home, we found my parents sitting on the couch, drinking their morning coffee. But something was off. Something was wrong.

"Good morning," my dad said with a forced smile.

"Auden, can Hadley call you later? We need to talk to her... as a family," my mom asked, her eyes red and puffy. Had I misunderstood my lack of a curfew? I was pretty certain they approved of my staying at Joe's. And I didn't have any messages on my phone. Oh no, a divorce? Were they getting a divorce? Starting the new year apart? My heart pounded in my chest.

Auden pulled me in for a brief hug. "Call me later."

Her words were soft, gentle. She knew something was wrong as much as I did.

When Auden left, my parents sat in silence as I joined them in the living room. They glanced at each other with questioning eyes and furrowed brows.

"Are you guys getting a divorce?" I asked, eager to get the discussion over with.

"Oh god, no," my mom said, pursing her lips and looking at my dad.

"Sweetheart, I... I have cancer," my dad said softly.

"What? No... no." Bile rose to my throat. I covered my mouth with my hand, pleading with it to go back down.

"The next few months are going to be hard," he continued.

"What kind?" I asked.

"Pancreatic."

"That's a bad one, right?" I asked, turning to my mom.

"It is," she said, tears threatening to run from her eyes.

"So, what are we going to do?"

"Chemo, radiation. Whatever my doctor suggests."

"Okay," I replied.

"But there are no guarantees," my dad said, his voice choking up. "You need to know that, sweetheart."

"Okay," I said again. I was still trying to process the words. Pancreatic cancer. Even as a self-involved college kid, I knew that diagnosis was fatal. I knew his chances were low. But I had had no idea just how little time I had left with him.

That afternoon, a hung over and remorseful Tucker showed up at my door. When he saw what a mess I was, he assumed it was about him. He apologized, he groveled, he made tons of promises to be better. Finally, I couldn't take it anymore. I broke down. I told him about my dad. And sweet Tucker returned. He held me as

I cried. He stroked my hair. All was forgiven. All was forgotten. I needed him and he was there.

∼

For years, what happened that morning overshadowed everything else in my life—the good and the bad. But now, I had to face the facts. Sweet Tucker was gone. Perhaps forever. It was time to let go. Eventually the soft sound of his breath lulled me back into a troubled sleep.

CHAPTER SEVEN

Hadley

I was late. And I was *never* late.
At first, when my period hadn't arrived two weeks ago, I hadn't noticed. Things were so busy at work since I had started planning the musical performance and the Valentine's Day dance that it never crossed my mind. Until I glanced at my desk calendar this morning, checking to see what time I needed to arrive for Auden's birthday dinner tonight. It was then that I saw the small red "x" that I had placed on January 14th. My heart skipped a beat looking at that simple marking. That date had come and gone with no sign of my period. I'd been on the pill for years, and month after month, it had arrived right on time without fail. Until that day.

"It's been three minutes," Ellie said, with hesitation in her voice, "do you want me to look?"

The small plastic pregnancy test sat on the ledge above the sink as Ellie and I stood in the employee restroom at Sunnyside. On my lunch break, Ellie had taken me to buy a test because, from the moment I'd walked into work on this snowy January morning, she could tell something was wrong.

"Hadley," Ellie whispered as she stroked my shoulder with her fingertips, prompting a response.

"Yes, please," I said, taking a deep breath in and out. "I can't look."

She sighed to herself.

"It's positive, isn't it?" I asked. My stomach flipped in my abdomen.

Ellie turned the plastic stick, revealing two very dark pink lines encased in the tiny plastic window. My heart thumped loudly, and I felt as if those lines were throbbing, moving to the beat of my pulse.

"Yeah, it is." She shrugged, rubbing my arm softly with her hand.

"What am I gonna do?"

This is not happening.

I searched her eyes for an answer, but I couldn't find one. She looked just as confused as I felt. We'd only been friends for a few months. She had no idea what to say. Then again, neither would Auden, and we'd known each other for years. Sometimes there are no easy answers.

"Why don't we go somewhere where you can sit and get your head together? Come on, let's go to the office."

Ellie took me by the hand, leading me to our office down the long corridor. Bryce waved and I offered him a weak smile. His face fell...he knew something was wrong. He removed his earbuds and ran to me.

"What's the matter?" he asked. His face turned a shade of pale that pulled at my heart.

"I'm...I'm okay—" I choked out.

"She isn't feeling well, Bryce. Please go back to work and you can check on her later, okay?" Ellie said in her sweet, calm voice as she placed her palm on his shoulder.

"Yeah...okay. Take care of her," he said in a protective voice. And despite all of the anxiety in my chest, despite all of the fear in my heart, those words soothed me in a way I had never imagined. I was loved. I was appreciated. I was *home* at Sunnyside.

Ellie closed our office door as I slumped at my desk and placed my head in my hands. As I breathed in and out, my lungs felt tense as I fought against the emotion that was struggling to escape my chest.

"What are you going to do? Are you going to tell Tucker?" she asked.

"Of course," I replied, feeling puzzled. *Why would she ask me that?* We stared at each other for a brief moment before she spoke.

"I—I'm sorry. It just seems like things have been weird for you two. And obviously you didn't plan for this..."

"And?" I asked, still confused.

"Well, you have options."

"Oh...you mean an abortion..." I said, looking down at my clammy hands.

"Yeah," she said, her voice timid and meek. "Did I offend you?"

"No," I said, shaking my head. "That's not it. It just hadn't crossed my mind, that's all."

"I'm sorry. We don't know each other that well. I shouldn't have said anything," she said, rubbing her hand against her forehead. Tension hung in the air between us. But at least it was a distraction from the racing thoughts of *baby, baby, baby* that were circling through my head like a clogged drain.

"It's okay," I replied. "You're just looking out for me. I know that."

"Pamela will understand if you need to take the rest of the day off."

"No, I need to get through the day. I have Auden's dinner tonight."

"Can you skip it?" Ellie asked.

"No, Auden really needs this. She's been really off lately. I need to be there."

"You need to take care of yourself, too," Ellie said softly.

"I know." I nodded, closing my eyes.

"Is Tucker going with you?"

"No, he has a business dinner. Thank God. Not sure I can face him yet," I said, wringing my hands. "Hey, would you be willing to take my exercise class this afternoon? I'm not sure I'm up for that group today."

"Absolutely." Ellie smiled as she gathered my folders. "You hang out in here for a while and I'll cover your groups. I'll see you for bus duty at the end of the day."

"Great." I nodded. Ellie walked towards the door.

"Ellie?"

"Yeah?"

"Thanks. For everything." A tear dropped down my cheek and landed on my sweater. Ellie tilted her head, let out a sigh and walked back to me. She knelt down in front of my chair and took my hands in hers.

"I know this wasn't in your plans. And I know I haven't known you long. But if you have this child, I know you'll be a wonderful mother."

"Thank you," I said, choking on the tears that poured from my eyes.

"I mean it," she said as she stood, wrapping her arms around me as I sobbed. She held me for a few minutes, rocking me steadily back and forth, calming me gently until the tears stopped running from my eyes.

~

Hours later, with a fresh layer of makeup on my splotchy red face, I was feeling somewhat ready to attend Auden's birthday dinner at La Hacienda restaurant. Taking off my coat, I sat on the wooden bench near the host's desk, glancing around at the stucco walls and terracotta pots in the waiting area.

"Haddie."

I turned to see Jason as he walked through the door. A huge grin was plastered on his face as he removed his coat and sat down beside me.

"Hey there," I said, pulling on the neck of my sweater.

"No one else is here yet, huh?" he observed, looking around.

"We're the first."

"I'm sure they'll all be here soon. My parents are kinda infamous for being fashionably late."

I nodded, not knowing quite how to do small talk yet, especially with the guy who controlled my heart for years.

"So, did you have a nice Christmas?" he asked tentatively, filling the awkward void.

"It was nice, pretty quiet."

"And your New Year's?" His words stung as my brain flashed back to New Year's Eve. It was the night I got pregnant. My hand touched my belly inadvertently as I pondered how to answer him.

"That was nice, too. I can't believe it's a new year already."

"Tell me about it." He nodded. We sat in silence. The last thing I wanted to do was be dismissive towards Jason, but seeing him today of all days was unbelievably awkward. Too many feelings to process. Feelings I had been trying to suppress for almost a decade.

"So," he continued, "it was great running into you at the coffee shop. I keep hoping you'll stop back in," he said, adjusting his tortoiseshell glasses.

"I really need to schedule another field trip. Thanks for reminding me." I smiled, knowing my cheeks were turning a very bright shade of red.

"I'd love to hear about your job. Your clients seemed awesome."

"I feel very comfortable there. I really love it."

"Maybe you can tell me about it during dinner?" he asked, tilting his head to the side. His dimples called to me from his tan cheeks. I used to daydream about those dimples.

"Looks like the birthday girl is here," I said, gesturing to the door.

Auden entered wearing a crimson red pea coat, a black hat and a gorgeous hand-woven black scarf. She looked as beautiful as always. But there was something sullen in her eyes. They'd been lifeless for months, ever since we'd boarded the plane back to Chicago. I'd tried to give her the space she needed. Auden had always been very open about her feelings. So I knew that if something was bothering her, she'd tell me eventually.

The sadness in her eyes lingered as she walked towards Jason and me. We greeted her with hugs and birthday wishes. She raised an eyebrow at me after our hug as she peered into my bloodshot eyes. She was on to me. *Damn it.* I needed to get a better poker face.

After hugging Jason, Auden chuckled as she pointed to the t-shirt under his black and white plaid button-down. "Save Ferris?"

Jason laughed and looked down at his shirt. "Yep."

"I love that you're still wearing your t-shirts after all these years," I said with a laugh. I hadn't noticed his t-shirt when he'd first sat down a few minutes ago. But when I pictured Jason in my head, he was always wearing a t-shirt...always. T-shirts with movie quotes, t-shirts with quirky sayings, t-shirts with song lyrics. I had given him a t-shirt a very long time ago. He had probably forgotten all about it and given it to charity or thrown it away. But I remembered it like it was yesterday.

∼

I was twelve years old and finally brave enough to be in the same room as Jason without blushing and acting like a fool. It was his birthday and Auden had invited me over for a sleepover. While Jason was out with his friends, I left the t-shirt in a small gift bag in front of his bedroom door. And even though I was hesitant to do it, I signed the card. There was no going back and I was scared to death. It was my do-or-die moment. He had to know I cared about him.

The next morning, while I was sitting at the breakfast table with Auden, Jason strolled out of his room wearing his dimpled grin and the "Camp North Star" t-shirt that I had bought for him at Spencer Gifts. Underneath the symbol for Camp North Star, it simply read, "It Just Doesn't Matter."

At the time, Jason was obsessed with the Bill Murray movie called Meatballs *and his very favorite scene was when Murray rallied the entire camp to chant "It Just Doesn't Matter!" I saw that shirt hanging in the store and knew he needed to have it. But seeing him wear it made my cheeks blush to a horrible shade of crimson.*

"Nice shirt," Auden said with a laugh, having no idea that I was the one who had purchased it. I had seen it while shopping with her at the mall, but had made a special trip back to buy it alone. I didn't want her to make fun of me. This gesture meant way too much to me.

"Isn't it?" Jason said, smoothing the cotton of the navy blue t-shirt. "It's my new favorite shirt."

"Where'd you get it?" Auden persisted.

Jason grinned at me, his dimple showing as it always did, before he directed his attention back to his sister. "Someone pretty awesome gave it to me. And that's all you need to know."

"Mmm-hmmm," their older sister Maya said as she took a sip of her coffee. A wave of embarrassment swept through me and I hung my head, looking down at my bowl of Cheerios. Auden turned to look at me. Her gaze made my cheeks burn but I continued to stare at the blue bowl in front of me.

"Okay, whatever," she said, finally dropping it. I went back to eating my cereal as Jason took a seat at the table. Mrs. Kelly placed a cup of orange juice in front of him.

"C'mon, let's go listen to CDs in my room," Auden said, pulling me up from the table. I could feel Jason's eyes on me as we walked out of the kitchen. I'll never forget that smile.

Auden closed the door and glared at me.

"Did you give my brother that shirt?"

"What does it matter?" I asked, my pulse racing. I had no idea if Auden would be upset or feel threatened by my feelings for Jason. All I knew was that I wanted to keep them to myself.

"*Just tell me. C'mon, vault.*" That was our word. The word we always used when we were promising not to tell a secret. We'd put it in our "*vault*" and never breathe a word to another person.

"*Vault?*" I asked her with terrified eyes.

"*Yes, vault. I promise,*" she said before narrowing her eyes at me. "*Are you in love with my brother?*" She was always the dramatic one.

"*Ummm,*" I started.

"*I knew it!*" she yelled, pointing her finger at me. "*Why didn't you tell me? You're my best friend! I need to know these things. All this time, I've been thinking you had a crush on Daniel McMillan.*"

"*From ceramics class?*" I winced. "*Um, no, that's gross.*"

She rolled her eyes as she sat down on her bed. "*Well, you're always super nice to him.*"

"*That's because he doesn't have any friends.*"

"*Yeah, because his breath smells.*"

"*Auden!*" I yelled, my eyes wide.

"*What? It does!*" She shrugged. "*Anyway, I totally thought you liked him because you always sit with him in class.*"

"*I do not like Daniel.*" I shook my head with certainty.

"*Well, that's a relief... although I have to say, liking my brother is kinda up there as far as the ick factor goes. I mean, c'mon, it's Jason. I mean, ew.*"

"*He's not 'ew' to me.*"

"*How long has this been going on?*"

"*Umm, I kinda lost track.*"

"*Seriously?*" A look of absolute betrayal crossed her melodramatic face.

"*It's been a while, all right? Remember, vault.*"

"*Vault, I know. Okay, so you got him the shirt. What else have you done for him?*"

"*Nothing.*"

"Well, he seemed to like it."

"I know, right?" I said, finally smiling as I remembered the sweet expression of gratitude on Jason's handsome fifteen-year-old face.

I looked to my best friend for approval, "Are you sure it's okay?"

"You liking my brother?" she asked, wrinkling her nose.

"Yes." I nodded.

"Yeah, I guess." She shrugged again. "I mean, ick. But fine."

"Vault?"

"Vault. I promise."

∽

Jason grinned as he looked down at his t-shirt. "Yep, still haven't kicked the habit."

Auden rolled her eyes. I had to laugh at their rapport. So close one minute, and embarrassed of each other the next. It made me long for a sibling.

As soon as Auden's parents and her sister Maya arrived, we were seated at a large table with brightly colored wooden chairs. Quickly, Auden ordered two pitchers of margaritas for the table. I ordered myself a Sprite, knowing alcohol was no longer an option. That was just the beginning of the many changes I would have to make. I wasn't a huge drinker, but abstaining was something that I'd never had to worry about before. I'd never had to protect another life before. I'd never had to put the needs of a tiny, helpless human above my own. The realization of that responsibility rolled over me like a wave. I could feel the blood draining from my cheeks.

"Haddie," Jason whispered from the seat next to mine, "is everything all right? You don't look so good."

I shook my head, staring off into space as I reached for my water glass. It was Auden's night and I would *not* spoil it.

"Oh geez, sorry. I'm just getting over a bug."

"No, you're not," Auden interrupted, suspicion written all over her face.

"Auden," Mrs. Kelly snapped.

Auden raised her arms in front of her. "I just don't remember you being sick."

"It's no big deal," I said, taking another sip. "I'm fine. Totally fine."

As the family caught up on the day's events, I was able to take several deep breaths. I could feel my body relaxing. When the margaritas arrived, Auden poured me a glass automatically. I didn't stop her or turn the glass away. I hoped that if I just let the glass sit in front of my place setting, no one would notice that it was still full at the end of our meal.

My plan was working well. The Kelly family imbibed their cocktails and ordered food. Small talk was heard around the table as well as funny stories about Auden's childhood. When our food arrived, though, Jason leaned in close.

"So... how's your job?"

In between bites, I said, "It's wonderful. I love it."

"Awesome," he said, smiling at me. "I know you take your clients on field trips, but what else are you doing for Sunnyside?"

He seemed genuinely interested in my work and I loved that. Tucker had barely asked me a handful of questions about my work since I had accepted the job. He didn't think it was "worthy" of my education.

"I teach basic skills like coin recognition and telling time. I love teaching exercise class; we go for long walks in the trails outside or we make up aerobic routines."

"Sounds fun." He chuckled, taking a sip of his margarita.

"It is! It's more fun than I ever expected. Right now, I'm planning the Valentine's Day dance and I get to choose the music. I'm excited about it."

"Oh, look out. It'll be nothing but '80s songs the entire night," Jason said, casually nudging me with his elbow.

He remembered the music I liked. I felt such conflict brewing within me. The butterflies were stirring in my abdomen, just as they always did when I was near him. Knowing I was pregnant with Tucker's child, though, stopped them immediately.

Get rid of those feelings, Hadley. It's not going to happen. It can't happen.

"I do love that decade." I nodded, picking at my chicken fajitas.

"I remember," Jason said before biting into his burrito. "You know, I used to DJ a little bit in college. I'm happy to help if you need it."

"Really?" I asked, stunned. Weeks ago, I'd asked Tucker if he'd like to be my date for the dance and he still hadn't given me a straight answer. Jason was just so...different from the man I was dating.

"Are you kidding? Of course. Just tell me what you need me to do."

His green eyes were wide as he placed his elbow on the table and perched his chin on his hand, giving me his undivided attention.

"Well, I do have a client who loves music. Would you be willing to work with him? He could be your assistant or something. I think it'd make his entire year."

"Sure." Jason nodded, still watching me intently.

"Awesome," I said, my heart once again aflutter. I took another bite of chicken just to break eye contact with the handsome man who was just inches away from me. His eyes were pulling me in. I was overwhelmed, bewildered and completely in awe of how he *still* made me feel after all those years apart.

"Maybe you could stop by the center a couple of days before the dance. I can introduce you to Bryce and you two can talk shop," I said, running my fingers through my hair. Jason's eyes followed my hand as it flowed from root to tip. I almost lost my breath.

"I'll be there," he said, reaching into his pocket for his cell phone. "Let me get your number and we'll set something up."

Once I finished giving Jason my cell number, Auden interrupted us.

"Will you come with me to the bathroom? I need to pee." Auden pushed herself up into a standing position. There was no doubt she'd had way too much to drink. Several pitchers of margaritas had been served to our table and the only one who had been drinking consistently was Auden.

"Of course," I said, standing and walking towards her, offering my arm. She looked relieved as she reached out for me and grasped my arm for support. She was even more buzzed than I thought

"Shh," she faux-whispered quite loudly into my ear. "I don't want my mother to know I'm drunk."

I turned back, glancing at her family. Her parents were busy in conversation, her mother playfully wiping the salsa from her husband as he spoke. Maya was checking her cell phone with a furrowed brow. Her husband was home with their sick baby. It was obvious she'd rather be there with them. Jason was sitting with his elbows on the table, still looking my way. When our eyes met, he grinned at me. Quickly I looked away, before rounding the corner to the bathroom. All of the attention from Jason was messing with my head.

Once the door to the bathroom closed, Auden turned to me and placed her hands on both sides of my head. She smoothed my hair down to the tips and a giggle escaped me. I hadn't seen her that drunk in months. Again and again, she ran her hands down the sides of my head, as she stared at me blankly, sweat building on her forehead.

"Sweetie," I said, tipping my chin, attempting to make eye contact with her. She glanced at me before throwing her head back in hysterics. If I had been the least bit tipsy, I'm sure I'd find her hilarious. But being completely sober and having had one of the strangest days of my life made it difficult to relate to Auden's laughter.

"I am drunkety, drunk, drunk, drunk," Auden said, her volume increasing each time she repeated the word. Twirling around the bathroom, pinching the fabric of her sweater dress, Auden spun herself through the air before bumping into the wall.

"Whoops."

Auden laughed again as she entered the largest stall of the bathroom. She closed the door behind her and giggled to herself as she used the toilet.

I stood at the sink, waiting for her to emerge from the stall. The toilet flushed, but she didn't move. Her charcoal ballet slippers were still pressed to the floor. She was still sitting on the toilet.

"Aud?" I said, knocking on the door of the stall. "You okay?"

"I think I'm gonna puke," she whimpered.

"Oh." That's all I could think to say. Auden had a tried and true phobia when it came to vomiting. She was terrified of it and would do anything and everything in her power not to do it. Snapping into caregiver mode, I walked to the stall door. We'd been here many times before during our college years. I took a deep breath and asked, "What can I do, sweetie?"

The latch loosened on the large stall door and it slowly creaked open. Auden was fully dressed, sitting on the toilet. Her skin was ashen and she clutched the handicap bar at her side.

"I don't wanna do it," she whined, her brow knitted, her hair disheveled.

"Shh," I said, smoothing down her hair. "Do you want me to get your mom? Or Maya?"

"No!" she shouted, grabbing onto my forearm.

"Okay, okay," I said, pushing her hair behind her ears.

"Just stay here with me... please," she whimpered, a tear slowly dropping from her eye.

"Of course, sweetie," I replied, squeezing her hand.

"I'm gonna sit down now," she said, pulling herself up and sitting down on the terracotta tile. Following her lead, I placed the latch back on the door and sat beside her on the floor. Auden placed her elbows on the seat of the toilet and leaned against her folded arms.

"Breathe in and out," I said softly as I rubbed her back. Taking deep breaths in and out, in and out, I tried to get Auden to follow my lead. After several minutes of this, Auden tugged at the neck of her sweater as sweat trickled down her neck. Yep, she was gonna vomit.

"I don't wanna, I don't wanna, I don't wanna," she whined as she shook her head vigorously back and forth. Doing my best to stifle my laughter, I just kept thinking about how grateful I was for the distraction. Auden was always entertaining, even when she didn't mean to be. She attempted to swat me when she heard my chuckles.

"You're a brat."

"Sorry, sweetie."

"I have to lie down," she said. And as much as I wanted to stop my best friend from lying down in a public bathroom, I said nothing. I simply moved out of the way and let her rest. She laid her head on her arm and closed her eyes.

I sat back against the wall, resting my head against the stucco-textured paint. Just when I thought Auden had fallen asleep, she whispered, "I think it's passing."

"Maybe your food is settling," I offered, rubbing her calf gently to comfort her.

"Maybe," she replied. "This sucks."

"I know. Puking is the worst."

"Can I tell you something?" Auden croaked out.

"Of course," I said, lightly rubbing her leg.

"I'm not happy. Ever since we got back from Europe. Something is just...not right."

"Is it your job?" I asked, hoping she'd give me more information. I wanted my best friend to be happy again and

I wasn't sure her current job in sales was really the right route for her. When she'd first told me she wanted to go into pharmaceutical sales, I was floored. It was so competitive. So cutthroat. But Auden loved a challenge. And talking with people had never been her weakness. But maybe it wasn't all she'd hoped it would be.

"Maybe, I don't know," she mumbled. "I just feel like I don't belong anymore."

"Don't belong where?"

"Here...I don't know. Anywhere, I guess. I just feel weird, like I'm failing."

"Not true," I argued. "You're one of the most outgoing people I know. You're anything but a failure."

"I don't know what it is. But I'm miserable."

"I'm here for you, honey. We'll figure this out together."

"Okay," she said, her voice soft as she drifted into sleep.

"Auden?" I said, touching her lightly on the leg.

"Mmmm," she said, eyes and lips closed.

"I need to tell you something. It's big. And I'm probably only telling you this because I'm pretty sure you won't remember tomorrow."

She mouthed the word "vault" as her eyes stayed shut. God, I loved her. Even in her state of drunkenness, she lived and breathed by our code.

"I'm pregnant," I said, my voice faltering. "And I have no idea what to do."

"Ohhhh, that's nice," Auden said, her voice trailing off. And within two seconds, she was snoring. I shook my head and let out another uncomfortable laugh, sitting back against the wall wondering what the hell I was going to do with my passed-out friend.

Just then, there was a knock on the stall door. Climbing to my feet, I opened the large metal door. An irritated Maya stared down at her sister in disbelief.

"Oh, for God's sake," she muttered. "Did she throw up?" Maya placed her hands on her hips.

"No, but I thought she might."

"Good. The world would've come to an end if Auden Kelly had to vomit," she said, rolling her eyes. "I'll get Jason and we'll carry her drunk ass out of here. I have to get home anyway."

"Okay." I gave her a half smile as I looked back down at the snoring Auden.

Jason walked in, trying not to laugh at his sister. He was trying *really* hard. He was such a good guy.

"I'm gonna drive her home. You okay to drive?" Jason asked, looking concerned.

"Me? Oh, yeah. Fine, totally," I stammered. Why did I embarrass myself like this around him?

Jason bit his lip and smiled, holding back a chuckle. Completely mortified, I was certain I was blushing again. Could he sense just how much he still affected me after all this time? *Lord, help me.*

"I'll call you about the dance stuff," he said, patting his cell phone in his pocket.

"Great," I said, helping him pull Auden to a standing position. She opened her eyes and let out a small burp. I smelled the tequila on her breath and had to turn my head as my stomach threatened to turn in my belly. If there had been any part of me that wanted to drink tonight, that part had just gone running from the room. Holding my breath, avoiding the smell of tequila, Jason and I locked eyes.

"Niiiice, sis," Jason said to Auden, shaking his head.

"Oops, sorry." Auden smiled before leaning her head on Jason's shoulder. "Thanks."

"No worries. I got ya." He put his arm around her hip and guided her out of the bathroom. I followed him back to the table to gather my things and say my goodbyes. Mr. and Mrs. Kelly didn't say much, obviously embarrassed for Auden. But I suspected they were also concerned about their daughter. She wasn't happy... not at all. And now we all knew it.

CHAPTER EIGHT

Jason

Her number had been programmed into my phone for days and I was finally getting enough nerve to call her. I'd known her for most of my life; why was I so nervous? I picked up my cell and dialed her number.

She answered after three rings, just when I thought it would go to voicemail. I had to clear my throat before speaking. *God, what is this girl doing to me?*

"Haddie?" I asked, embarrassed. *Pull it together, Kelly.*

"Jason, hi," she said. Her voice cracked and for some reason, I felt like she might have been crying.

"Everything okay?" I asked, concerned.

"Oh sure. Just watching a movie."

"Which one?" I asked, secretly hoping it was a certain John Hughes movie we'd watched together years ago.

"*Pretty in Pink*," she answered.

That's it. That's the one. And I don't think I'll ever forget it.

"*Jason, get out of here,*" *Auden said, her hands on her hips, staring down at me as I lounged on the couch in the basement. It was my favorite spot. It's where our big-screen TV was and everybody knows movies and video games are much better on a bigger screen.*

My dad let me help him pick it out at Best Buy. Since then, it had become my favorite spot in the house.

"No, I'm good," I said with a smirk. I crossed my arms in front of me in defiance. I was so tired of my stupid middle school younger sister always telling me what to do, as if she was in charge, as if I cared what she wanted.

"I'm serious. We want to watch a movie."

"Who's 'we'?" I asked.

"Hadley's sleeping over. She'll be here in a few minutes."

Haddie. I was hoping that Auden had no idea how I felt about her best friend. Ever since she had given me my favorite t-shirt, I couldn't get her out of my head. My friends had been pushing me to date a girl named Heather, but I wasn't interested. She was pretty and all, but she just didn't do it for me. And I didn't want to be one of those dick guys who dated girls just to get something from them. That just wasn't my style. My friends probably thought I was gay or something because I didn't really date a lot of girls that school year. But I was hung up on a thirteen-year-old. How pathetic was that? I knew how she felt about me, but I was always afraid of doing anything to show her how I felt. Probably because Auden was always around.

No matter what, Auden was always there. I never had a chance to talk to her without my sister breathing down our necks, annoying the hell out of me. Every once in a while, we'd share a laugh or a quick conversation about music or movies. But usually it was over as quickly as it started, with Auden walking back into a room or putting down her cell phone and focusing her attention back our way.

"Fine, you guys can watch down here," I said, acting more put out than I really felt. I was excited to see her again.

"Don't do me any favors," Auden said, rolling her eyes. When I didn't move from the sofa, she glared at me.

"What?" I asked, exasperated.
"Aren't you going to go park your ass somewhere else?"
"No, I told you that already."
"Whitman!"
"Don't call me that, you little shit!"
"Why not? It's your name!" She always knew exactly how to push my buttons. She and Maya both. Stuck between two hormonal pain-in-the ass sisters. Life would've been so much better if I'd had a brother.
"Shut up," I groaned, picking up the book I had to read for Lit class.
"You're seriously not going to leave?"
"Nope." I smiled wide, purposely trying to piss her off.
"Fine, whatever. Don't bug us."
"Wasn't planning on it," I said with a smirk.
"Riiiight," Auden said, rolling her eyes, placing a DVD into the player.
"Shouldn't you wait for Haddie?" I asked, regretting it right away.
"What is your deal with her? Do you like her or something?" Before I was able to answer her, I heard the door to the basement open and footsteps starting down the stairs. I put my nose back in my book, knowing it was Haddie.
"Hey guys," Haddie said, placing her duffle bag and backpack by the stairs. I waved silently from the couch, my eyes never leaving my book. I wasn't trying to be a dick, but I couldn't face her after what Auden had just said.
"My mom let me buy that Molly Ringwald movie," Auden said, flipping her hair.
"Really?" Haddie asked, "The one with Blaine?"
"Pretty in Pink," Auden said with a snip.
"I know what it's called. I just wanted to make sure," Haddie said, taking a seat on the couch. Auden sat between us and I wanted to groan.

"She was in a lot of movies before she dropped off the face of the earth," I added.

"True," Haddie smiled, "and I love her."

"Why?" I asked her, placing my finger in my book, holding my place.

"Because she was just a normal girl. She's not like all these gorgeous actresses who just pretend to be the average girl. She really was."

Good point. I was kind of tired of the fake ugly duckling movies where you seriously put some makeup on a chick and she was magically transformed into a beauty queen. Molly was pretty, but not hot like the girls I was used to seeing at the movies.

"Shut up! It's starting," Auden said, pushing the bowl of popcorn onto Haddie's lap.

Thirty minutes later, Auden's cell phone rang and she whispered to Haddie that it was some guy named Chad. Auden squealed a little bit before hopping off the couch and walking into our father's office on the other side of the basement.

"Who was that?" I asked.

"He's in her algebra class. She's been into him for a while."

"Do I need to be concerned? Kick his ass maybe?" I asked, laughing, karate chopping the air, which probably made me look like a total dork. I wasn't exactly the guy that got into fights. I pretty much lived by the mantra "live and let live." Haddie knew that about me. Her small giggle said it all. She got my humor. She ran her fingers through her hair and placed the popcorn bowl on the coffee table.

"Nah, he's fine."

We didn't say anything else for a little while. As much as I hated to admit it, the movie sucked me in. I really wanted this Andie girl to get the guy. And it pissed me off that she didn't think she was *good enough for him.* When I scoffed at Blaine for the third time, Haddie laughed and turned towards me.

"You're really into this," she said.

"It's all right." I shrugged. Lie. I was totally into it. There was no way I was going to miss the ending.

"It'll end happily, don't worry," she teased me. Her golden hair was hanging in loose curls down past her shoulders and I wished I could run my fingers through it. Instead, I kept my hands in my lap, waiting for Auden to walk back in and destroy my night entirely.

A loud laugh came from Dad's office and Haddie shook her head knowingly.

"She's going to be in there for a while," she said, smiling.

"Good." I smiled and watched as Haddie's pale cheeks turned a pretty shade of pink.

Without wanting to seem too obvious, I sat up on the sofa, shifting so I was a few inches closer to her. She swallowed hard as I moved closer and I knew I was making her nervous. I didn't want that so I didn't get any closer. After a few minutes, her breath seemed to even out and she seemed to be engrossed in the movie once again.

When the final scene came on the screen, I watched Haddie smile as Blaine professed his love to Andie and gasp as Andie followed him out to the parking lot for their big kiss. God, I wanted to kiss her.

When the credits rolled, Haddie reached for a tissue to wipe her soaked cheeks. Even when she cried, she looked beautiful.

"Did you know that John Hughes changed the ending?" she asked, turning her body to me, moving a few inches closer.

"Really?" I was intrigued.

"Yeah. In the original ending, Duckie got the girl."

"Duckie? Seriously?"

"Mmm-hmm." She smiled proudly. "But test audiences hated it. They wanted her to be with Blaine."

"Interesting," I said, leaning my body to face hers, putting my head on my elbow.

"What?" Haddie asked, her cheeks getting redder by the second.

"Well, you tell me. Blaine or Duckie?" I asked.

"Blaine." She smiled, and her cheeks turned red.

"Why?" I'd always been fascinated by stories and characters. No wonder I became a writer.

"Because he's romantic and handsome. Because he deserves her, even though he doesn't think he's good enough. And because everyone else pales in comparison," she said, looking into my eyes. Her forehead creased with anxiety.

"Good point." I nodded.

"Do you think she should've been with Duckie?"

"No, I don't," I answered honestly. "The entire movie is about her and her feelings for the popular guy. For her to end up with the geeky best friend, that'd just be weird."

Leave it to me to dissect the plot. I knew that wasn't what Haddie was really asking me. But my writer brain always seemed to take over.

"I agree. She didn't like him like that."

"Exactly." I nodded. A long pause hung in the air as I tried to decide what to do. Just as I was getting the balls to tell her that I liked her. That I would never treat her the way Blaine treated Andie. That she was the coolest girl I knew, that everyone else paled in comparison... Auden walked out of the office. I heard the creaking of the door and knew she'd be in the room with us in just a few seconds. I picked my book back up from the coffee table and went back to my assignment. Wishing I had grown a pair.

"Oh my god," Auden shrieked as she ran over to Haddie, pulling her from the couch. "Movie's over, right? I need to talk to you!"

She dragged Haddie up the stairs and I didn't see her again for the rest of the night. Damn my sister.

∽

"How many times have you seen that movie?" I asked with a hearty laugh, remembering the tears streaking down her young face and picturing similar tears on her face right now.

"Too many to count," she replied.

"I believe it," I teased. "You always had a thing for that guy... Blake...."

"Blaine," she corrected me, so much sarcasm in her dainty voice.

"I know," I said with a cocky grin. "I remember watching it with you."

"You do?" she asked, sounding surprised, which gave me pause. Was she oblivious to how I felt about her?

"Oh yeah," I said, running my fingers through my hair. "Auden spent the entire movie in my dad's office."

Haddie's voice was soft and almost hesitant, "Yeah, she did." A long pause sat in the air, as heavy as a boulder sitting on the phone line.

"I remember," I insisted. More silence hovered between us. I must've been making her uncomfortable. "Do you still need help with your Valentine's Day dance?"

"Oh," she paused, "yes, definitely."

"Cool," I said, unable to control my smile.

"Can you come by Sunnyside sometime this week?"

"How's Thursday?"

"Perfect. Any time in the afternoon works for me."

"I'll see you then," I said.

"Thanks," Haddie replied. Her voice sounded a little sad.
"Oh, Haddie?"
"Yes?"
"Enjoy the movie. I hear the guy gets the girl," I said, my tone bold and flirtatious.
"Which guy?" She laughed, playing along. I could hear her smile through the phone. It felt good to make her smile. Really good.
I paused before answering, "The one who deserves her."
Silence. Beautiful silence. I think I stunned her. I hope I did, anyway.
"Good night, Haddie," I said, grinning from ear to ear.
"Night."
I hung up the phone, smiling to myself. I knew she had a boyfriend, but things can always change. We had a past, we had a history and I was now convinced that we could also have a future.

～

Hadley

My stomach was in knots as I hung up the phone.

I knew he was planning to call about volunteering at Sunnyside, but I didn't expect him to say those words.

I hear the guy gets the girl.
The one who deserves her.

Jason Kelly was into me. He was *really* into me. There was no other way to interpret those words. The thirteen-year-old girl in me wanted to bounce off the walls. But the grown-up took over and knew it was never going to happen.

In eight short months, I would be a mother. I would have a *child*. And even if Tucker wasn't in the picture, it was hard to believe that any single guy would want to take on that burden. A new girlfriend *and* a brand new baby? It'd be foolish of me to think anyone, even a kind, generous soul like Jason, would want that. I had no idea if Jason ever wanted to be a father, let alone date a woman who was carrying a child who wasn't his.

Too many thoughts rushed through my brain. My stomach flipped again and again. I turned off the television and ran down the hall to the bathroom. I made it there just in time. Unfortunately, my mom was walking down the long hallway and heard me emptying the contents of my stomach.

"Honey, are you okay?" my mom asked, tapping lightly on the door. I wasn't ready to tell her. I wasn't ready to admit that I had morning sickness or that my relationship with Tucker was unraveling.

The old Allison could've handled it. The mom I had had for nineteen years would have been the first person I would've gone to. Allison and Martin Foster would've supported me, no matter what. But this Allison—I wasn't sure about this Allison. The new version of my mother was another person entirely. And news like this might shake her too drastically. The thought gave me a panic attack and I just knew I couldn't tell her. Not yet.

"I'm fine," I said, standing up to rinse out my mouth.

"You don't look good."

"It's just a bug. I'll be okay."

"Can I help?"

"No, thanks. I'll be in my room."

I escaped into the comfort and solace of my bedroom, knowing the new Allison wouldn't pursue it further. She'd shrug her shoulders and go about her business. She'd take my words at face value and not push any further. But my mom—the mom I used to know—would be knocking on my door, insisting there was more to discuss. God, I missed her. I needed her so badly right now.

Instead of seeking the comfort of my mother's arms, these days I was seeking comfort in movies. As silly as that might sound, watching a movie from my childhood was soothing in a way I never expected. And one of my all-time favorites, *Pretty in Pink*, was quickly becoming my go-to movie since I'd discovered I was pregnant. Things were so unsettled in Andie's life. She didn't think things could possibly work out. But they did. And I clung to the hope that, like they did for Andie, things could possibly work out for me.

Jason's words were more than unsettling. For years, I had literally dreamed of the day that Jason Kelly would pursue a relationship with me. But now? Seriously?

Turning the TV back on, I escaped back into the world of Andie and Blaine, where at least I knew they would get their happily ever after.

CHAPTER NINE

Hadley
Seven weeks pregnant

"Hey," Tucker said as he entered the townhouse on a cold and bleak February evening. He took off his ski coat and draped it over the nearest stool at the breakfast bar. Tonight was the night. I had to tell him that he was going to be a father.

But I was terrified. Even before I took several pregnancy tests, I was pretty sure that Tucker and I were headed for a breakup. But now... now we would be linked for the rest of our lives. The baby was developing and growing each day. And every single day, I became more and more attached to the tiny life inside of me. I was still just as scared as I was the day I realized just how late my period was. But in very small ways, my maternal instincts were taking over, and I was falling in love with the idea of a child. Maybe I was naive. I didn't know. But I did know that Tucker had a right to know what was going on. And that I was scared as hell.

I kissed him lightly on the cheek before offering him something to drink. He gave me a slight, forced smile and I felt my stomach drop to my knees. Perhaps we were closer to a breakup than I had first expected.

"I'll have a beer," he said, sitting down on the couch. "Your house is quiet."

"Mom's working tonight," I said, sliding onto the plush fabric of the sofa. The smell of Tuck's beer caused my stomach to do tiny flip-flops. My gut instinct was to take a few deep breaths...but that was the last thing I should do. It would only make the smell stronger.

I'd been lucky. No routine morning sickness yet. Granted, it was still really early, according to the *What to Expect* book I'd picked up at the local bookstore. But I was getting sensitive to smells and tastes. Each day, my sensitivity grew and I dreaded how things would smell to me in a few weeks when my first trimester was in full swing. The thought made me shudder.

"So," Tucker said, taking a sip of his beer, "what's up? You said you needed to talk."

"Yes, I do," I said, my voice cracking. I cleared my throat and shifted my body to face him. He relaxed back into the couch, putting his arm against the back of the cushion.

"And?" He looked impatient with bulging eyes and pursed lips. Part of me wanted to avoid the truth and not tell him anything just yet. Keep it to myself just a little bit longer. But I couldn't. I knew it had to be today. *Here we go...*

"I...I—"

"Jesus, Hadley, just spit it out," he said, looking exasperated.

"I'm pregnant," I said. Silence.

"You're *what?*" he asked, raising his voice. His eyes bulged even further and his chest heaved up and down, up and down.

"Pregnant. As in 'with child,'" I said impatiently. Did he want me to spell it out for him?

"I don't understand." He shook his head. "You're on the pill. You've *always* been on the pill. How is that even possible?"

"I know I am, but—"

"What the fuck?" he yelled, pushing himself off of the couch. He paced the small living room, his long legs stopping at the wall before he turned to walk back in the other direction. His eyes darted between me and the front door. I couldn't believe what I was seeing. I knew he'd be shocked. I knew he wouldn't be happy. But this? I'd never expected this.

The nausea I felt from the smell of his beer was nothing compared to the butterflies bouncing around my belly. I knew I was going to be sick.

I ran to the bathroom and emptied my dinner into the toilet, doing my best to keep the tears from streaming down my face.

"Fuck! Look, I'm sorry," Tucker said from the hallway. I was unable to look at him. Quickly, I flushed the toilet and rinsed my mouth out with cold water. I walked past him into the kitchen, grabbing an Altoid from my purse.

The cool peppermint eased my throat and stomach. The burn from my sickness began to calm and a slight sense of peace washed over me, combined with a new sense of purpose. I needed to be strong for the baby and myself. And if Tucker couldn't be strong right along with me, then I guess that was how things would have to be.

"You should go," I said, unable to look him in the eye. He touched my arm—a light touch of his cold, hard fingertips.

"Sorry, I just—I came here because you wanted to talk. I thought we needed a break or something... and then you tell me you're pregnant! I mean, come on! How do you *expect* me to react?" His voice had risen to a shout. He placed both hands behind his neck and stared up at the ceiling. More silence.

"I'm in shock, Hadley. What in the hell are we going to do?"

"I can't...I don't...want to have this conversation anymore."

"Do you *want* this baby?"

"What kind of question is that?" I asked, the fear puddling in my mouth. *Don't ask me to do it, Tuck. Don't.*

He raised his eyebrows and pursed his lips, tipping his chin forward slightly. I knew exactly what that meant. When Tucker made that face, it's because he thought I was up to no good. Usually he made that face when we were joking around, when he'd had too many beers and I was giving him shit. But not about something like this.

"Do you think I *planned* this? Like I'm trying to trap you?" I spit the words out, disgusted and mortified at the same time.

"Well, the timing is really fucking weird," he said. "Can you blame me for being suspicious?"

"So you came over to break up with me?" I asked, not terribly shocked.

"I wasn't sure yet. But yeah, I thought we might be ending it." His unemotional shrug ran chills down my spine.

"And what? You think I got knocked up on purpose?"

He shrugged and pursed his lips again. "I don't know. I mean, yeah, it did cross my mind. I hear about these girls who stop taking their birth control to get pregnant, and the poor schmuck has no clue!"

"Need I remind you that you didn't use a condom on New Years? We've always used condoms! Always! I was drunk out of my mind! And it's your responsibility, too!"

"You're on the fucking pill, Hadley!" he screamed.

"Get out!" I hollered at the top of my lungs, grabbing his coat, opening the front door and throwing it onto a large pile of snow outside the townhouse.

"Goddammit!" he yelled, rushing to pick up the jacket, smacking it roughly to get the snow off the leather.

"Go home, Tucker. I have nothing else to say to you."

"Fine, but you're going to have to talk to me sooner or later."

"We'll see about that," I said as I slammed the door, quickly snapping the lock into place. Sinking to my knees, I placed my forehead in my shaking hands. I didn't expect tonight to be an easy conversation—I'd be really naive to think that way. But I'd spent six years of my life dating Tucker. Six years of loyalty, six years of monogamy. Six years of putting his needs ahead of my own. But now it wasn't about him and it wasn't even about me. It was about this baby. And that's how it had to be from now on.

CHAPTER TEN

Hadley
Eight weeks pregnant

Streamers and balloons hung from the small rec room of Sunnyside. Papier mâché hearts hung from the light fixtures by red, curly ribbons.

"It looks great," Pamela said as she walked into the room. "When does our DJ arrive?"

"He should be here pretty soon," I said, glancing at the clock. *Forty-two minutes. He'll be here in approximately forty-two minutes.*

Jason had visited Sunnyside twice since offering to help with tonight's dance. He impressed everyone with his friendly and outgoing personality. He was eager to talk to all of the clients. Little did he know that Lucy, Riley and many of the other women had been asking for him almost daily. I think some of them were hoping he'd get a permanent job here.

I was doing my best to view Jason as a volunteer who was simply helping the center. But with Jason it had always been so much more. My stomach flipped in anticipation of seeing him. And I hated myself a little bit for feeling that way. Maybe it was just hormones. Maybe they were messing with my head.

I'd lost five pounds so far during my few short weeks of pregnancy. My appetite was almost nonexistent and I was nauseated easily. Ellie kept our office stocked with ginger ale and saltines. She'd been great. Aside from Tucker, she was the only one who knew about the baby. I hadn't had the nerve to tell my mom yet, and Auden didn't remember a thing I said to her in the bathroom.

Tucker and I hadn't spoken since I threw him out two weeks ago. He'd called me a half-dozen times and sent me a bunch of text messages, but I just wasn't ready. I couldn't bring myself to answer the phone when I saw his number and I couldn't read his texts either. At that point, I wanted nothing to do with him. But he was right. I'd have to speak to him sooner or later. It was his baby, too.

"The clients are really excited for tonight," Pamela said with a smile.

"Oh good," I replied, stacking the CDs that Jason had dropped off earlier that morning. I was pleasantly surprised to see quite a bit of '80s music in the stacks. It brought a smile to my lips, which was a big freaking deal. I felt like I hadn't smiled all month. It was nice.

"We're really happy to have you here," Pamela said, biting her lower lip. And suddenly I realized that my sullen attitude might have given my boss mixed messages.

"Pamela, I—"

"I think you probably know that we have a really high turnover rate. I hope you'll be with us for a while."

"I hope so, too," I said, looking her directly in the eye. I wanted her to know my sincerity about working here. I wished I could tell her that my mood changes had nothing to do with Sunnyside. I couldn't possibly share my pregnancy with her, though. My first doctor appointment wasn't until next week. I didn't even know when I was due. I needed time to process all of it before my employer knew my situation.

Pamela sighed loudly before giving me a genuine grin. "I'm so happy to hear that. I'm sure tonight will be a huge success."

"I hope so. I know how much the clients have been looking forward to it."

"Nice touch, letting Bryce help with the DJ responsibilities."

"He's very excited."

"Jason seems nice."

"He is," I said with a nod.

"You've known each other for a long time, right? Since you were kids?"

"That's right. Did he tell you that?" I asked, confused. I was certain I'd never told Pamela anything about our past.

"Yeah, we talked for a bit in the break room this morning. He's a very nice young man." She winked at me. Pamela really didn't know anything about my personal life. She didn't even know I'd had a boyfriend. I kinda liked having a clean slate there. But obviously she'd picked up on something.

"What was that about?" I narrowed my eyes at her, referring to the wink.

"I'm just saying he seems nice. I'll be back in a bit."

Right when the room looked perfect for the dance, Jason knocked on the door. He was holding a small plastic container and my heart skipped a beat.

"Hey there," he said softly. "You look very pretty."

"Thanks," I said, trying really hard not to blush as he walked toward me. "What's that?"

"Just a little something I got for you," he said as he opened the container, revealing a sweet white calla lily corsage.

"You didn't have to do that," I said, holding out my wrist. Gently, he slid the elegant corsage over my hand. Goose bumps ran up my arms as his hand touched my skin.

"It's a dance, isn't it? You need a corsage." His green eyes locked with mine. I could hear my shallow breathing as I stared at him.

"It's gorgeous," I said, looking down at the flower. Calla lilies are so elegant. I'd always been fascinated by them. They almost look fake—that's how beautiful and elegant they are at first glance. But when you touch one and feel its delicate spathe, you know you're holding something so real, something so unique and lovely. I ran my fingers across the flower, taking in its smooth texture. It was breathtaking.

"Then it's perfect," Jason said, looking into my eyes and taking my hand in his. The walls felt like they were closing in on me. I had to get out of here. Right away.

"I—I'll be right back. I left something in my office." Quickly, I pulled my hand from his and Jason's smile disappeared.

"Sure," he said, as I offered him the best uncomfortable smile I could muster. Quickly, I walked out of the rec room and down the hall to one of the side doors. Pushing open the door, I stepped into the bitter February air, gasping for breath. Tears were threatening to spill, but I couldn't let that happen. I couldn't have red, blotchy skin. He would know.

This can't be happening. I can't be with Jason. I just can't.

But as I looked down at the corsage on my wrist, I knew that what I'd wanted for fourteen years was finally in my grasp. It felt like a cruel joke, one that I couldn't escape.
What in the hell am I going to do?
The clients were arriving one by one. I needed to pull myself together and get back to the rec room. By the time I took a few breaths and walked back inside, the disco lights were on and music was playing. Jason had taken charge in my absence.
I'm so lucky he's here.
One thing I'd learned during my time at Sunnyside—our clients loved to dance. They danced whenever they had the chance: at their work stations, when they finished eating lunch...anywhere, anytime. It didn't surprise me to see a large group already on the dance floor, swaying to the music pumping out of the speakers.

Jason had his headphones on and was busy talking to Bryce, his assistant DJ. When our eyes met, he smiled warmly at me. Guilt filled me from head to toe. There was nothing I'd rather do than be near him, to talk to him and learn more about him and his writing. His hopes and desires. I wanted to know if this gravitational pull I felt towards him was the real thing. I wanted to know if the right guy really did get the girl. But I couldn't bring myself to cross the dance floor and take that leap. I was too afraid. Lucy, Sam and Riley were standing in the center of the dance floor, swaying as they held each other's hands. They made my heart melt. I walked to them as the song switched to one of their all-time favorites, "Greased Lightning" from the *Grease* soundtrack.

Warren and Brian jumped up and down. They ran to the girls, showing off their T-Birds leather jackets. Bryce left Jason behind to join his friends on the dance floor with his matching black jacket. They immediately started lip-syncing to the song, doing the T-bird arm movements right along with John Travolta's Danny Zuko. The girls were swooning—they were literally standing off to the side, watching their friends serenade them. They were in heaven and so was I. It had to be one of the most adorable things I had ever seen in my life.

Without even thinking about it, I walked to Jason who was also watching them in awe.

"They are too cool," he said, shaking his head.

"I know," I replied, taking in the scene straight out of a musical.

"I'm glad I brought this," he said, raising his eyebrows, holding up the empty case for the *Grease* soundtrack. "There's more where that came from."

"You will have quite a few fans by the end of the night, Mr. Kelly."

"Will I?" His eyes brightened as he looked at me. And even though the look on his handsome face was genuine and sweet, I just couldn't handle it. If he knew my secret, he wouldn't look at me that way. I knew it. I felt it in my bones.

Casually, I nodded before heading back to the dance floor to stand with Nick, Ellie and a few other employees. Jason went back to his DJ duties.

"There's something there," Ellie whispered into my ear.

"I know."

"Just making sure you knew," she said, rubbing my arm.

"Yep, I know. And I have absolutely no idea what to do."

"Give it time. You'll figure it out."

"Thanks," I said, biting my lower lip, trying to keep the tears from leaving my eyes. Luckily the darkness of the room was the only camouflage I needed.

Several songs later, Jason handed off the headphones to Bryce, who smiled widely before placing them on his head. The two men talked briefly before Bryce grabbed the microphone.

"This one goes out to Hadley from Jason," Bryce said in a perfect DJ voice.

The notes of a familiar song spilled from the speakers and my breath was taken from my lungs. The song. *Our song.* The only song we had ever danced to. My fingers went numb as Jason walked around the DJ booth and stood in front of me.

"Shall we?" he asked, holding out his hand. I placed my hand in his and followed him onto the dance floor, just as the sound of the keyboard subsided and Susanna Hoffs' distinctive voice filled the air.

Close your eyes
Give me your hand,
Darlin...

Jason's lips formed a shy smile as he placed one hand on my waist and the other in my hand. We swayed together on the dance floor. Neither of us said a word. And as I listened to the lyrics, I was transported back to the first time we danced to this song.

It was my freshman year of high school and my very first high school dance. Auden and I didn't want to go stag. Girls who did that were usually ridiculed pretty badly. We'd agreed to go with two of our friends, Jay and Ryan. They were both awkward, skinny freshman who played for the water polo team. But we'd known them for years and thought we'd all have fun together.

My mom helped me pick the prettiest dress at Nordstrom. She curled my hair and applied my makeup. I felt so grown up. When Jay forgot to bring me a corsage, I didn't even care. I just wanted to go to the dance.

I knew Jason was going with his girlfriend of about a month and I was terrified to have to see them together. Her name was Brooke and I loathed her. I mean, I really despised the girl. She was all wrong for him. She was a junior and a member of the football cheerleading squad. She didn't study and didn't like to read. Jason didn't belong with someone like that. He needed someone who understood him. Who liked to read and to learn and who was fascinated by all of the things he was fascinated by. Why couldn't he see that girl was me?

We hadn't spoken in a long time. His parents had bought him an old Honda CRV and he was usually out with friends whenever I slept at Auden's. He was too cool for me. He was seventeen and driving, going on dates and staying out until curfew. I was just a loser freshman with a crush that wouldn't go away.

When Auden told me that his car was so old it didn't even have a CD player, I saw this as an opportunity to try one last time. I knew it was sad and pathetic. But I was a melodramatic adolescent and felt I needed to express myself through song. I used my parents' old stereo and created three mix tapes for him, full of my favorite '80s love songs. Some fast, some slow. Some sappy, some New Age. I'd written out the names of the songs on the cassette memo paper. I had no idea if he'd know my handwriting, so I left a note inside the cases.

"For Jason: Happy Driving. Love, Haddie"

Just like the t-shirt I'd given him two years before, I left the cassettes in a small gift bag in front of his bedroom door during a sleepover with Auden. When she returned from the bathroom, my best friend rolled her eyes at me, but said nothing. She knew there was nothing she could say or do to stop the way I felt. I guess she thought if she gave me enough rope, I'd simply hang myself.

Jason never thanked me for those tapes. And it broke my heart. That had been three months before and I'd avoided him ever since. But I knew I'd see him at the dance. Luckily, our gymnasium was large enough that I could dodge him whenever necessary.

The dance was okay. Auden and I joked about how similar it was to middle school dances. For some reason, we thought it'd be different somehow... more grown up, more refined, more mature. But it wasn't. Just a bunch of kids standing around in dresses and shirts and ties. About an hour into the evening, Jay and Ryan disappeared to joke around with a few of their water polo buddies. And Auden was gossiping with Leah, a girl from our history class. I stared off into space, watching the upperclassmen dance. When the song came to an end, the familiar sound of the Bangles filled the air and I felt a tap on my shoulder.

"Would you like to dance?" Jason asked. He was standing in front of me, his hand reaching out to mine.

"Sure," I said, barely able to choke the word out. He placed his hands on my waist and I put my hands up on his shoulders and we swayed. Back and forth. Back and forth.

"You don't have a corsage," he finally said, looking down at my hand.

"My date forgot," I said, shrugging.

"That sucks. You should have one."

"That's okay."

"Thanks for the tapes, Haddie."

"What?"

"The mix tapes."

"Oh... right."

"They're really good. I've been listening to them... a lot, actually." His eyes widened as he said that. And my heart skipped a beat.

"Thanks," I said. He stared into my eyes as if he had more to say but couldn't find the words. My heart was pounding so hard in my chest I was convinced he could hear it. In fact, I was convinced everyone in that gymnasium could hear it.

We swayed in silence for another minute until the song came to an end. As soon as the final note played, Jason released his hands from my waist and took a step back.

"Thanks for the dance," he said softly.

"Sure," I said. He smiled and walked away.

Soon Auden was at my side.

"Did you just dance with my brother?"

"Yes," I said, in a daze.

"Are you okay?"

"Better than okay." I smiled, holding my hand against my chest like the dramatic fourteen-year-old that I was.

The rest of the night was a blur. I think I danced with Jay and I'm pretty sure I danced with a few other boys from my class. But nothing else mattered. That simple dance with Jason was the best four minutes of my night.

"Do you remember this song?" Jason asked, looking into my eyes, drawing me back into the present.

"Of course I do," I said, swaying to the music with Jason. The lyrics of "Eternal Flame" bounced around and around inside my head. Tiny beads of sweat formed behind my neck. Electricity from his touch was shooting through my veins and I'd never felt so alive. Not even that night eight years ago at the Homecoming dance. This was more—so much more.

"We danced to it at Homecoming," I finally said.

"Yep, I requested it," Jason said with a smirk.

"You what?"

"I requested it that night."

"You did? Wait...why?"

"It was on one of the mix tapes."

Holy crap. It was on one of the tapes? I can't believe I hadn't realized that all those years ago. I was so stunned that it was completely lost on me when he asked me to dance.

"And I think you know why," Jason said, pulling me closer and pressing his head to mine. We swayed to the song, as I dreaded the familiar chords of the final verse.

"Jase, I—"

"I know you have a boyfriend," Jason said softly into my ear. "But I'm not giving up."

"You're not?" I asked, feeling like the wind had been knocked out of me.

"Nope."

"What do you mean?"

"The right guy gets the girl, remember? I'm going to show you who that guy is."

So desperately I wanted to kiss him. I wanted to pretend that our future wasn't already doomed from the start. I wanted to tell him that I had been in love with him for fourteen years. Instead, I glanced at the lily on my wrist.

"You bought me a corsage tonight because I didn't have one at Homecoming?" I said, a tear forming in my eye.

"Yep."

"You remember so much."

"I remember everything, Haddie. Everything."

The song ended, and I forced myself to pull away. Before I was able to utter a word, Warren tapped Jason's shoulder.

"May I cut in?" he asked. Jason smiled widely and patted him on the shoulder. He was so gracious even in times of thick, unfathomable tension.

"Of course, buddy."

Jason kissed my hand.

"Another dance later, perhaps?"

Unable to resist smiling at his charm, I nodded.

"Perhaps," I replied, a tear rolling down my cheek.

And just like that night fourteen years ago, the rest of the evening was a total blur. I know I danced with Warren, and I'm pretty sure I danced with several other clients. But the best four minutes of the evening was the short time Jason Kelly held me in his arms.

CHAPTER ELEVEN

Hadley
Nine weeks pregnant

Barry Manilow sang softly through the speakers of my gynecologist's office. I had just been here for my annual exam several months ago and truthfully, I was embarrassed to be back again so soon. Most of the women in the waiting area were in their late twenties or thirties. Most of them appeared to be pregnant. Some looked uncomfortable with large, bulging bellies. One woman had a tiny little bump but was clearly ready for people to acknowledge her pregnancy. She was wearing a maternity blouse that accentuated her belly, and she continuously rubbed her tummy as she waited to be called back to an exam room.

The paperwork was ridiculous. Questions about screenings, blood tests, ultrasounds, etc. My head was swimming as I paged through it all. I wished my mom were there to know which boxes to check. Better safe than sorry. Checking all the boxes, I signed off on every screening possible. When I finished checking the final box, a nurse called me back. Before even saying a word, she placed a plastic cup in my hand.

"We need a sample from you. Write your name on the cup, put the cap back on and leave it in the window inside the bathroom. Then meet me in Room Four."

"All right."

Geez, that was a lot of instructions. My brain was on overload. And as silly as it may sound, I felt like the nurse was judging me with her eyes. Thinking about how stupid young people are these days, having unprotected sex, blah blah blah. I forced myself to take a deep breath and followed the directions I was given.

After leaving my urine sample, I made my way to Room four. The nurse was waiting for me. She took my blood pressure and weight before asking me to remove my sweatshirt. It was time for blood work. Vial after vial sat on the table, taunting me.

"Um, are you going to fill all of those?" The blood drained from my face.

"It's not as much as it seems. Can you make a fist for me?"

The nurse pressed on my skin to find a vein. Turning my head, I stared at the wall, feeling a pinch.

"Okay, open your hand," she said softly. Her voice was surprisingly soothing.

She finished filling several vials before applying a Band-Aid and patting me gently on the forearm. Next, she handed me a gown. I noticed a large machine in the room with a projection screen on the wall.

"Dr. Myers is going to give you an internal ultrasound. You'll need to remove your pants and underwear. There's a sheet for you to cover up."

"All right." I felt like that was the only phrase in my current vocabulary. My brain was too scattered to think of anything else to say.

Dr. Myers walked in just a few minutes after I perched myself on the exam table. She was a woman in her mid-thirties with long brown hair and bright blue eyes. I'd always found her beautiful. But today, she looked stunning, almost as if she was glowing.

"Hadley, back so soon? You were here—" she paused to glance at my chart, "in November, right? Is everything okay?"

"I'm pretty sure I'm pregnant," I muttered.

"Ohhh," she said, pulling her stool up to the table where I sat, almost squirming. "I'm guessing this wasn't planned?"

I shook my head while pursing my lips.

"I see...well, now I know why we're in Room Four." She looked back to my chart. "Okay, so the first day of your last period was December seventeenth."

"Right."

"So you're about two months pregnant, assuming you *are* pregnant."

"Is it possible that I'm not?"

"Yes. Missed periods usually do mean pregnancy, but there's always a chance that something else is happening. Stress, a hormonal imbalance. You've lost weight, and you've always been trim...it could be that you're not storing enough fat to get your period. Have you started a new exercise regimen?"

"No. But I've been throwing up a lot."

"Ahh. Did you leave a urine sample?"

"Yes." I nodded.

"I'll be right back. You just sit tight."

Dr. Myers patted me gently on the knee before walking out of the room. About five minutes later she returned, looking serious. She sat back down on the stool and patted my knee again.

"Your urine test was positive. You are definitely pregnant."

"All right." There was that word again.

"Do you want to talk about it?" Dr. Myers asked.

"Um... not sure what to say."

"Well, we can discuss your options...." Her words trailed off.

"I don't want an abortion."

"Okay, I respect that," she said with a warm smile. "Lie back; we're going to do an internal ultrasound."

She sat down, pulling the large machine towards us. Placing latex gloves on her hands, she then selected a plastic wand from the side of the machine.

"This is going to go inside of you. It's a little uncomfortable, but as you can see, it's no larger than a penis. Just remember to breathe, okay?"

"Okay," I replied, shaking my head at myself.

"Let's get started," she said. I took a deep breath and stared at the projection screen on the wall. The wand was uncomfortable, but I was so focused on the little *thump thump thump* on the screen that I barely even noticed it.

"What is that?" I asked, pointing at the little circle that was throbbing out of control.

"That's the heartbeat."

"Ohhh," I said, left speechless. My baby had a heartbeat. My baby had a *heartbeat*.

"I'm going to do some measurements, but I'm pretty sure everything is right on schedule. You appear to be nine weeks along."

"So, that means I'm due in..."

"We'll take a look at the calendar in a moment. Just relax and look at your baby."

"It's so small."

"That's normal," she reassured me as she clicked the buttons on the keyboard, measuring the different dimensions of the baby.

"Can you tell if it's a boy or a girl?"

"Not yet. We'll be able to see that around twenty weeks or so."

"Sorry, stupid question, I guess." My cheeks reddened with embarrassment.

"There are no stupid questions during pregnancy. If you're curious about something, just ask. And you'll want a copy of *What to Expect When You're Expecting*."

"I bought it."

"Good. Then you're on the right track." She removed the wand and told me to sit back up.

"Everything looks good. Let's figure out your due date."

"All right."

She looked down at a calendar on the desk.

"September twenty-third."

"Really? That's so soon." My heart was pounding and I felt faint. Suddenly, it was hard to swallow. And the room felt smaller somehow. Smaller and warmer. Yes, someone had definitely turned up the heat in this tiny shoebox of a room.

"Believe me, it's longer than it seems. By the end of July you'll realize just how long nine months is." Dr. Myers chuckled as she patted my leg. Despite the fact that she was obviously attempting to comfort me, the constant patting of my leg was really starting to annoy me.

"Whenever you're ready, you can get dressed. And I'd like to see you back here in four weeks."

"Thanks."

"Sure...and Hadley, I know this is a lot to take in. Make sure you get a support system in place."

"Right." My teeth clamped onto my bottom lip.

"You're gonna need supportive people in your life."

"I know."

"I know I shouldn't pry, but I've known you since you were seventeen. The father? Will he be involved?"

"Honestly...I have no idea." I said, as tears formed quickly in my already wet eyes.

"That's the first step. Figure that out first and you can handle the rest as it comes."

"Thanks, Dr. Myers."

"Of course. Take care and we'll see you in a month."

Once the door had closed behind her, I got dressed and walked to the front desk to make my next appointment. When she asked for my insurance card, I panicked. Reality check number God-knows-how-many for this incredibly surreal day. I wouldn't be able to hide this from my mother for long. I had to tell her before any bills arrived from the office. This was getting more and more overwhelming by the minute. But that tiny little beating heart had found its way into mine.

∼

I walked to the phone and made the call I'd been dreading since I had seen that tiny little person on the screen. I owed it to that little person to make this call.

"Hey," he said, answering after several rings.

"Hey." Silence.
"You're going to talk to me now?"
"I think I have to."
"Yeah." More silence.
"I'm due September twenty-third."
"So you're definitely having it?"
"Tucker!"
"I'm serious. You should think about it, at least!"
"I have thought about it."
"And?"
"I saw the heartbeat."
"What? Already?"
"Yes."
"Oh," he paused, "what about us?"

"What do you mean?" I asked, hoping to stall. I wasn't in love with Tucker. Of this, I was certain. "Do you love me?" I decided to cut to the chase.

Another pause. A very long pause.
"Had..."
"Just answer. Don't worry about hurting me. Answer."
"I don't think so, no." Instead of feeling anxious or hurt or sad, I felt relief. Unbelievable relief.
"Okay then."
"And you?" he asked.
"No," I said as gently as I could.
"Wow." I could hear the relief in his voice, as well. Although he seemed genuinely surprised. Asshole.
"Think about it. I won't pressure you. I know you aren't ready to be a father."
"Right, but I should help you. I mean, what are you gonna do?"

"You know money isn't an issue," I said.

"Oh right, the money from your dad."

"Yeah." When my father passed away, he had had a substantial life insurance policy. My mom and I were very well taken care of. But that didn't make me miss him any less. I still ached for my dad...every single day.

"Don't feel obligated," I added.

"I don't...I mean. You know what I mean."

"Yeah."

"I'm sorry," he said, clearing his throat after saying the words. As if they tasted terrible coming out of his mouth. Tucker doesn't like to admit he's wrong.

"For what?" I asked.

"You know—for thinking you did this on purpose. That was fucked up."

"It was," I scoffed.

"Do you forgive me?"

"Not yet," I said, matter of fact. It was the truth.

"I'm not sure I'm ready to be a dad."

"I know."

"We're only twenty-two. I just finished college. I just started this job. And things are going really well. I just don't—"

"Tuck, stop." I couldn't listen anymore. I knew all the reasons why this baby wasn't planned. I didn't need to hear them listed for me again and again. It wouldn't change the way I felt.

"All right."

"I have my next appointment in a month. I'll call you after that and we'll see how we feel about things."

"Fine, okay. But what about you and me?"

"I think it's pretty obvious."

An uncomfortable pause took over the already tense conversation. He was making *me* say it. Tucker never did well with guilt either.

I sighed and told him what he wanted to hear. "We're over, Tuck. We both know it."

"I guess I needed to hear *you* say it."

"So you won't feel like the asshole who dumped his pregnant girlfriend?"

"No. I swear. I just... you know, I had to know for sure. That you'd be okay without me."

"I'll survive without you, Tuck," I scoffed again.

"I know."

"And we're not going to stay together just for the baby. He deserves better than that."

"It's a boy?" he asked, his voice hopeful for the first time during this entire conversation.

"No. I mean, maybe. I don't know yet. It's too early."

"Oh." He sounded disappointed.

"Do you want a boy?" I asked, confused.

"Shit, I don't know." His voice turned defensive and I knew this conversation had run its course.

"Right. I should go," I said.

"Call me next month?"

"Sure, bye."

I sank down to my bed, hugging my stomach and crying. Hard. An ugly cry that hadn't happened in years... not since Dad had died. I needed to let Tucker go. But he'd been my lifeline, my safety net, my life preserver... for years. Literally years of my life had been spent depending on Tucker. Turning to him when I needed to cry, when I needed to throw things because I missed my dad so goddamn much. He had been there for me. Always. He'd hold my hair when I threw up after drinking my sorrows away. He'd hold my hand as I sobbed. He was just... there.

And because of that, I'd felt indebted to him. I'd felt like I was his to take or leave... like our entire relationship was up to him. But it wasn't about me anymore. And it wasn't about Tucker. It was about that tiny little life on the screen. That fluttering little heart.

I pushed up on my elbows and reached for the phone on my bedside table. It was time to tell her. I needed her with me, desperately.

Sobbing into the phone, I choked on the words, "Can you come over?"

Without skipping a beat, Auden answered, "Give me ten minutes."

~

Auden held me, stroking my hair as I wailed into her chest, grabbing on to her sleeves for dear life. She'd been holding me like this for at least twenty minutes and hadn't pushed me to tell her what was going on. She knew I had to get it out.

Finally, when I was completely exhausted from crying, I managed to find the words.

"I'm pregnant," I whispered.

A long pause went by. And then a deep sigh. Not one of disappointment. Of that I was sure. It was a sigh of contemplation. She wanted to help me, but had no idea how.

"Tucker?" she asked.

"Yes."

"Are you sure?"

"I haven't been with anyone else. And the doctor confirmed it today."

"How far along are you?" she asked calmly, still threading her fingers through my hair.

"Nine weeks. I'm due September twenty-third."

"Wow," she whispered.

"I know... it's so soon," I said. Another tear slipped from my eye. It landed heavily on my hand, and I wiped it away with the sleeve tucked around my hand. Whenever I'm upset, my shirts get wrapped up like that. My mom says I've done it since I was really young. And here I was again... tucked up like a child, crying on my best friend as a child grew inside of me. It was all too surreal.

"Do you know what you're gonna do?" she asked.

"I'm going to keep it."

"You know you don't *have* to, right?" Auden asked, no judgment in her voice.

I sat up and looked her square in the eyes. "What do you mean?"

"You know..." her voice trailed off as she raised an eyebrow, looking at my stomach. "You're only twenty-two. You have so much you still want to do."

I shook my head, "That's not what I want."

"I just want you to be sure. This is a huge decision."

"Believe me, I know that," I said, feeling myself getting defensive.

"What did Tucker say?"

"He doesn't want it." I shrugged.

"Can you blame him, sweetheart? You two have been sketchy at best."

"I know, but—I just can't. I can't do that."

"Look, you took care of your dad, and now you take care of your mom. When are you going to take care of *you*? When does your life get to be about *you*, Hadley?"

"I don't know." More tears rushed out as I scrunched my eyes together in frustration. "When did my life spin so out of control? I had plans. And those plans made sense. None of this makes sense to me. None of it."

"Maybe that's the beauty of it."

"What do you mean?"

"You've always been scheduled; you've had routines that made sense. Things are a little crazy right now, but maybe that's how it's supposed to be...maybe you weren't shaking things up enough on your own. Someone else is shaking them up for you."

Auden shrugged and looked up at the ceiling. But I didn't want to talk about God. I didn't want to talk about fate. I just wanted things to make sense again. I wanted my life to fit the picture I had in my head...and it was panning out to be nothing like that picture. Not at all.

"Whatever you decide, I'm here for you. You know that," Auden said, squeezing my hand.

"I do."

"So, what's next?"

"I see the doctor in a month."

"Okay."

"And I broke up with Tucker."

"I've been waiting for that," she said with a smile.

"It's like a part of me has died."

"Six years is a long time...and those last three were brutal. But he's not the one, sweetheart."

"I know," I said, curling up and placing my head on Auden's crisscrossed legs. She instinctively rubbed my back and hummed a song.

Tucker had been my safe place for three years, my secure dock in a sea of indecision as I dealt with my father's illness and death. And now I had to sink or swim. It was time to let go and move on. Slowly, I pushed off from the dock that was Tucker Montgomery and prepared to swim...praying I wouldn't drown.

CHAPTER TWELVE

Jason
Six weeks later

I didn't mean to make Hadley uncomfortable that night at the dance. But I'm pretty sure that's exactly what I did. Something came over me and I just had to tell her how I felt... that she was worth fighting for. I was determined to show her that we're a good fit, a good match. I knew she felt something for me. I knew she'd felt that way for years. But maybe I'd just missed my chance. Maybe I'd waited too long and managed to lose her.

But I was *not* giving up.

I'd meant every single word I said.

Completely and entirely.

I was done pushing my feelings away.

Haddie and I were emailing practically every day, but we hadn't actually spoken since the dance. Madeline had finally started to cooperate, so I'd been writing like crazy, funneling all of my frustration and emotions over my feelings for Haddie into my novel. I was almost there, almost finished. My editor was expecting it by May 1st, which gave me just a couple more weeks.

I was nervous as hell to see Haddie. I was volunteering at Sunnyside for the next several months until the big performance in August. I was excited to see her weekly. And if I was being honest with myself, I really was looking forward to volunteering at the center. Her clients were so full of life, so lighthearted and fun. I had had such a great time at that dance, even when I wasn't with Haddie. Bryce was a killer DJ's assistant, so eager to help keep our audience entertained. I looked forward to helping them select songs for the big performance. I suspected Bryce would be instrumental in that.

Haddie had also asked me to assist her with choreography, props and costumes. Oh, and sets, too. So, pretty much every aspect of the show, which was just fine with me. Each Thursday, I'd be there for about four hours, assisting with all of those things.

I was happy to have the opportunity to spend more time with her, to show her how much I cared and that this thing between us was far from over. With every fiber of my being, I felt like our story had just begun.

I tried my best to calm my nerves as I walked through the doors of Sunnyside. The receptionist gave me a smile and directed me to the rec room where Haddie and Ellie were meeting. I was right on time.

They sat at a long wooden table, looking at Haddie's laptop. I assumed they were looking at playlists because each of them took turns pointing at the screen and laughing about songs and singers. Just as I was about to say hello, Haddie looked up, as if she could feel my presence.

Her cheeks turned a gorgeous shade of pink and she pushed her hair behind her ears. She looked different, but I couldn't quite put my finger on it. Was it the tone of her skin, maybe the style of her hair? I swear she may have even had a few new freckles on her cheeks. No matter what the changes were, she looked stunning.

"Hey," she said. She didn't stand up, and pulled nervously on her shirt as she gave me a shy smile.

"Great seeing you again." Ellie stood to greet me, shaking my hand.

"Thanks," I said, pulling up a chair and joining them at the table, purposely sitting opposite Haddie so I could have the best possible view of her. It had been way too long since I'd seen those sky blue eyes and that golden hair.

"We're choosing the music for the show. We'll need to have about eight songs in all. And they have to fit our theme."

"Let me guess—the '80s?"

"Pretty close," Ellie said, rolling her eyes.

"John Hughes?"

Haddie's cheeks grew crimson as she closed her eyes tight. That grimace made it obvious. My guesses were *really* close.

"The theme is Soundtrack of the '80s. All of the songs will be from the '80s and many of them will be from movies of the decade. And there may be a song or two from John Hughes' movies."

"Of course," I said with a grin. "Simple Minds is a must."

"Absolutely," Haddie said, typing on her laptop.

"Who are they again?" Ellie said, looking confused.

"'Don't You Forget About Me'?" Haddie asked, pretending to be irritated. "It's the song at the end of *The Breakfast Club*. It's genius."

"Oh...right," Ellie said. "What else should we have?"

"'If You Leave'," I suggested and Haddie stopped dead in her tracks. This was the second time *Pretty in Pink* had come up in our conversations. I wasn't trying to put her on the spot... well, maybe I was. It worked. She tucked her hair behind her ear and looked back at her laptop without making eye contact.

"Yeah, that could be a good one," she said softly, glancing quickly in my direction before staring back at the screen, completely dodging my stare. It was a good time to change the subject.

"I'm guessing you're not a huge fan of the '80s?" I asked Ellie.

"That's right. Because I'm a normal twenty-five-year-old. I'm a child of the '90s. If it was up to me, the entire show would be Counting Crows music."

"Yuck," Haddie said. "They're depressing. This show needs to be fun and upbeat. Music that makes you want to dance."

"Fine, whatever," Ellie said. Just then, her husband Nick popped his head in.

"Ells, I need you for a minute."

Ellie hopped up from her seat, gave us a wave and followed Nick out the door. Their voices trailed off as they walked down the main hall of Sunnyside, leaving Haddie and me with the silence lingering between us.

"How've you been?" I asked, leaning in towards her. More than anything, I hoped to break her shyness with my persistence.

"Fine," she said with a nod, avoiding eye contact. Maybe I had pushed too hard at the dance. Maybe I'd invented the connection between us. Maybe I was making her uncomfortable. The thought made my stomach churn.

"'In Your Eyes'?" I asked, getting back to the task at hand.

"Huh?" She looked flustered as she put her hands up near her eyes.

"The song," I said, unable to hide my smirk.

"Oh." She laughed. "I guess I misunderstood," she said, looking back down at her keyboard, shaking her head at herself.

"Your eyes are gorgeous. But when I'm talking about them, you'll know."

Haddie lifted her chin so that her eyes locked with mine. My pulse was surprisingly calm as a satisfied smile crossed my face. She opened her mouth to speak, but said nothing. The tension was palpable. I could hear the soft rise and fall of her chest. She was trying her best to hide it, but I knew I'd rattled her. And in the best possible way. None of this was in my head. *None of it.*

Ellie returned just as Haddie's cheeks returned to their normal porcelain shade. We brainstormed the list of songs to use and, I had to admit, we had a really great program planned. I could practically see Bryce, Warren and the other guys dressed up like *Ghostbusters* singing, "Who ya gonna call?"

At three o'clock, it was time for me to go. I wanted to stick around, to spend just a few more minutes with her. Haddie and Ellie had bus duty, though, so I packed up my things and threw my backpack over my shoulder.

"I'll walk you out," Haddie said, finally rising to her feet. She wore a flowing shirt and leggings. She looked gorgeous, but even more self-conscious than usual. She grabbed her notebooks and binders and pressed them to her chest. Did she think I would try to check out her boobs in the middle of Sunnyside? I was into her, but I was no pig.

We walked in silence towards the exit. Before I lost my nerve, I took her hand in mine. Haddie looked down at our joined fingers and didn't pull away. It was a start.

"Auden told me," I paused. Her eyes widened and her mouth opened. I waited for her to speak, but no words came out. So I continued, "About you and Tucker."

"Oh," she said, looking relieved. Her reaction left me confused. What else would there be to tell?

"Do you have plans this Saturday night?"

"I—um..." Haddie said, looking around her, blushing again.

"I know you haven't been single for very long—"

"That's...um. That's not it."

"What am I missing?"

"Are you sure Auden didn't tell you anything else?" She looked serious...and terrified.

"Absolutely. Is there something else I should know?" I asked, suddenly nervous as I gazed into her eyes. God, she was so beautiful. I wanted to go back to the seventeen-year-old version of myself and punch him in the face for letting her slip through his fingers. Idiot.

"Hadley Foster, you're needed in Area C," a voice said into the intercom above us. Damn it.

"I have to go, I'm sorry. I'll see you next week."

And with that, she turned and walked down the long hallway of Sunnyside. I'd come here determined to ask her out, get answers and have something to look forward to. But I was leaving more confused than I'd ever been.

CHAPTER THIRTEEN

Hadley
Sixteen weeks pregnant

Tick. Tock. Tick. Tock. The large clock in Dr. Myers's office was the only thing I could focus on. My heart was pounding so fast and I had an empty feeling in the pit of my stomach. When the doctor had called and asked that I come in this morning, I knew something was wrong. I had had a normal appointment last week. I'd heard the heartbeat, and everything had measured normal. My vitals were okay and there seemed to be nothing to worry about. So why the hell did they need to see me?

Dr. Myers entered the office, a grim look upon her face. I forced myself to take a deep breath as I shifted back and forth in the uncomfortable chair.

"Good morning," she said, sitting in her chair and opening my chart. "Hadley, I asked you to come in this morning so that we can discuss the results of your triple screen."

"My what?"

"At your last appointment, we did several standard blood tests for this stage of your pregnancy. One of those tests is the triple screen. You signed off on it on your first visit. We use it to classify a patient as either high-risk or low-risk for chromosomal abnormalities and neural tube defects like Down syndrome and Trisomy 18. After your first trimester neural tube screening, it was recommended that you have the triple screen. Do you remember?"

"Yeah, I, um...I guess I forgot. It's been a lot to take in." My mouth was dry and swallowing was difficult. Had I put my baby at risk? I remembered the phone call. I remembered the nurse explaining that they'd be drawing more blood. But I didn't understand why. I should've asked questions. I should've done more.

"I understand," she said. "All of this can be very overwhelming." She stared at me for a moment, her mouth open slightly. "You're very pale. Can I get you a glass of water?"

I shook my head no and my eyes began to water.

"My baby is sick?" I asked, my heart exploding in my chest.

"No, not necessarily. This test just showed that you are at a high risk for a diagnosis of Down syndrome. We'll know more in a few weeks when we give you another ultrasound. You also have the option of an amniocentesis."

"That's dangerous, right?" I'd watched enough *Grey's Anatomy* to know what an amnio was, and that it wasn't an ideal test for the mother or baby.

"There are risks, yes. But then you'd know for sure and can make a decision."

"A decision?" God, I felt so naive. Everyone was hinting that I consider terminating the pregnancy. Yet, I walked around like a deer in headlights, not even considering it an option. "I don't understand. I'm in my second trimester."

"It can still be done. In fact, many women choose to terminate...after careful consideration, of course."

"Many women...?" I stammered, unable to put a coherent thought together.

"We can schedule an amnio at the hospital and then you can make a decision."

"Or?"

Dr. Myers's lips formed a tight line. She inhaled deeply before speaking, "Or, we can wait a few more weeks and give you an ultrasound. It's not as definitive as an amnio, but we can measure the skin on the fetus's neck as well as the length of his femur. There are many soft signs of Down's that can be indicated on an ultrasound. But I must warn you, Hadley. It's not one hundred per cent accurate. Just last week, I delivered a baby whose ultrasound showed he'd be at least ten pounds. That baby was barely eight pounds. Ultrasound is a beneficial tool, but it is not diagnostic."

"Okay," I said, my hands sweating and my mind racing. "Can I think about it?"

"Of course. Call the office by Monday, please. If you want an amnio, it's best to get it as soon as possible."

"Thanks," I muttered, walking out of the office. Once in my car, I sat in silence, unable to focus. I couldn't even begin to wrap my mind around everything she'd said.

The baby may have Down syndrome.
But then again, the baby may be just fine.
The baby could have neural tube effects—I don't even know what that means.
The baby may have Trisomy 18. I don't know what that means either.
I can find out what those things mean if I agree to an amnio.
I can also find out if my baby is okay.

I work with developmentally disabled adults.
I love my job. More than I ever imagined I could.
And yet the thought of raising a developmentally disabled child terrifies me to my very core.
Can I handle this? Am I good enough to handle it?
Am I a hypocrite for wanting a healthy baby?
When did my life start spinning so out of control?
And when will it ever make sense again?

So many thoughts, racing through in the swirling mess that was my brain. I glanced at the clock, knowing I needed to get back to work. As much as I wanted to take a sick day and curl up in my bed for the rest of the morning, I was certain that would only make me feel worse. I needed to be where things made a little bit of sense to me...and that was at Sunnyside. It was a perfect distraction.

I was so frazzled, I couldn't even remember how I got back to work as I pulled into a parking spot at the center. I parked the car and somehow made it to my office without breaking down. Closing the door behind me, I sank into the couch, leaning my elbow on the soft fabric; I rested my head on my hand as I gazed out the window. Tears streamed down my cheeks. I wiped them away with my sweater as I watched the tree branches bump against the window. I was so focused on the branches being pushed back and forth by the wind that I missed the sound of my office door opening.

"Haddie?" a familiar voice said, shocking me back to reality. I wiped my face and turned to see Jason.

He's here. Why on earth is he here?

"Hey," I managed to say.

"I shouldn't have walked in, I'm sorry. You weren't in the conference room, so..."

"Oh God. It's Thursday, isn't it?" I said in a panic. Of course Jason was here. He was here every Thursday to help with the show. When my doctor had called early that morning, I'd completely lost track of everything else, including the day of the week. Mortified at my gigantic oversight, I covered my face with my hands. I didn't want him to see me like that.

"What's going on?" he asked, sitting next to me on the couch, placing his hand on my knee. His fingertips stroked my kneecap back and forth as he peered into my eyes. And suddenly, I felt safe. I felt like I could tell him anything, share anything, confess *everything*.

"I'm having a baby," I said, pressing my lips together to keep the tears from spilling from my eyes. Jason's eyes widened for a second. He opened his mouth, but then closed it again and continued to stroke my knee.

"I had no idea," he said. The sincerity in his voice was unmistakable. Auden hadn't told him. It was still locked up tight in her vault.

"One of the screenings came back positive. And I don't know what to do," I said, looking into his eyes, hoping he'd have an answer for me.

"Positive? For what?"

"Down syndrome or something called Trisomy 18. I don't even know what that is. But something could be wrong with my baby," I choked on the words. Jason jumped up from the couch, grabbed the box of tissue from Ellie's desk and sat back down, handing me a tissue.

"I'm so sorry," he said, stroking my knee once again.

"What am I gonna do?" Pulling on the neck of my shirt so hard, I was afraid the top button might pop.

"What did your doctor say?" Jason asked, gently prying my hand from my shirt and holding it in his own.

"She wants me to have an amnio. But I don't think I want to."

"So don't," he said matter-of-factly.

"It's not that simple."

"It's not?" Jason asked. His voice was gentle but confident. He was pushing me to figure this out for myself.

"What if the baby is sick?"

He looked me dead in the eye before he spoke, "Will you love the baby any less?"

"I don't know," I replied, shaking my head.

"I do." He nodded. "I've seen you with these clients. You're a natural. You're patient and kind. And they all love you for it."

"But that's not the same. I get to go home at the end of the day. Being a mother is all the time. Twenty-four, seven."

"I have total faith in you. But really think about this.... Will you love this child less if it has Down syndrome or some other health condition? Will this baby be any less a part of you if that should happen?"

"No," I managed a weak smile as a fresh tear rolled down my cheek, "I won't love it any less."

Jason nodded as he pressed his hand to my scalp and smoothed down my hair, tucking it behind my ears.

"You can handle this; I feel it in my gut. You can do this."

"Thanks for having faith in me," I replied, overwhelmed at how kind and gentle Jason Kelly continued to be. "I just keep thinking that I'm only twenty-two."

Jason chuckled. "My mom was nineteen."

"Really?" Auden had never mentioned how old her mother was when she became pregnant with Maya.

"Yep. And I think we all turned out okay," he said, nudging me gently in the arm. "Look, age doesn't matter at times like this. What matters is character. And I have no doubt about yours."

"Wow, I don't know what to say," I said, looking into his deep green eyes. His demeanor changed slightly and he cracked his knuckles. I'd made him uncomfortable. What on earth was going through his head?

"Can I ask you something?" he asked finally, shifting a little in his seat.

"Sure. I don't have anything to hide anymore." I laughed.

"Last week, when I asked you out...you said no. Is this why?"

"Yes." I nodded.

"That makes me feel a little better," he said with a shy, lopsided grin.

"I'm sorry," I said. Jason shook his head and glared at me.

"No...don't be sorry. You've done *nothing* wrong. That's my stuff, not yours."

"It's just so overwhelming.... I mean, I waited years for you to ask me out. Literally, years. And now, I can't possibly do it. Not that you'd want to anymore, anyway."

He tilted his head and licked his lips, placing both of his hands on my knee.

"It doesn't change anything—not for me," he said.

"What?" My hand flew to my chest.

"Maybe it sounds crazy, but I still want to take you out on that date."

"I don't know..."

"Think about it. I'll respect whatever you want. I've been waiting to ask you out for six years, though. I'm not giving up so easily."

"You're kidding, right?" I laughed. I couldn't believe he was able to make me smile and laugh at that moment. This man had a power over me that no one else ever did. That was clear.

"Not at all. But I'm not going to pressure you."

"Thanks. That means a lot."

"I just want to know you better." He shrugged.

"I want that, too," I said. My resolve began to slip away.

"Just think about it and let me know. If you want to be friends, then that's what we'll be. I want to spend time with you no matter what. We've spent too much time apart already," he said with a chuckle.

"That sounds nice."

Somehow, Jason managed to keep my tears from returning. Eventually we made our way to the conference room to meet with Ellie about the show. And as we discussed the performance, the music and the props, I found myself getting lost in Jason's handsome features. The two little freckles on his neck that I always fixated on when he'd sit on the couch in his basement, reading a book or watching a movie....I loved those two little brown flecks on his pale skin. Being friends with Jason wouldn't be easy, but the thought of not having him in my life scared me to death. He believed in me. He had faith in me. And that gave me hope. Maybe I could handle all of this. Maybe...just maybe.

Allison Foster's mouth was agape as she stared at me from the couch across the small living room. The silence that hovered over us was killing me.

"Say something. Please, Mom..."

"I—I don't know...." Her face was puzzled, conflicted...and full of emotion. Wow. Who knew that all I had to do to get my mother to feel again was to get pregnant?

"Something, anything, please," I pleaded.

"You're so young...you had plans, I—"

"I know."

"And you're so far along. Why didn't you tell me? Why?" Her forehead creased for the first time in years.

"I didn't know what to tell you and I didn't know how you'd react. But now, with these test results.... I'm overwhelmed. I *need* you, Mom."

She breathed in deeply, staring off into space for several seconds before standing up. My heart ached with dread. Was she going to walk away from me now when I needed her the most?

A concerned expression spread across her lips and she crossed the room to sit next to me. She placed her arm around me in an awkward motion, almost like that of a marionette. But I embraced the gesture and leaned into her shoulder, tears spilling from my eyes. I hadn't felt the safety of her arms for so long...since before Dad died. Before she'd retreated into herself. Before she'd stopped being the mom I knew and loved so deeply.

My mom had been a different woman since my father passed away. He had been sick for my entire freshman year in college, battling the cancer that had invaded his pancreas. She knew the day was inevitable when we'd have to say goodbye to him, having gone to each chemotherapy appointment and every appointment with the oncologist, who delivered bad news again and again when the cancer refused to stop spreading. But it didn't matter. She had had a breakdown and been placed into psychiatric care for several months. Those were the worst months of both of our lives. She and I had both been fighting with reality.

She had wanted to live in a reality where Martin Foster was still with us. And I had been fighting to maintain his memory without completely losing her as well. During those months, I would visit her at the facility. They were some of the scariest, most uncomfortable times I'd ever experienced.

"Mom," I said. It was the middle of July and I was home for the summer. She'd been at the psychiatric treatment center for three weeks and looked more like a zombie than ever before. She was wearing the same pajamas she'd worn the last time I'd visited. Her hair looked stringy and unwashed.

"Can I braid your hair, Ma?" I asked, holding up her hairbrush and a tiny plastic elastic that had been given to me by the nurses. No belts, no shoelaces, nothing that a patient could use to harm themselves. This tiny little elastic couldn't be used to aid my mother in hurting herself. It pained me that something so tiny and seemingly insignificant had now become a part of our lives. I was only nineteen years old and I had to worry about which hair accessories could be used to help my mother do something suicidal.

Mom nodded and turned her body so I could sit next to her on the bed. She stared at the walls as I talked to her about school and friends and the steady stream of flowers and well-wishes we'd received from friends and family in her absence. At times, she'd respond with a small "hmm" and at least I knew she was listening.

When I finished weaving her blond hair into a braid, we sat in silence for a minute or two. Feeling brave, I wrapped my arm around her shoulder, hoping to comfort her as she had always comforted me. She didn't cry, she didn't yell, she just stared at that cold, concrete wall. And I mourned the woman she used to be.

The pads of my mother's fingers pressed into my shoulder, bringing me back to my current reality. My emotions were a whirlwind. My baby could be sick and I was the most frightened I'd ever been. Possibly more frightened than the day my parents told me about Dad's cancer or the day my mom was admitted to the treatment center. The responsibility of it all, the responsibility of another life inside of mine was the most intimidating and overwhelming thing I'd ever experienced. But my mother was comforting me, and I clung to the idea of the old Allison Foster being there with me again. Relief covered me like a blanket and I clutched it with every ounce of strength remaining inside me.

CHAPTER FOURTEEN

Hadley
Eighteen weeks pregnant

"It's nothing, really."

Making eye contact with Ellie was impossible. I had been avoiding her for two weeks. My feelings of hypocrisy had consumed me since I'd spoken to Dr. Myers. Since the day I'd realized I was living a lie. I adored my clients, but was terrified to have a child with special needs. It'd taken everything in me not to give Pamela my notice just so I could escape the guilt that weighed so heavily on my shoulders.

"Lies," she said, with a shake of her head. "I'm not leaving until you talk. You've been a zombie for days. I know I'm not your best friend or anything, but I'm really worried."

"I don't want you to worry," I said. My eyes darted away from hers again.

"Too late," she said, her voice stern.

"I don't know how to tell you. I... I'm a horrible person."

"Oh puh-lease. If you're a horrible person, then this world is full of utter scumbags. Now, talk."

"My triple screen blood test was positive... which means the baby may have Down's or a couple of other genetic disorders."

"Oh shit," she said, instantly covering her mouth after saying the words.

"I know," I nodded, "And I don't want that. I'm selfish. I want a healthy baby. I know that makes me such a hypocrite. God, I don't deserve to work here anymore, do I?"

"Oh my God, you can't be serious." She pulled her chair to mine, sitting to face me. "Look at me, Hadley. You are *not* a bad person...you're just scared. Everyone wants their baby to be healthy. *Everyone.*"

"Our clients are healthy." I raised an eyebrow as I said the words.

"To a degree, yes. But Violet has a heart condition that's tied to her Down syndrome. And I'm pretty sure you knew that."

"Yeah," I said with a conciliatory nod.

"What pregnant woman doesn't want a healthy baby with no special circumstances? Stop demonizing yourself. I mean it."

"I can't help it...every time I look at Warren, I want to cry. I adore him. I'd be lucky to have a child like him."

"He's not a child," she asserted.

"I know." Silence hovered in the air.

"So, how many false positives happen with this test?" The optimism was building in her eyes. She was looking for the bright side of things. Something I usually did. But not this time.

"A lot."

"So everything *could* be just fine?"

"Yeah."

"When will you know more?"

"In two weeks...hopefully. I have my twenty-week ultrasound. They'll be able to check certain things to see if they match up with the screening."

"Okay. So, in two weeks—"

A knock came from the office door. Nick peeked his head in. His carefree expression was wiped away the moment he locked eyes with his wife.

"Oh, sorry," he said as he closed the door quickly. Ellie rolled her eyes, jumped out of her seat and opened the door.

"Get in here, Miller." She waved him into the office. I did my best to mask the distraught expression on my face. Not that I had any kind of poker face whatsoever.

"Didn't mean to interrupt," he said, walking into the office without looking me in the eye. Such a guy. They never quite know how to deal with an upset woman. Sitting on the couch, he rested his elbows on his knees, focusing his attention on Ellie.

"We need your opinion on something."

"Ellie, no—" I started to protest. She raised her hand up to me with a reassuring nod.

"When you and I get pregnant," she began. Nick's eyebrows shot up.

"Are you?" he asked her, placing his hand on her stomach.

"No. Not yet. We just started trying, babe. It takes time," she said, taking his hand in hers. "But when we do get preggers, we'll want a healthy baby, right?"

"Of course," Nick said. "That's a no-brainer, Ells."

"Okay, so...if I had a test done—a standard pregnancy blood test—and that blood test showed signs of the baby having Down's..." she tipped her head to Nick, hoping he'd fill in the blanks on what she was inferring.

"It'd freak me out." He put his hands up in front of his face in mock surrender. "I'm sorry. Maybe that makes me a dickhead. But..."

"No, it doesn't," Ellie said with a smile.

Nick Miller was Sunnyside's star employee. He loved those clients with all that he was. Working with them was his life's work, his passion. He was there day in and day out, spending his time making the clients' lives as fun and productive as possible. He was an exceptional human being.

"It makes you honest," I said. "Thanks, Nick."

Nick's eyes finally found mine. They looked pained.

"Is everything all right? Is the baby okay?"

"I'm not sure yet." I shrugged, pursing my lips together.

"She'll know more in a couple weeks. I just wanted her to see that she's normal. Her reaction is normal."

"So, I was your guinea pig?" Nick asked, turning back to his wife. "Geez, Ells, what if I had said the wrong thing?"

"Impossible." She shook her head. "I know you too well."

"All right... now you're starting to mess with my head." He laughed and walked to the door.

As he placed his hand on the door, he turned back to me. "You know we're here for you, right?"

"I do," I said with a smile.

"Good."

Ellie looked back to me. "Have you told Tucker... or Jason?"

"I'm waiting to tell Tucker. I want to have more info first. But Jason knows."

"And? What does he think?"

"He's so wonderful. He's doing lots of research. He won't let me Google anything myself. But he's constantly looking things up. He wants the baby to have the best life possible. And he's not pushing me the way Tucker does."

"He's a good guy."

"I know."

"Hold onto that one."

"He's not mine to hold onto."

"We'll see."

CHAPTER FIFTEEN

Hadley
Twenty weeks pregnant

My belly flinched as the cold gel made contact with my skin. My heart was racing like crazy. Jason was right. The love I felt for this child was unwavering. Regardless of what the tech said, I was completely and utterly in love with my baby. But I wanted him (or her) to be as healthy as possible.

My mom held my hand, her best reassuring smile plastered to her face. Relieved to have her there with me, I was able to relax slightly. Auden had offered to come, but I wanted my mom and I to take this step together. Luckily, Auden understood. Besides, I think the entire idea of an ultrasound would have been a little overwhelming for my best friend. She was nowhere near ready for this step in her life. Even though she'd been supportive, my being pregnant was still surreal to her. I kept telling her to "join the club." It was still surreal to me each morning when I felt the baby move within my belly.

The tech focused on the screen, humming as she took measurements of the fetus. I hated that word. He or she is a *baby*, a *person*, a *human being*... the word *fetus* was just too clinical for the life growing inside of me. I tried not to take it personally since she spent her days looking at images on ultrasound screens. But to me, this was everything. This was my present, my future, my life-changing moment.

"Have you thought about names?" the tech asked as she typed in more measurements, never looking away from the screen.

"Yes," I said, nodding and wiping the sweat from my brow.

"You have?" my mother asked.

"Marty," I said softly, looking into her clear blue eyes. She gasped softly.

"For your dad?" She looked surprised and...genuinely happy. Her eyes glistened and I stared at her in disbelief. Tears hadn't fallen from Allison's eyes in three very long years. Her grip tightened on my hand and she placed her other hand on top of mine. "If it's a boy, it'll be perfect. Martin would've loved that. But what if it's a girl?"

"Martie." I shrugged. "She'll be Martina or Marta or something like that. But to me, she'll be Martie. No matter what, I'm naming the baby after Dad."

"I can tell you if you'd like to know," the tech said. I smiled and nodded eagerly. "Do you see this?" she asked, pointing at the screen.

"It looks like a little turtle," I said, scrunching my nose. "So, it's a..."

"Boy," my mom said softly next to me.

"Yep, it sure is," the tech said. She wiped the gel from my belly as I continued to stare at the screen. "Everything looks good, but I'm going to give the measurements to Dr. Myers. You can meet her in her office."

"Thanks," I said, my pulse was racing again with those words. I gathered my things, and Mom and I walked down the hall to the doctor's office.

A framed copy of an ultrasound photo sat on her desk. I hadn't realized Dr. Myers was a mother. The door swung open and Dr. Myers entered the office. For the first time, I noticed that she had a very small baby bump. My doctor was pregnant herself.

"Hello, ladies," she said as she took her seat. My mom nodded at her. She'd been my mother's gynecologist for years, too. Regardless of the familiarity in the room, I was still on edge. I needed her to talk to me about Marty. I needed to know he would be okay.

"As you know, ultrasound is not a diagnostic test. But I must tell you that everything looks normal. His femur measures at an average length, as does the skin behind his neck. There is no indication of any heart defects or anything else that, at this stage, would indicate Down syndrome. There is also nothing to indicate Trisomy 18."

A huge sigh of relief left my mouth. My mom squeezed my hand as I took another deep breath in.

"Oh my god, thank you," I said.

"The only thing I'm concerned about is your placenta. As pregnancies progress, the placenta should move towards the lower region of your uterus, up towards the top. Yours hasn't moved as much as it should. So we're going to keep an eye on that."

"What does that mean?"

"For some women, it can lead to placenta previa. If you have any bleeding, I want you to call the office immediately. Other than that, just be sure to take it easy as much as possible."

"If she had placenta previa," my mom said, clearing her throat, "what would that mean? For the baby, I mean."

"It can be dangerous and would mean bed rest until the bleeding stopped. And if you're past thirty-six weeks, it might mean delivering the baby. It would certainly be a C-section delivery, as well."

"Oh," I replied, clutching my belly, doing my best to process all the information given to me.

"As long as you communicate with me and take care of yourself, there should be nothing to worry about." Her smile reassured me. Somehow knowing she was pregnant too was comforting. *She understood.* She understood my worries and my concerns. I had to trust that she'd take care of Marty and me.

~

An hour later, my mom and I were enjoying a quiet dinner at a restaurant near the condo. I sent Tucker a text the moment we left the doctor's office, but there was no response. I couldn't say I was surprised. Any time I sent him a text or left a voicemail about the baby, he didn't respond. *Message received, Tucker. You son of a bitch.*

A feeling of calm was finally running through my body, despite my slight fears regarding the possible placenta previa.

But there was something else bothering me. Something that only my mother and I could fix. Together.

"I need to talk to you, Mom. But first, I want to thank you for today. It was so nice having you there with me."

"Of course," she said. Her brow creased as her cautious eyes gazed into mine. This was going to be difficult.

"I need to get my own place."

"I—I don't understand," she said, placing her fork on the table and her hands in her lap.

"You're not well, Mom. Not really. I know you're trying your hardest. But with the baby coming...it's just not enough. I'm going to use the money that Dad left me."

"Hadley, I'm really not sure that's the right decision."

"Mom, I love you. But I'm not asking permission. I'm twenty-two years old and I'm going to be a mother now. I have to do what's best for the baby. And for myself."

"But I want to help you."

"I know, but you have to help yourself first. It's time, Mom," I said, giving her the softest expression I could as I extended my hand across the table, hoping she'd take it. She hesitated at first, but took it in her own, squeezing tight.

"Your father *would* be disappointed at how I've carried on, wouldn't he?" she asked. She looked ready to accept the conversation.

"He'd *want* you to move on. He'd *want* you to be happy. I know it may seem like a weird time for me to move out, but I think it's for the best."

"Okay." She nodded.

"I miss him, too," I said, looking into her eyes as they continued to water. She squeezed them tight and nodded, tightening her grip on my hand.

"I missed him so much it physically hurt. *Every single day.* I thought it would get easier, but it didn't. The meds help me get through the day...and I'm terrified to go off them. I don't know if I can do it, honey."

"I know, but there's got to be a better way. You need to *feel* again. The baby deserves the best of you."

"And so do you," she said, tears spilling from her eyes. "God, I've been awful, haven't I?"

"Not awful...just not you. And I *need* you."

"I can do this," she said, taking a deep breath in and smiling a brave smile. "I can. I will. I promise."

CHAPTER SIXTEEN

Jason

"Where would you like this box?" I asked Haddie, holding a bundle of her belongings in my arms. She had moved into a small apartment complex in a quiet, safe area of town. It backed to a beautiful wooded area and her small balcony had a really nice view. I felt good about her living here.

"Um..." she said as she searched the box for clues. "Oh, living room. It's picture frames and stuff."

"Got it," I said, placing it on the coffee table.

"This place is gorgeous," Auden said, carrying a lamp into the spare bedroom/future nursery.

"Thanks...I think it'll be good place for the baby," Haddie said, looking guilty. I knew she felt like she was letting her mom down, but I was proud of her for putting the baby first. That's the kind of thing good mothers did.

Just then, her mother walked into the living room, carrying several shopping bags.

"Groceries," she said with a weak smile. "I thought we could stock your fridge."

"Thanks, Mom," Haddie said, taking a few bags from her mom. I took them from her, giving her a wink, and placed them on the kitchen counter. I was being a little overprotective, but I didn't want her lifting anything too heavy or putting any strain on her body. Not when I was there to help.

It took a few hours, but eventually all of Haddie's belongings were moved to her new place. Auden and I offered to take her out to dinner, but she was too wiped.

"We can order a pizza," her mom suggested. Haddie looked pleased. I knew Haddie wanted to connect with her. The fact that she was reaching out was making an impact. Auden and I exchanged a glance, knowing we needed to give them some time together.

We said our goodbyes and walked to our cars. I was feeling really unsettled, but I wasn't quite able to put my finger on the reason.

"What's going on in there?" Auden asked, tapping her fingers lightly on the side of my head.

"I don't know...just confused, I guess," I said, placing my hands in my pockets.

"Wanna grab a bite? Talk about it? Maybe I can help."

No one who knew us would describe our sibling relationship as close. But my feelings for Haddie seemed to be bringing us closer for once in our lives. She wasn't the bratty kid sister who used to drive me crazy. Instead, she was the best friend of the girl I was absolutely crazy about. Auden knew Haddie like no one else and she actually wanted to help me. I'd be a dumbass if I turned her down.

⁓

Thirty minutes later, Auden and I were eating sub sandwiches and making small talk. For some reason, I chose not to start the conversation looming around us. Luckily, Auden seemed to sense that. She finished chewing, took a sip of her Diet Coke and simply said, "She's just as confused as you are."

I nodded, knowing that Haddie was overwhelmed.

"I don't want to make things worse for her."

"I know that...she does, too. Just be patient. It'll happen."

"I keep waiting for the other shoe to drop, ya know? I keep waiting for Tucker to come back into her life. I'd be a shit if I stood in the way of her having a family."

"He's not coming back," she said with a confident shake of her head.

"But does she *want* him to?"

"Honestly, no. They were falling apart for months before she got pregnant. The baby just made it more complicated."

"Much more," I said before taking a few more bites of sandwich. Our meal became eerily silent. I looked up at my sister. Auden bit her lip and scrunched her nose. *Why is she nervous?*

"What?" I asked with a mouth full of food.

"I have a confession to make." She twiddled her thumbs in a frantic way. She used to do that when my parents caught her in a lie.

"You do?" What could Auden possibly have to confess that was making her freak out? I hadn't seen her panic like that in years.

"I'm the one who pushed her to date Tucker. It's my fault she was ever with that asshole. It's my fault she's having his kid."

"Hardly," I scoffed.

"No, seriously."

"They dated for six years—you're not responsible for that. She could've broken up with him."

"I know, but her dad died...and he was there for her. She needed him after all that happened. And he stepped up. But in the beginning, she was hung up on someone else."

"Who?"

"Don't be a dumbass."

"Me?" I asked, in shock. I knew she had cared about me when we were younger. But I hadn't realized it had continued for that long. I couldn't believe what I was hearing.

"You were away at school and I told her she needed to get over you. She was pissed for a while, but eventually she let me set her up with Tuck."

"Wow."

"Are you pissed?" Auden winced, stirring her drink. "I just wanted her to be happy...with someone."

"Of course not," I said with a furrowed brow. "Just a little shocked."

"She's been crazy about you since we were, like, eight." She rolled her eyes and I kinda wanted to smack her. Sometimes she was still my little pain-in-the-ass sister. But her stance on Haddie and I being together was refreshing. I didn't expect her to feel that way. At all. Especially given our history.

"Can we change the subject? I feel like we're just going round and round and getting nowhere."

She shrugged as she wiped her mouth. "I just feel bad, that's all."

"I know." It was usually our unspoken topic. We were finally talking about it without *really* talking about it. Haddie had been our divide for a long time. But, ironically, she was actually pulling us together now.

Auden changed the subject after an uncomfortable silence lingered at our table. She hated her job and was content to tell me all about it...which was really nothing new. She'd been in a mood for months. Nothing seemed to make her happy. As Auden began to retell a story I'd already heard last week at our Sunday dinner, I zoned out. Realizing how Haddie felt all along brought up so many thoughts and answered so many questions. All I could think about was the day I discovered that Haddie was dating Tucker. I would never forget that day.

It was my first Christmas home with my family after starting college. Awesome smells filled the house. My mom's famous brined turkey and garlic mashed potatoes. Cornbread stuffing and cherry pie. I couldn't wait. My school cafeteria wasn't the best and instead of gaining the freshman fifteen, I had lost weight during that first semester at school. I was homesick, yes. But I was missing someone specific. Haddie.

It was pretty ridiculous, really. I had gone on several dates with girls from my dorm. And they were all pretty cool. But none of them really did it for me. I would be home for three full weeks and I had made up my mind...I was going to ask Haddie out on a date. A real date. No more avoiding, no more ignoring how I felt about that girl. She was a junior in high school, and before I'd left for college, she had never really dated anyone aside from the occasional dance at school. I really wanted a fresh start with the only girl who every really had my full attention.

My plan was to show up at her house that night, after my aunts and uncles had all gone home. Auden had mentioned to my mom that Haddie and her parents were having a quiet holiday at home. It would be perfect. I'd made several mix CDs for her... songs that had made me think of her while I was at school. I'd burned them on my computer and made copies for myself. I listened to them all the time.

My roommate was the one who'd planted the seed in my mind. He was having a long-distance relationship with a girl who was still in high school. They had been dating for years and were still making it work. I'd always heard horror stories about long-distance relationships, but after watching Pete and his girlfriend, I'd decided to be impulsive and follow my heart.

That evening, I drove to Haddie's house. Large snowflakes were falling on the ground, and I started to have visions of kissing Haddie in the snow. When I reached her house, though, I saw a car parked in her driveway. I parked the car, turned off my headlights and focused on her front door. A guy I didn't recognize was standing on her front porch, holding a bouquet of roses. I watched, my mouth agape, as Haddie answered the door. She covered her mouth in surprise before taking the bouquet and wrapping her arms around him.

My heart sank. After she took his hand and led him inside, I drove away. She'd given up on me. She'd found someone else. And for me... well, it was time to let go. Maybe I'd get another chance with her in the future. I just had to be patient.

CHAPTER SEVENTEEN

Hadley
Twenty-six weeks pregnant

Jason and I were spending the day together and I was terribly excited. Our friendship had grown significantly and I found myself looking forward to hearing his voice, spending hours chatting on park benches and walking through my neighborhood on lazy Sunday afternoons. He hadn't told me yet where we were going, but I had been told to dress in my "Sunday best."

My hair was curled in loose waves down my back and I wore my favorite maternity dress. It was light and airy and I wore it as often as possible. Auden had given me a gorgeous jade necklace for my birthday and it sat perfectly on my chest. I was fixing my hair when I felt a familiar push inside my belly.

"Hey there, baby boy," I said, rubbing my tummy. Pushing slightly into my baby bump with the tips of my fingers, I waited for him to respond. He did, just as I'd hoped, with another nudge of his foot or elbow. It was impossible to know exactly what my busy boy was up to, but I loved that we were able to communicate.

"We're spending the day with Jason, sweet pea. You will love him...just wait and see." My son pushed against me again, bringing another smile to my face. I heard a knock and I couldn't get to the door fast enough.

When I looked through the peephole, an unfamiliar face smiled back at me. A petite woman with chocolate brown hair, porcelain skin and dark brown eyes.

"Hello," she said with a kind smile, as I opened the door. "My name is Kate Maxwell. I'm a friend of Jason's."

"Oh," I said, slightly confused. "Um, Jason's not here, but he should be any minute."

"Actually, he's not coming."

"I don't understand," I said. I was disappointed. So disappointed... not to mention confused.

"Jason sent me as a gift. He wanted to surprise you with a maternity photo session. That's where I come in. I'm a photographer," she said, motioning to the large camera bag around her left shoulder.

"You're kidding," I said, aghast. When would this man stop surprising me?

"Nope, dead serious. Here," she said, reaching into her bag, "this is for you."

A simple unmarked envelope was placed in my hands. Quickly, I flipped it over, pulling the white card stock out of its envelope.

Dear Haddie,
I know you were hesitant to have something like this done. But I want you to embrace the love and joy that you feel for that baby inside of you. You deserve a keepsake, photos to keep with you as he grows from a baby to a boy, from a boy to a man.
Kate is a genius and will take wonderful care of you.

If you aren't too tired after your session, I'd love to take you out to dinner.
Call me later.
—Jason

"Wow," I muttered, staring off into space, trying desperately to wrap my mind around the kindness and generosity that Jason continued to show me.

"He's got it bad," Kate said with a devilish grin.

"I'm starting to see that," I said. Gesturing for Kate to come in, I looked down at my dress, a little bit panicked. Was I dressed right for this?

"You look gorgeous," Kate said. "And based on your outfit, I have the perfect spot in mind."

"Really?" I had no idea where she was thinking we'd go. I knew nothing about photography.

"I arrived early and scoped out your neighborhood. There's a small wooded area behind your complex. I thought we could get some beautiful shots out there. I also brought a backdrop in case you'd like some general studio-type shots."

"Natural sounds good." I followed Kate out of the apartment, thinking only of a man named Jason Kelly.

∼

Two hours later, Kate and I made our way back to my apartment. As Jason had predicted, I was exhausted. But that wasn't going to stop me from calling him. I was practically giddy at the thought of seeing him, hugging him tight and thanking him for his incredible gift.

"I'll go through all the photos, do some editing and send them to you in an email. Sound good?"

"Absolutely," I said, rubbing my stomach gently. "Thank you so much."

Kate smiled warmly. "It was my pleasure. Jason's a great guy. You make him very happy."

"Oh, um...we're not dating," I said, suddenly embarrassed of my baby bump. How ridiculous she must think I was, carrying another man's baby as we discussed Jason's feelings for me.

"That doesn't matter. He's crazy about you." She raises an eyebrow and I felt the heat rushing to my cheeks. It was getting harder and harder to deny my feelings for him.

Kate smiled as I shrugged my shoulders, looking all kinds of embarrassed.

"And I him," I whispered.

"I can tell." She smiled again.

"But how could he...? Never mind." I waved my hand dismissively in front of my face.

Kate looked concerned, so I did my best to gather my thoughts before speaking. I barely knew this person, and yet, I felt if I didn't tell her how I felt about him, it would be a betrayal of some kind. That I would be denying him somehow. And that was the *last* thing I wanted to do.

"The baby isn't his," I said simply.

"I know. And I know how confusing that must make it for you."

I nodded in response. My cheeks were hot. Thank goodness she had finished taking the pictures.

"I know what it's like to be without the person you love. My husband and I were apart for a long time and it was awful. I don't want that for Jason. Nor you."

"You barely know me," I said, confused again.

"I know that Jason is smitten and I know he's felt this way for a long time."

"But how could he love a baby that isn't his?"

"He already does."

"He does?" I couldn't believe my ears. It had never crossed my mind that Jason would be falling in love with the baby just as I was.

She smiled gently. "He loves you *and* he loves the baby. Can't you see that?"

I shook my head back and forth, almost in denial. I knew Jason had feelings for me. I'd known that since the night of the Valentine's Dance. But the thought of him actually being able to love my baby had to be the most beautiful thing I'd ever heard. I couldn't get my hopes up. It wasn't fair to the baby... or to me. I had to stay strong for the two of us. I couldn't allow myself to have a broken heart.

"We're friends." I shrugged. "Right now, that's all we can be."

"Okay." Kate's eyebrows knitted together as she gathered her things. "Well, I should go. I hope to see you again, Hadley."

"Thank you again for this wonderful gift. I can't wait to see the pictures."

I walked Kate to the door, shutting it behind her, terrified to pick up the phone. Ten minutes ago, I couldn't wait to see Jason, but now... now, I was an overwhelmed mess. I needed to do the right thing for the baby and I didn't know what that was. I had allowed my naïve self to get wrapped up in a relationship that could blow up in my face. My focus should be solely on the baby. Becoming a mother was such an incredible responsibility and I needed to honor that. I had to focus on the boy whose life was entirely in my hands. I refused to screw that up.

Reaching for the phone, I dialed Jason's number, hoping for voicemail. He answered right away. Damn it.

"Hey, how'd it go?" He sounded so happy, so satisfied, so proud. It killed me to have to do what I was about to do.

"It was great," I replied. Silence filled the air. "Thank you so much."

"Of course. I want you to have memories of this. You're radiant, you know."

"Thanks," I whispered, pressing my eyes tight, pulling on the strap of my dress.

"So, are you hungry?" His voice was eager.

"I'm actually really tired. I think I'm gonna lie down, maybe go to bed early."

"Oh," Jason said, sighing softly into his phone. "Do you want some company? I could bring a movie and a pizza."

"Jase," I said gently, my heart sinking as I said his name. *I hate this.*

Jason sighed again. He understood what I was doing. He knew I was pushing him away. I was scared to death and he probably knew that, too.

"Yeah, sure. Um...I guess I'll see you on Thursday, then?" he said as he cleared his throat.

"Thank you for the gift. I can't even express to you how much it meant to me."

"You're welcome, Haddie."

I placed my phone on the counter and walked like a zombie back to my room. Turning on the shower, I climbed in to wash the smell of fresh pine and grass from my hair and body. Smelling like the photo shoot would only make me think of Jason and how much he loved me. How much he would do to make me happy. How I wouldn't allow him to do anything else because of how much I loved him in return.

My tears joined the hot water as it spilled down my chest and swollen belly. The baby kicked against my side. And it was the only thing that kept me from sinking to my knees.

"Hi, sweet pea." I said through my sobs, pressing my fingers into my belly.

This tiny person was my first priority. He had to come first, no matter what. I would worry about my own happiness later.

CHAPTER EIGHTEEN

Hadley
Thirty weeks pregnant

What the hell is that?
I gasped in horror. There was blood in my underpants. Not a lot of blood, just a few spots. But my heart raced and my stomach dropped to my knees. *When was the last time the baby kicked?* I honestly didn't remember. *Oh my god, oh my god, oh my god.*

I raced to my kitchen and dialed the emergency line for Dr. Myers' office. The nurse on duty instructed me to come in right away for an ultrasound. I took a fast shower, got dressed, and grabbed a banana from the kitchen.

On my way to the hospital, I called Ellie. I had no idea if I'd be able to go to work today... physically or mentally. Every time I came to grips with the pregnancy, I was thrown another curve ball—another crisis or critical moment that made me question whether or not I was cut out to be a mother.

I arrived at the office and was taken promptly to an examination room. Dr. Myers was already waiting for me. Her face was painted with concern and it scared me to death.

"Okay, let's take a look," she said, placing the gel on the plastic device in her hand. She rubbed the gel onto my belly as well.

"Are you still bleeding?"

"No," I replied.

"Have you felt much movement this morning?" she asked.

"No, none," I said, choking out the words.

"Deep breaths," she said with a reassuring expression that, unfortunately, did absolutely nothing to reassure me.

Within seconds, she located the baby. I took a deep breath just as the corners of her mouth curled towards her nose. The heart was beating like crazy and I saw my boy moving his tiny fingers.

"Is he okay?" I asked. "Is he going to be okay?"

"He appears to be just fine. And some other good news is that your placenta has moved higher inside your uterus, which is what we were hoping for."

"So, there's nothing to worry about?"

"Well," she began, "the bleeding was probably from the recent movement of your placenta. Or, it could be stress induced. Have you done anything out of the ordinary?"

"I moved into my own place not too long ago."

"Well, that could do it. I'd like to put you on temporary bed rest. I'd also like to do some tests on your urine and blood just to be safe."

"Bed rest? For how long?"

"Let's do two weeks for now. As long as the bleeding doesn't come back, you can go back to work. But for now, you need to have your feet up and avoid stress whenever you can."

My heart sank knowing that I'd be away from Sunnyside. The performance was in just a few weeks and I needed to make sure Lucy was conquering her stage fright. We needed costumes and props. There were still *so* many things to be done. I wondered how much, if anything, could be done from my apartment....

CHAPTER NINETEEN

Hadley
Thirty-two weeks pregnant

Ding-dong. The ring of the doorbell woke me from my nap. I'd been sleeping a lot that week. I was bored out of my mind—wishing I was at work, with my clients, planning the big performance and teaching my daily classes. Instead, I was following doctor's orders, lying in bed for most of the day, checking Facebook way too often and reading books on my Kindle. I was hoping and praying Dr. Myers would let me return to work since the bleeding had completely stopped days ago. I missed work so much. And the show was quickly approaching. They needed me.

Mom was worried since I was no longer living with her. She wanted to take care of me, which meant more than she could possibly understand. But the fact remained that the baby and I needed a place that was just for us...away from her uncertainty and muted moods. I wanted my baby to feel loved...all the time. And living with my mother made that a lofty goal.

Making my way to the front door of my apartment, I opened it and yawned. There was no one there. But when I looked down, I found a large basket filled with all sorts of things: movies, candy, and other items. But what jumped out at me were the large paperback novels front and center in the basket. My breath hitched as I picked up the basket and placed it on my kitchen counter. A card with my name faced me. I knew who it was from. As much as I tried to fight it, I was falling in love with Jason more and more with each passing day. And I was pretty sure this basket would send me over the edge.

Opening the pastel blue envelope with shaky hands, I removed the card. Ferris Bueller was flashing his signature grin at me, with his arms crossed. When I opened it, I heard the "Oh Yeah" song play. A simple note was written on the inside of the card, "H, I know you're bored. Hoping to help you pass the time." It was unsigned but I knew *exactly* who it was from.

Placing the card on the Formica, my hands glossed over the three paperbacks written by Whitman Kelly. Out of curiosity, I opened the first one. As I'd hoped, there was a note.

"For Hadley. I hope you enjoy my writing." Silly man had no idea that I'd already read every one of his books. But I'd happily read them again. The other two books had notes as well. I hugged them to my chest as I walked to my bookshelf. Gingerly, I placed them on the top shelf, giving them a spot of prominence in the room before heading back to the basket and all the undiscovered goodies that still awaited me.

My three favorite candies were the next things I discovered: Swedish Fish, Twizzlers and Reese's Pieces. Yum. The man really did pay attention! Either that or he had gathered really good intel from his sister. Two gossip magazines were next. He knew I was addicted to Hollywood gossip. Two '80s movie packs were next...with Post-It notes that said, "Hope you don't already own these!"

Man, he made me smile like no one else could. As I stared at the Post-It note in my hand, the bright square brought me to an odd sense of déjà vu. My heart raced and memories bounced around clumsily in my brain.

Post-It notes. Post-It notes.

Tucker had always used Post-It notes when he left me gifts...didn't he? Supporting myself against the counter, I walked unsteadily to the bedroom, struggling to breathe.

Carefully, I lowered myself to the floor and pulled a small shoebox out from under the bed. I had been tempted to throw these away after our breakup, but wanted to remember the good in Tucker. I wanted to have something to go to in the future when he inevitably let me down or let our child down. Because I knew it *would* happen. I wanted to remember a time when he was supportive and thoughtful, kind and adoring. But it wasn't him. He wasn't that person. And things were suddenly becoming clear.

Removing the lid of the box, I sifted through the Post-It notes. One after another with similar, unsigned messages. In the exact same handwriting as today's green Post-It stuck to the movie boxes. I was elated, yet destroyed. I was thrilled, yet betrayed.

"Hadley, something just arrived for you," my mother said from the kitchen. I raced down the steps. I hoped it was another care package. Tucker had been leaving care packages on our doorstep every few days since my dad had started chemo. Movies, candy, books, flowers. Every time, it was different. But aside from making my dad

smile, these packages were what I lived for. I was home for the summer and it was a lovely June afternoon.

My mom gave me a weak smile as she placed the basket in my hands. A simple green Post-It note sat on today's package... a gift card to a local bookstore as well as two boxes of my favorite green tea and a plastic bear filled with honey. I had the best boyfriend in the world. The Post-It simply read, "H, enjoy a book and a warm drink. Lose yourself in fiction." It wasn't signed, but I knew who it was from. Every time a gift arrived, I'd call Tucker and thank him for his latest generosity. And every week, he always said, "You're welcome" or "No need to thank me" or "I love you, baby." And every night, I'd go to sleep knowing just how lucky I was to have a boyfriend who cared enough to show me over and over again. He knew how much my father's illness was hurting me. He knew how much my father meant to me. And he was determined to put a smile on my face, even if it was only once every few days.

For years, I'd thought Tucker was the one who was thinking of me, supporting me, loving me through his gifts and surprises. But it had been Jason. He didn't want recognition—he didn't need it. He was just trying to take care of me. Just as he was now. Grabbing on to the bedframe, I pulled myself up off the floor and picked up the phone. He answered after two rings.

"It was you," I said.

"Guilty as charged. I thought you might want to read my stuff. And I've heard pregnant women love candy." I could hear his smile through the phone.

I'm in love with him. Completely head over heels in love with this man.

A moment passed and I still didn't know what to say. I didn't know how to collect my thoughts or my emotions. I was awestruck.

"Haddie, what's the matter? I was just trying to cheer you up."

"And take care of me," I added.

"Well...yeah. Is that okay?" Nervous laughter escaped his mouth. He didn't understand the discovery I'd just made. The absolutely overwhelming realization that I had finally come to after three years of false memories.

"When my dad was sick...the presents...that was you." The other end of the phone line held only silence. "Jase!"

"Yeah, that was me." His words were soft and hesitant. "But...I thought you knew that."

"No. I thought it was Tucker...for years. Until this afternoon."

"Oh," he said with a sigh. "Well, I guess I'm glad you know now."

"I wish I'd realized it then. I'm...I'm so sorry, Jase."

"Don't apologize. I just wanted to take care of you."

"You still do," I replied.

"Yeah," he said, and I could hear his smile return. Relief filled my lungs as I took a deep breath in and out.

"I'm done pushing you away," I said, matter of fact.

"What? No, Haddie. Don't do this out of guilt. Don't feel sorry for me."

"No, no. That's not it. I've been fighting myself for months and I don't want to do it anymore. I want to be with you, Jase. If you still want me."

"Of course I do. But I think we should wait till after the baby's born. You're so full of emotions and hormones right now... especially being on bed rest. I want you to be sure."

"Oh," I said, taken aback at how much this man cared for me... that he'd prolong his own happiness just to make sure I was certain in my decision.

I'm so lucky.

"It doesn't change how I feel about you. I promise."

I smiled into the phone. "Me neither."

"And when you're ready, after he's born, I'll take you on a proper date."

"Sounds good to me," I said with a smile. Jason Kelly warmed my heart in a way I didn't know was possible.

"Are your feet up?" His voice changed. He sounded fatherly and stern.

"No, but I'm going to put them up and read as soon as we hang up. I promise."

"Okay. I'll check on you later."

~

I hung up the phone and walked, almost in a daze, to the living room. Removing one of his books from the shelf, I retreated back to my bedroom. I pulled the covers up, basking in the chilly air conditioning. I spent the rest of the afternoon with Madeline Kramer, Jason's book heroine. I got lost in her world, lost in the world that was his imagination. And with each page, I fell deeper and deeper in love with the man who had had my heart since I was eight years old.

CHAPTER TWENTY

Jason

I've been fighting myself for months and I don't want to do it anymore. I want to be with you, Jase. If you still want me.
Holy shit.
She wants me.
She wants to be with me.

I was getting another chance with her. But as much as I wanted to drive to her apartment, bang on the door and kiss her hard once she answered, we had to do this the right way. She'd never been more vulnerable than she was right now. I couldn't take advantage of that. I refused to screw things up. She meant way too much to me and I'd wanted her far too long to mess things up now.

I had no idea how I was going to get back to my writing. I put my phone back on the café table. Beans had become my favorite writing spot for several reasons. Their French Roast was the best in town, but it was more than that. This is where I had seen her last fall. This is where things had started for us. And so, every morning when I set off to write, I found myself at Beans. Every. Single. Time.

I stared at the screen but was jumping out of my skin. I had to call someone.

Kate answered on the second ring. "What's up, t-shirt guy?"

"She wants me. I thought she didn't, but she does." I'm sure I sounded like a crazed lunatic. I could practically hear her rolling her eyes at me on the other end of the line.

"Hadley?"

"Yeah."

"Oh, thank God. After the photo shoot, I was freaking out. I thought I did or said something wrong."

"I think she just felt guilty... and weird."

"It's not a traditional situation, but that's okay. I knew she was into you... even after just a couple of hours. It was obvious."

Her words struck such a chord with me. I loved that Haddie's feelings for me were obvious... but it also helped me understand why she had pushed me away so suddenly. Kate had picked up on it and it freaked her out. She was just trying to do the right thing... the honorable thing.

"Her hormones are all over the place. Be careful with her," Kate's voice was soft, but confident. Insistent.

"What do you mean?"

"Pregnant women are moody messes. You're a sweet guy, Jase. Just be gentle with her. Let her bitch you out if she needs to, or change her mind a million times in an hour. Just be there for her."

"I got it," I said, waiting for her to confess a pregnancy of her own. She seemed to know an awful lot about the experience. She didn't say anything, though, so I assumed she'd just had a lot of experience with other women in her life.

After discussing Hadley, Kate told me all about her next photo assignment. She was getting a four-page spread, which was such an accomplishment for someone so young. She would be shooting photos of a television show cast. They were filming in Chicago and wanted to promote the latest season of the show. I was excited for her.

Kate was an artist like me, and she understood me in a way that others hadn't during my years as a struggling writer. It felt good to have a friend who comprehended the highs and lows of putting yourself out there artistically. My novels were an extension of myself, just as photos were an extension of Kate. We weren't typical nine-to-fivers, and in some ways, I think that messed with our heads. But it also provided us with so many feelings of accomplishment when people loved and appreciated our work. I was happy to have her in my life.

CHAPTER TWENTY-ONE

Hadley
Thirty-three weeks pregnant

Auden was acting weird. She had picked me up to have tea with her mom at The Drake Hotel downtown. I felt sort of foolish dressed up like this to sit in a stuffy hotel restaurant drinking tea and eating delicate, crumbly cookies while we discussed baby names and Diaper Genies. Secretly, though, I felt lucky to have such support and enthusiasm from Mrs. Kelly. My mom was trying...she really was. But she was focused more on the practical side of things rather than the excitement.

Sometimes it was nice to be surrounded by excitement and enthusiasm. I was so scared all the time...afraid I'd be terrible at motherhood. Afraid I'd drop the baby, forget to feed the baby, forget to change the baby, run out of diapers in the middle of the night, not be able to nurse properly...the list went on and on. But when I was with Auden and her mom, I was able to forget those fears, if only for a little while. I got to think about the special moments that Mrs. Kelly told me about...the first time he'd smile, laugh and say a word. I couldn't wait for those moments. I couldn't wait to *live for* those moments.

"Tell me again...why The Drake?"

"You forgot, didn't you?" Auden said with a crooked smile.

"I guess so," I said, my brow wrinkled in confusion. I had no idea what she was talking about.

"When we were in, like, fourth grade, my mom took us there."

"Yeah, I know...." I tipped my head, waiting for the significance of it all.

"The entire time we were there, you went on and on and on about how beautiful it was. How much you wanted to come back again and again."

"I remember going. I remember it being pretty."

"You were in awe. Seriously. So, Mom wanted to take you back there."

"It's been a while," I said with a nod.

I was nine years old in fourth grade. And, newly twenty-three, I was going to be a mother. It was terrifying. Things were so easy when I was nine. Sometimes, I wished I could go back to the simplicities of childhood.

"Put a smile on your face or Mom's feelings will be hurt. This means a lot to her." Auden was suddenly serious.

"Of course," I said, trying to reassure her. I would never want to upset Mrs. Kelly. She'd always welcomed me into her family with open arms.

∽

After parking the car, we made our way into the lobby of the hotel. Instantly, I was taken back to age nine, dazzled by this elaborate and gorgeous hotel. Glistening chandeliers adorned the tray ceiling. Marble tabletops with dazzling bouquets of flowers were spread throughout the lobby. The blue and gold signature carpet brought a smile to my face. I was distracted, though, by a familiar face, walking quickly away from us. I stopped dead in my tracks and peered at Auden. Suddenly, I knew why I was there.

"Why is my co-worker, Ellie, here?"

"Shit." Her nose wrinkled. "*Pretend* to be surprised, okay? Our moms worked really hard on this."

"Is this my baby shower?" My heart fluttered. Why hadn't I figured that out? Tea at The Drake really did seem like an odd way to spend a Sunday afternoon.

"Yes and you *have to* act surprised. They'll be heartbroken...." Auden's words trailed off as she searched the lobby for a sign of our mothers.

"The coast is clear. Let's go. I'll be fine."

"All right," Auden said. "Let's do this."

Shaking my head, I followed Auden to the room and instantly, I was nine years old again. Memories of sipping tea had a whole new meaning once I was inside the room... once I took in the sights and smells of the beautiful room with fancy table linens, harp music and bouquets and bouquets of fresh cut flowers.

The first face I saw was Ellie's. Her bright red cheeks stood out in the crowd. Giving her an unsuspecting warm smile, I turned my attention to the hostesses of this event. My mom and Mrs. Kelly were standing, their arms linked, and ready to greet me at the door to the private room.

"Surprise," my mom said, looking apprehensive. Did she think this would be too much for me? She was trying to get to know me again and didn't always know how I'd react. But Mrs. Kelly was glowing as she set her kind eyes on me. She could tell that I was taking it all in... the experience of it all.

"You did this for me?" I asked, looking back and forth between the two women. They both nodded. I hugged my mom first and she grasped me tight.

"Is this okay?"

"It's beyond my wildest dreams, Mom. *Thank you.*" Her grip tightened as I said those words, and I pressed my eyelids closed as tight as possible to prevent tears from spilling. The combination of hormones and emotions was bubbling to the surface. As we pulled away from our embrace, my mom's eyes shone with moisture. Every little sign of emotion was a sign of improvement. And I'd take as much as I could get of them. Especially today.

Mrs. Kelly hugged me tight and whispered into my ear, "You deserve this, sweetheart."

"Thank you," I said, as she lightly patted me on the back.

"Come, sit," Auden said, taking my hand and leading me to a table.

"I want to say hello to everyone first," I insisted.

Looking around, I saw so many friends and family members. Aunts, cousins and co-workers from Sunnyside. College friends, high school friends and two very special friends, Violet and Lucy. When I spied them sitting at their table, I almost jumped up and down. I was so happy to have them there.

"Hey girlies," I said, sitting down next to Lucy who leaned over to hug me and rub my belly gently.

"Surprise," Violet said. "We didn't spoil it. Aren't you proud?"

"I'm always proud of you," I said, running my hand across Violet's cheek. She leaned into my touch and closed her eyes briefly.

"This was Ellie's idea, huh?" I asked my clients as Ellie approached us.

"Yep. She picked me up at my house," Violet responded.

"Me too," Lucy said, twirling her hair in her fingers.

"Well, I'm so happy you're here."

∽

Two hours later, we'd had tea, tiny sandwiches and a gorgeous baby shower cake that looked just like large blue alphabet blocks. It was so pretty I actually felt bad eating it. But considering how much this baby enjoyed sugar, I was happy to indulge in a piece... okay, two pieces of delicious buttercream decadence.

Auden announced it was time to open the gifts. I had almost forgotten about that part! I'd been so wrapped up in catching up with everyone over delicious food that the reason for the event had practically escaped me.

Gift after gift was unwrapped and celebrated. Baby blankets, bibs, a high chair, and a car seat. I felt so lucky and so loved. When I reached the end of the pile, there was a simple basket and I knew who it was from. Inside the basket was a selection of children's books... some of my all-time favorites. *The Wizard of Oz*, *The Velveteen Rabbit*, and Richard Scarry's *Best Storybook Ever*.

I held the books tight to my chest. He always knew the way into my heart. Always.

"Who are they from?" Violet asked.

"Jason."

"Ooooh, I like him," Lucy said.

"I do, too." I smiled at her, before locking eyes with Mrs. Kelly. "So much."

CHAPTER TWENTY-TWO

Hadley
Thirty-four weeks pregnant

The big performance was finally upon us. Jason surprised me two weeks ago by convincing a local high school to allow us to use their auditorium for the show. Sunnyside usually performed in the gymnasium with chairs set up for audience members. But this year, the clients would be on a stage and they couldn't have been more excited about it.

Bryce wasn't sleeping. He was too excited about his solo for "Thriller." Nick had taught him how to moonwalk and he'd been doing it in his work area for weeks. Nick would try to get serious and remind Bryce that there was work to be done in Area C, but just like the rest of us, he saw how much joy the show was bringing him. Bryce and his mother were waiting for us when Jason and I pulled into the parking lot of the school. He was already wearing his red and black pleather jacket and sparkling white glove.

Bryce's mother wore an exhausted smile. "He had to be the first one here," she said as we approached them on the sidewalk in front of the building.

Pulling the earbuds out of his ears, Bryce gave me a devilish grin.

I tilted my head towards him. "Are you ready, Freddy?"

"You know it!" he said, moonwalking to the front door of the building.

Jason chuckled as he unlocked the door to the school. In just two short hours, we were hoping to fill the entire auditorium with family members and friends who were important to the clients.

"I'm here! I'm here!" Auden shouted from her convertible as she pulled into the nearest parking space. She looked happy and excited, which meant a lot to me. I hadn't seen too much happiness from my best friend during the past months. Despite the fact that everything was ridiculously uncertain in my life, I was genuinely happy. Happier than I'd ever been. It was odd.

Whereas Auden, who had next to no responsibilities outside of her career, seemed lost. As happy as she was that I'd come to appreciate my pregnancy, and that her brother and I were moving toward being a couple, she wasn't content. In fact, she was as unsettled as I'd ever seen her. I wanted so much for her to just be happy. But whenever I brought it up, she grew defensive and said she felt guilty complaining because of everything I had on my plate. And no amount of reassurance from me seemed to change her mind. Maybe once the baby was born, she'd finally open up to me.

Auden quickly removed two large paper bags filled with costumes from her trunk, slammed it shut and jogged to us. She gave me a quick kiss on the cheek and a pat to my belly. She nodded "sup" to her brother and I had to roll my eyes. She hadn't quite figured out how to handle Jason and me. She said she was thrilled for us. And I believed her since she was the most straightforward person in my life. Auden had always told it like it is, and always would. She didn't hold back when it came to revealing her opinions. She just hadn't quite figured out how to act around Jason and me. Considering we'd yet to even kiss, I was still trying to figure it out myself. But when he and I were together, things fell into place. It was soothing and comforting, with a hint of butterflies and delicious stomach flipping. What more could I ask for?

We made our way to the enormous auditorium. There were over 300 seats for our audience and I hoped we would fill most of them. Jason took my hand in his and helped me up the rickety back stairs that led backstage. We'd had two dress rehearsals this week, so most of our props and costumes were already there. After climbing the stairs, I had to sit down. My lungs felt squished by the baby boy who was getting bigger every day. These days, when he moved, I could feel him stretching out as he pushed against me. It was a fascinating feeling and different from the flutters of my second trimester.

"You okay?" Auden asked, placing her hand on my shoulder.

"The stairs are rough for her," Jason said, giving me a supportive wink.

"Ugh, I am never getting pregnant. It's like you've been invaded by a parasite... or an alien."

"Watch it," Jason warned and I couldn't help but laugh at his protective nature.

"It's fine. Sometimes that *is* how it feels."

When my heart rate returned to normal and my breathing slowed, I started organizing costumes according to musical number. Jason placed my index cards on the podium down stage. We would be taking turns introducing the songs and helping the clients prepare for each number. We had practiced it this week, and although it was exhausting for me, it was the best way to do it. I couldn't just stand near a podium all evening. I had to be backstage, helping everyone get ready, to calm their nerves and fix their hair. Remind them of the lyrics and reassure them that they could do this. Luckily, most of my clients felt they were born to perform. They weren't nearly as nervous as I was. I had so many butterflies in my stomach, I felt like I might be sick. I wanted to do this right.

Little by little, clients arrived for the show. Violet strolled in with a feather boa around her neck. She waved to the invisible audience as she sauntered down the center aisle. Jason chuckled, jogged down to her and bowed before offering her his arm. God, he made my heart melt.

On the total opposite side of the spectrum, Lucy walked in, her head down, staring at the floor as she walked. She was terrified and I knew it. I'd been talking to her for weeks, trying desperately to reassure her of her dancing abilities, but she was an introvert and wasn't as comfortable as Violet and Bryce when it came to situations like this. Her parents wanted her to be involved in the performance, so in many ways, she was doing this under protest. But I was determined to change her mind. When the night was over, I hoped to see a genuine smile on Lucy's adorable face.

"I love Lucy," I called out to her. Her eyes darted in the other direction, but she couldn't keep the corners of her mouth from turning up in response. "I need your help with something, darlin'. Come on up."

Her pace increased slightly, a hint of a spring to her step as she made her way to the staging area. I had a job waiting for her that I knew she would enjoy. It would keep her focused and less apt to worry as time continued to press forward. She began separating the pom-poms for the "Mickey" cheerleading song. She paired them together for each of the performers, looking to me for reassurance. I nodded and smiled widely for her. She grinned before going back to her work.

Sam arrived and was eager to start the performance. He was another natural performer, and although he'd been irritated with me for some time regarding the theme of the show, I was finally forgiven. He was beyond pleased to utilize his T-Birds leather jacket for the show. Sam and a few of the other guys would be lip-synching "Living on a Prayer," each of them decked out in leather and mullet wigs. He had arrived wearing his extremely bushy wig and was ready to roll. He was also wearing acid-washed jeans and high-top sneakers. In a word? Awesome.

Five minutes before introducing the first act, Jason called everyone in for a group huddle. The clients gathered together in a large circle backstage. We took one another's hands and stood in silence. Jason looked at me, awaiting my instructions. I nodded and began.

"I'm so proud of all of you," I began. Riley cut me off.

"But we haven't done anything yet," she said with a huff. Riley was extremely literal. Jason squeezed her hand gently and gestured for her to go back to listening. He was such a natural with my clients. It was truly incredible.

"But you will. And in one hour, you will all be stars. Your friends and family are so excited to watch you tonight. And

I know you will all make them proud. Remember, if you make a mistake, if you flub a line, that's okay. Just keep going. And most importantly, have fun. Jason, Auden and I are all here if you need help with your costumes and props."

Sighs of relief filled the stage, followed by silly giggles. Taking two big, deep breaths, I placed my arm in the center. The clients followed my lead, most of them placing their arms in as well.

"On three...." Jason said.

One.
Two.
Three.

"Go Sunnyside!" everyone yelled.

"Okay, places for the first song. Go!" I said in a very coach-like manner. The clients scattered to their places and I was filled with so much pride it hurt. All of a sudden, I remembered that it was my turn to be nervous. I had to step out on stage, stand behind the podium and face a crowd of hundreds.

"You've got this," Jason said from across the stage. I was starting to think he could read my mind. His green eyes were shining underneath the bright stage lights. His smile was subtle and comforting. We each took a deep breath. He waved before turning his attention back to the clients. They were already made up to look like zombies for the big opening "Thriller" number. They looked fantastic.

"Follow my lead," Bryce said over and over again. Jason patted him on the back as he helped the clients find their places.

I stepped out onto the stage and, even though the lights were blaring, I could see that we had packed the house. Not only was every seat filled, but we had standing room only in the back of the auditorium. It was truly a sight to behold. I took one more giant breath as I felt Marty kicking inside me.

"Here we go, buddy," I whispered, picking up the index cards written carefully in Jason's masculine handwriting. My fingers were shaking, but I did my best to focus on Bryce and the rest of the zombies who were ready to dance the night away.

"Good evening, ladies and gentlemen. Thank you for joining us tonight. My name is Hadley Foster and I'm the activities coordinator for Sunnyside Association. We've been working so hard on this performance, and it is with great pleasure that we share it with you now. Our first song is one that everyone remembers from the 1980s. Eighties music began and ended with Michael Jackson. And it seemed fitting that we should begin the show with his biggest hit of all time. So, sit back, relax and enjoy the show."

The crowd erupted in applause as the heavy red curtain opened, revealing our first performance. The familiar gong of Michael Jackson's "Thriller" began as I joined everyone backstage. Standing next to Jason, I watched as Bryce and the eight other zombies danced and sang to the creepy but upbeat song. Children were dancing in the aisles. And the audience stood up to clap before the song reached its end. If this was any indication of how the show was going to be received, my confidence had just received the biggest boost possible.

"They're loving it," Jason said, stroking my arm gently. He wiped a tear from my cheek... one that I didn't even realize was there. "You did good," he said with a decisive nod.

"Thanks... couldn't have done it without you, though."

He shrugged, brushing it off, but deep down we both knew that he had been an integral part of this show. The look of pride in his eyes was obvious as he watched the number he choreographed.

"He's nailing it," Jason said, watching Bryce move his body back and forth, just like in the original video. The other clients weren't nearly as into it as he was, but that was okay. This was his moment and he was making the most of it.

We heard Vincent Price's voice pour through the speakers, our cue to prepare for the next number. Jason walked to the podium as I gathered up the pom-poms for "Mickey." I closed the curtain just as Mr. Price's evil laugh came to a close. Bryce jumped up and down as he ran to me.

"Did you see me? Did you see me? I was AWESOME!"

"You were absolutely awesome! Congratulations, buddy. Okay, go grab a bottle of water and take a break. You have four songs before you're on stage again. I have to get the girls ready for this one," I said, guiding him towards the rest area.

As soon as the cheerleaders were in position and ready to sing all about how fine Mickey was, I heard Jason wrapping up the intro. Giving the girls a nod, I pressed play on the sound system and opened the curtain.

∼

The night continued in this way and before I knew it, we were finishing the show with "Love Shack" by the B-52s. All of the clients had decided to participate in the closing number, so the stage was packed. My grin was stretching across my face as I watched them, confident in themselves and having the time of their lives as they danced and sang, wearing brightly colored wigs, confetti, feather boas, leather jackets and everything else you could imagine from the '80s. I stared at them in awe, knowing we had pulled it off and that they had enjoyed themselves doing it.

I looked around, realizing I hadn't seen Auden or Jason for a couple of songs. Part of me wondered if Jason was dancing on the stage. I could imagine him bouncing around in a bright orange wig and glow necklace. With fifty people dancing and laughing on the stage, it was impossible for me to find him, so I just enjoyed the last minute of the show.

"Tinnnnnn roof—rusted." That was my cue. The song would be over soon. I walked back to the curtain, ready to pull it down. The baby was kicking like crazy. Eighties music was obviously in his genes. I smiled, rubbing my belly as "Love Shack" faded out. As the curtain met in the center of the stage, my clients yelled, laughed and hugged. They all looked so happy, so content, and so *proud*.

"May I have everyone's attention." I heard Auden at the podium. We hadn't discussed doing a closing for the show. I was relieved she thought of it. I'd been so wrapped up in the emotions of the last number, I'd forgotten about the audience.

Jason slid up next to me, winked and pulled the curtain open before disappearing around the corner. I raised a confused eyebrow.

What is going on?

"None of this would've been possible without the hard work and dedication from a certain activities coordinator. Hadley, will you join us at the podium, please?"

My heart was booming in my chest as I walked on stage. Pamela was standing next to Jason. She had tears in her eyes and held a large bouquet. Behind Pamela, Jason was passing each one of my clients a single flower. Pamela took the microphone and addressed the audience, pulling me next to her, placing the flowers in my arms. As she spoke, describing how proud she was of the performance, of our dedication and hard work, Jason gave the clients a nod. One by one, they each placed a flower in my hands. Some hugged me; others planted kisses on my cheek. Bryce kissed my belly after he kissed my cheek and the crowd roared in laughter. Tears poured from my eyes. The career I had never planned on, never even imagined, had become such an enormous part of my life. And I wouldn't have changed a thing.

CHAPTER TWENTY-THREE

Hadley
Thirty-eight weeks pregnant

Oh my god.
    I had wet myself. I had literally peed on my bed while I was sleeping. How gross.
What is this baby doing to me?
Using more effort than I'd like to admit, I pulled myself out of bed, leaning forward to anchor myself with the nightstand. A sharp pain crushed my abdomen as my belly turned rock hard.

Picking up the phone, I dialed Auden as quickly as I could without going into a panic. When she answered, I could tell she was rubbing the sleep from her eyes.

"I either peed myself or I'm in labor."

"What? You're not due for, like, three more weeks."

"Two. But I think my water broke. My bed is all wet."

"Yuck," she said. I pictured her lip curling in disgust. I rolled my eyes at my best friend. "Call your mom and get your ass to the hospital."

"She works Saturday mornings. I need you to take me."

"Have you called Jason?"

"Auden!"

"Right, right, okay. I'll be there in ten. But call Jase. He wants to be there, too. Never mind, I'll call him and pick him up on the way."

"Seriously, Auden. I need to go *now!*"

Just then, my other line beeped.

"Gotta go, get over here!"

"Good morning," Jason said in a sweet tone after I switched over to his line.

"I'm in labor.... I think," I said, starting to panic.

"Holy shit. I mean, okay...you sit tight. I'll be there in five minutes."

"Auden's going to leave any minute."

"Haddie, I'm on my way. Don't go *anywhere!*" The phone line clicked before I could utter another word. Quickly, I sent a text message to my mom, telling her to meet me at Lutheran General. I hopped in the shower to wash off the amniotic fluid. As I was getting dressed, I heard pounding on the door. That was fast.

"Haddie!" Bang, bang, bang went the door. "Haddie, I'm here!" Jason yelled from the hallway. His nervous demeanor was actually really cute. He was invested in me and the baby. It was a nice distraction from the intense pressure in my abdomen.

When I opened the door, his cheeks were bright red and he was wearing one of his movie t-shirts and jeans. He looked completely disheveled. His hipster glasses were slightly off kilter on his face, making him more adorable than ever before.

"Do you have your things? I already called Auden. She's meeting us there. How far apart are the contractions? Don't worry—these things usually take hours and hours. I'm sure there's plenty of time. Are you ready to go? Do you have your things?" He rambled as he took me by the arm and guided me to the door. I laughed and pointed to the small overnight bag on the kitchen table. He grabbed the bag just as I paused.

"What is it?" he asked. "Are you okay? Do you need anything?"

"Breathe, Jase. It's going to be all right. I promise." Running my hand up to his shoulder, I squeezed gently. The warmth of him radiated to me just as another contraction hit. I clutched my belly, gritting my teeth. Damn, that hurt like hell!

"How far apart did you say your contractions are?" he asked, wrapping his arm around my waist.

"I didn't. I have no idea."

"Haddie, didn't you learn all this stuff? You're supposed to time the contractions. I read it in the *What to Expect* book. The farther apart they are, the more time we have."

"Right. Um... I guess they're about ten minutes apart?" I said, completely unsure of my guesstimate.

"Okay, that's good. Ten is good. We'll have plenty of time. We should go, though." He looked flustered as he ran his fingers through his hair, supporting me as we walked out of the apartment, down the outside staircase and into his car.

He drove way too fast. I knew it. He knew it. But I didn't say a word. I knew that the quicker we got to the hospital, the more in control we'd both feel. I was terrified and that was not going to change, but I needed to know that I was surrounded by doctors and nurses who knew what they were doing. The thought of giving birth anywhere else but there gave me anxiety.

When we arrived at the hospital, Jason and I looked at each other as he took his key from the ignition. We both took a deep breath and the car was silent. A reassuring smile covered Jason's face before he took my hand in his.

"You're going to be the most incredible mother. And I just want you to go into that room knowing how much I care about you.... I think you're amazing, Haddie."

He exhaled, his eyebrows raised. He looked even more terrified than he had just moments before when he was racing down the road going twenty miles over the speed limit.

I opened my mouth to respond, but Jason held his hand up. "Let's get you inside before baby boy decides to arrive here in the parking lot!"

He jumped out of the car, running around to open my door. I smiled at him with such appreciation. He really was the most beautiful person on this earth. I wanted to tell him that, but I knew he didn't want me to say anything out of guilt or obligation. I had to wait. I knew that's how it had to be.

∼

An hour later, my contractions were closer together. My mom held my hand as Dr. Morgan checked my cervix. Dr. Myers had been held up, but was on her way up from the O.R. The idea of having another doctor with me during the delivery made me super uncomfortable. This was not at all how I thought the birth would take place. I hoped Marty would wait long enough for my doctor to show.

"You're at four centimeters and progressing nicely. Have you decided on whether or not you'd like an epidural?"

"Yes," I replied, nodding emphatically. "Bring on the drugs."

Dr. Morgan chuckled as she nodded to a nurse who quickly walked out of the room. "The anesthesiologist will be here in a few. You sit tight until then, okay?"

"How ya doin'?" Auden asked, putting her cell phone down. I didn't blame her for checking Facebook while the doctor was examining me. Jason excused himself to use the washroom. Doctor checks were awkward enough without having everyone staring at me.

"Oh, just peachy keen," I said, clutching my belly with one hand just as it tightened once again. The pressure was getting so intense, I felt like I was going to throw up. I grasped onto the side of the bed with my other hand, squeezing until my knuckles turned white. My mom glanced at her watch, holding up seven fingers. The contractions were getting closer and closer together. Mom gently pressed a cool washcloth against my forehead. It felt nice. Not as nice as I imagined the drugs would feel, but comforting just the same.

Jason walked in, following the anesthesiologist, a middle-aged man with a large smile.

"Somebody order an epidural?" he asked, holding up the needle. Jason turned and walked back out of the room. Auden threw her head back in laughter.

"Such a wimp," she said.

"Auden, will you please check on him?" I asked.

"Are you sure?"

"Yeah, Mom's here. You guys can come back in when this is done."

Auden looked relieved as she walked out of the room to find her brother, whose skin had turned so pale when he saw that needle that I honestly felt bad for him—even though I was the one doubled over in the fetal position. After washing my back with cold antiseptic, the doctor instructed me to lie on my side with my back curled in towards my belly. Mom held my hand as the needle was inserted into my back. It pinched and stung a little, but didn't last too long. I exhaled deeply as the anesthesiologist cleaned up his cart and walked to the nurse's station to inform Dr. Myers, who had just arrived on the labor and delivery floor. I was beyond thrilled to see my doctor.

"I'm here, I'm here. I'm so sorry. I was called in for an emergency C-section and was just going into surgery when you arrived. How are you feeling?"

"Um, the needle kinda hurt and the contractions have been intense."

"You should be feeling better very soon," she said, glancing down at my chart.

∾

My pain was gone. Completely. It was surreal, especially since it had taken less than fifteen minutes to feel relief. I was so comfortable that I drifted off for about an hour. I woke to the sound of Dr. Myers' voice.

"Hadley, sweetheart. You're dilated to nine. I need you to start waking up so you can push."

"Push? Now?" I asked, groggy and hazy. Jason's fingers pushed my bangs from my eyes.

"You can do this, Haddie," he said.

"I hate to do this, but there can only be two people in the delivery room when Hadley begins to push. I'm afraid one of you will have to wait outside."

"I'll go," Jason said, looking pained.

"No," I shook my head quickly from side to side. "I need you here."

Jason looked up at his sister, who shrugged, walked to the side of the bed and kissed me on the forehead.

"I...I'm so sorry, Auden." I could barely get the words out. I felt terrible that my best friend had to leave. She'd always been there for me. Always.

"Stop it," she said in a stern, confident voice. She leaned in and whispered in my ear, "This is how it should be."

She pursed her lips into a gracious smile. When she got to the doorway, she turned back, "I'll be right out here if you need me. Jase, give me an update when you can."

"You got it," he said, threading his fingers through my hair. After several attempts to braid it, he turned to my mom.

"Allison, would you help me with this?"

Mom smiled, chuckled to herself and walked to the other side of the bed, carefully braiding my hair and tying it with a small elastic. Instantly I was transported back to the facility where she had stayed for several months of our lives. Everything had changed so much since then. And for the first time, I realized I wouldn't change a thing. Not a single thing.

∽

"Okay, when I say go, you need to start pushing. We'll count to ten and then you can rest."

Those words, said with such delicate grace and ease were enough to send me into a tailspin. All of a sudden, I was completely and utterly terrified. The pain in my belly was gone, but I could still feel the pressure of Marty making his way into my lower abdomen. My breathing turned ragged and sweat collected on my forehead.

"It's going to be fine, honey," my mom said. But her voice didn't reassure me like I wished it would.

Jason quickly took my hand, squeezed it and brought it to his lips, kissing my skin gently.

"I'm right here. Let's do this together. You're so strong, Haddie. Stronger than anyone I've ever known. You can do this." He nodded at me as I whimpered. Those words, that nod—that's what I needed. Encouraging words from the man I loved.

I looked to Dr. Myers. "I'm ready."

"Okay, ready...go!"

I pushed down into my abdomen, with every ounce of strength within me. The lower half of my body was almost completely numb, but I could feel the exertion with every second they counted. I honestly didn't know if I was strong enough to make it to ten, but I kept pushing for as long as I could.

"Ten," the nurse said. I exhaled harshly and fell back in the bed. Jason wiped my forehead with a cold cloth and then kissed me softly. The warmth from his lips mixed with the cold left behind by the washcloth. It soothed me as I breathed in and out, preparing for the next push.

∽

In what felt like hours later, the nurse counted to ten again. I collapsed back onto the bed for the sixth time. I was exhausted as sweat poured from my face, my neck and my arms.

"Listen to me, Hadley. The baby is crowning. This is it. He's almost here. I know you're exhausted, but I need you to give me all the strength you have. Are you ready?"

I looked to Jason. His cheeks were red, his brow was damp and he was clutching my hand just as hard as I was clutching his. He pushed a few stray pieces of hair from my face, wiped me with a washcloth and nodded. I looked to my mom, and she repeated his actions. Pushing my hair behind my ears, wiping with the cloth and nodding. I felt strong. I felt ready. And damn it, I wanted to meet my son.

One.
Two.
Three.
Four.
Five.
"*C'mon, Hadley, don't give up on me.*"
Six.
Seven.
Eight.

"Here he is," Dr. Myers said as a primal grunt escaped my lips. My mom squealed, and I felt Jason's lips pressing to my forehead again and again.

"You did it," he said. "You did it."

Tears plummeted from my eyes as I heard the baby screaming bloody murder. Horrified that something was wrong, I looked to my mom in sheer panic. She just smiled as her eyes began to water.

"Totally normal," she said.

The nurse cleaned my son off, bundled him up and brought him to me. She placed him on my chest and he went silent, his eyes tightly shut. He was the most beautiful sight I could have ever imagined. His face was red and smooshed and kind of goopy at the eyes, but he was perfect. Insanely perfect. And he was all mine. His tiny fingers reached out from under the cotton blanket and I offered him my index finger. He grasped it, and the tiny movement made me gasp aloud.

"Oh my god," I said, looking to my right. Jason had tears streaming down his face. He looked at me with so much pride and so much care. It was overwhelming. And for a moment, I felt like we were a family. A real family.

"He's beautiful," Jason said, as he sniffed. He wiped his tears from his cheek and placed a hand on the outside of the baby's blanket. "As beautiful as his mom."

"Thank you for being here," I said through burning tears.

"There's nowhere else I'd rather be at this moment, Haddie. Nowhere."

"Would you like to hold him?" I asked, my eyes pleading. Hoping and praying he'd say yes.

"Are you kidding?" he said, grinning like a kid. "Of course. Let me wash my hands first. The books say it's the right thing to do." He jogged to the bathroom, washed his hands and returned to my side.

Carefully, I placed the baby in his arms. He gazed down at my son with admiration and joy. Just the way a father would look at his own child.

"What's his name?" Jason asked, looking to me again.

"Martin Whitman Foster," I said with a smile, knowing Jason would never expect the baby to bear his name in any way. But it was a gift that I wanted to give to him and my child.

His mouth opened in shock. He looked honored and overwhelmed and an entire batch of emotions that I wasn't even able to comprehend. But all of them were good.

"Are...are you sure?" he asked, his eyes welling up slightly, his nose getting red.

"Absolutely." I smiled, looking back down at my beautiful boy.

The knock at the door didn't startle me at all. I felt awful that no one had given Auden an update. She was standing at the door, but instead of looking happy for me, she looked sad, concerned, puzzled.

"Come and meet Marty," I said with a smile.

"Had, um...Tucker's here."

"What?" I screeched, unable to process what she'd just said. "I don't want him here."

"Honey," my mom said, "he's the father."

Guilt plagued her face as soon as she said the words. She looked to Jason with an apologetic glance and he froze. For the last few hours, we'd been able to deny the elephant in the room. But now, the father of the baby was here and he wanted to meet his son. And no matter what I wanted, I had to allow it.

"I'm going to step out for a little bit. Give you two a chance to..." Jason's voice trailed off as he looked down at the baby. Gently, he kissed Martin on the forehead and placed him in my arms.

"Please don't go," I begged, my voice trembling. I wanted him there with me. I *needed* him there.

"I can't be here. It'll be too awkward. But I won't leave the hospital, I promise. Okay?" he asked, smoothing my hair down. I took his hand in mine and kissed his palm, releasing him from me as my heart began to thud in my chest. I felt nothing for the man who was about to enter the room and absolutely everything for the one who was leaving it.

Tucker stood in the doorway. Jason walked to where he stood and extended his arm out to Tucker. Tucker was hesitant, but shook Jason's hand.

"Congratulations, man," Jason said before looking back at us one more time. He left the room, looking conflicted as he walked into the quiet hallway. Tucker didn't move. He just stood by the entrance of the room, his hands in his pockets.

"Can I come in?" he asked. His voice was husky and deep, with no trace of emotion whatsoever. It made me ill.

"Yeah," I said, looking down at our son. When Tucker stood next to me, it felt awkward and strained. Not at all like a family. I felt betrayed that someone had called him, even though he had every right to be there. I felt utterly lost.

"I'm going to give you two a minute, as well," my mom said, preparing to leave the room.

"Wait," I said, my eyes wide and desperate. I didn't want to be alone with Tucker. Not anymore.

"I'll be right outside the door. Just call out if you need me." She kissed me on the forehead, touched the baby gently and walked out of the room.

"How did you know? You haven't spoken to me in months."

"Your mom called me. She thought I should know." No wonder she had acted guilty and not at all surprised when he arrived.

Tucker and I sat in silence for several minutes. He watched the baby sleep, not asking to hold or touch him.

"Don't you want to know his name?" I asked, finally, after waiting for him to inquire on his own.

"Oh, god," he said, scratching his head, "Um, yeah. Does he have one?"

"Yes, he's Martin. But I'm calling him Marty."

"After your dad. That's great."

In that very moment, I realized that I hadn't yet confronted Tucker about the Post-It notes and the realization that I had had about his supposed gifts three years ago.

"I know they were never from you," I said through my teeth.

"What?"

"When my dad was sick. All those gifts. It wasn't you. None of them was."

He opened his mouth to speak, but hesitated.

"You never thought that would catch up to you, did you? Why the hell did you do that, Tucker?"

"I don't know—you were always so happy when they arrived. Whenever you called, I didn't want to spoil it. I knew I should probably tell you, but you were happy. I didn't wanna take that away."

"Or have someone else get the credit."

"Maybe, I don't know. It was a long time ago. Can we just focus on the kid?"

"I've done nothing but *focus on the kid* for months. Where have *you* been?"

I knew I shouldn't be raising my voice around my newborn son. But I was at my wits' end. I'd just given birth to a human being and I was feeling pretty invincible. Tucker had put me through way too much to receive a carefree welcome. I was angry and I wanted answers. I deserved them and so did our child. When Tucker said nothing, I raised my voice.

"I said, where have you been, Tucker?" I asked, glowering at him.

"What do you want me to say? That I'm an asshole? Fine, I'm an asshole. I still have a right to be here, to meet my kid."

"Okay fine. Then what?" I asked. Glaring into his lifeless brown eyes, I knew the answer to my question. And so did he, even if he didn't have the guts to say it out loud. I wish I could've said that I wasn't disappointed in him. But that would be a total lie. I'd known him for years and expected more. Instead of feeling cloaked and protected with love, I felt nothing but disdain and disappointment for Tucker. I could only hope, for Marty's sake, that one day he'd prove me wrong. Until then, my guard was up. And that's how things had to be.

CHAPTER TWENTY-FOUR

Jason

I had never held a brand-new baby before. I'd never felt the adrenaline of watching a new life enter the world. Was that all this feeling was? Because it felt like I'd fallen in love with that eight-pound little man. It felt like my world shifted for the better the moment I held him in my arms. And now... now I was sitting outside Hadley's room in an uncomfortable wooden chair in the waiting room, feeling like the walls were starting to close in on me.

Why is he here?

All of a sudden, without any sign or warning, Tucker had decided to be a part of all of this? It didn't make any sense to me. He didn't want Marty. I knew that in my gut. So why would he want to ruin things for Hadley? How selfish could someone *be*?

Auden rubbed my back as I sat with my head in my hands. My thoughts were racing through my head. I was completely and utterly head over heels in love with Haddie. I wanted her. And I wanted that baby. I wanted both of them for myself. And maybe that was the problem. Maybe *I* was the problem.

Hadley hadn't mentioned Tucker in months. I had got used to being the man in her life. I had got used to being the one who supported her, who held her hand when she was afraid. Hell, she had wanted me in the delivery room. But by replacing him with me, maybe she was just avoiding what had to eventually work itself out. Tucker was Marty's father. Not me.

A shot of adrenaline rushed through my veins and I popped out of my seat, pacing the floor. I couldn't keep up with my own thoughts, my own feelings. They zigzagged through my head and left me gasping for breath. It sucked. I wanted to stake my claim, beat the shit out of Tucker and kick his ass out of the hospital. I wanted to tell Haddie how I felt, ask her to be mine, and adopt that little man.

But then I realized that was all a fantasy. He wasn't mine. Haddie and I had never even been on a real date. Maybe I was just a distraction for her when things were out of control. Maybe she didn't have feelings for me at all. Maybe I was just kidding myself.

"Stop it," Auden said. Her voice was sharp, piercing my ears. I snapped my head towards her with a scowl on my face that felt permanent. I was beyond pissed. I wanted nothing more than to punch something. Hard.

"What?" I growled.

"Pacing, stomping around, acting like an alpha male," she said, her arms crossed in front of her chest, her eyebrow cocked. Was she enjoying my misery?

"Shut up, Auden," I said, shaking my head, looking away, pacing the floor again.

"I mean it, Whitman, knock it off. In a few minutes, Tucker will go and Hadley's going to need you."

"Are you sure about that?"

"Certain," Auden said with a sharp nod. "He doesn't love her. And he definitely doesn't want to be a father. The question is...do you?"

"I...I don't know."

"It's a big deal."

"Don't you think I know that? It's a big fucking deal. But I love her. I love her and I've never even kissed her. How fucking ridiculous is that?" I ran my hands through my hair so forcefully that a few strands were left between my fingers. A groan forced itself out of me as I sat back down in the chair.

"It's not. Not at all."

"Don't tell her I said that.... I don't wanna freak her out or anything."

"I know," Auden said, rubbing my back gently. My head fell back into my hands; my elbows were once again digging into my thighs.

"He doesn't deserve her."

"I know that, too," Auden said, her response dripping with sarcasm.

"There's something I just don't get," I said, turning to look at my sister's widened eyes.

"What?" Auden asked, tilting her head to the side and looking at me through the sides of her eyes.

"When her dad was sick...and I sent her those gifts. You should've told her they were from me. You *know* my handwriting."

"I never saw the gifts, I swear. She didn't want me coming to the house when Mr. Foster got sick. She was so protective of him...and he was so weak. She didn't want people looking at him weird...or feeling sorry for him."

"How could she think he would do all of that for her?"

"That was the lowest point in her life, Jase. And you weren't around...at all. Of course she thought it was all from her boyfriend. She needed someone to depend on. And for God's sake, he took credit for every single one of those presents. He makes me sick."

"He doesn't deserve her," I said, shaking my head.

"You said that already." She smiled weakly.

"But I do."

"Yes, you do."

"Do you think she loves me? Seriously, be real with me. I'm getting so wrapped up in her and in the baby that I can't even see straight. I need clear eyes to see for me."

Auden's smile grew and her eyes softened. "Big brother, that girl has been in love with you for most of our lives. That's not gonna change."

"So, tell me what to do. What do I do?" I said, removing my glasses and pinching the bridge of my nose.

"Sit here with me. Wait him out. I guarantee he'll be leaving soon."

"Okay. I can do that." I took a deep breath and sat back in the uncomfortable wooden chair. Staring at the door to Haddie's room, I just kept hoping Tucker would walk out, walk away, and be done.

Ten minutes.

Twenty.

Thirty.

He was still in there. I was doing my best not to feel insecure about any of it, but for god's sake, my mind was a whirlwind of all sorts of emotions. Was I supposed to be the better man and move aside? Did I need to give

Haddie a chance to make things work with Tucker? Would I be a total shit if I stood in the way of them becoming a family? My knuckles turned white as I grasped the arm of the chair. The thought of losing Haddie, and now Marty, made me feel physically sick. I felt trapped, out of control and desperate. Like an animal in a cage... only instead of being like Tucker and clawing to get out, I just wanted to get *in*.

They should be mine. And I should be theirs. I've never wanted anything more.

∼

I walked to the gift shop and picked up a balloon that said "It's a Boy" and a blue teddy bear wearing glasses. Auden laughed at the resemblance between the stuffed animal and me when I brought it back upstairs. I didn't even realize that I was drawn to a bear that looked like me.

"Marking your territory?" she asked with a smirk and one raised eyebrow. She's such a pain in the ass.

"No." Rolling my eyes, I sat back down, again watching the door. Tucker walked out just then. Without even realizing it, I was off the chair and walking towards him. My pace was determined. My mind was set. I had to fight for what I wanted.

Tucker's muscles stiffened the moment we made eye contact. His hands slid into his pockets. I held the bear close and the balloon drifted up to the ceiling. Tucker watched as it touched the white painted tiles.

"Hey," he said, making brief eye contact before looking past me. He was searching for Auden, assuming she'd come to his rescue. The dumbass didn't realize that my sister wasn't going to defend him anymore. She was done defending someone who had the nerve to treat Haddie and his own blood the way he had.

"Going so soon?" I asked with a smartass tone.

"Yeah, she doesn't want me here."

"And what about you? Did you hold your son?"

"No. I'm not so sure he's mine." He glowered at me.

"What? You think Haddie would lie to you?"

"How can you blame me? You're in the goddamn delivery room and now you're keeping guard for her. For all I know, you two have been fucking for months."

I grabbed him by the scruff of his neck and pressed him against the wall. Clipboards dropped at the nurses' station. The stuffed bear tumbled to our feet.

"Now you listen to me, shithead. I *wish* that were my kid in there. And if he were mine, I wouldn't let you near him...either of them. So, you better make a choice. Either be there for your kid or back the fuck off."

"If he's my kid, then that's not up to you, asshole," he said, just as a nurse stepped between us, pushing me back.

"Figure it out," I said, glaring into his eyes, "Quick. Or next time I won't be so nice."

Tucker let out a grunt and kicked the bear across the floor as he stomped down the hallway. The little stuffed animal bounced off the wall. The balloon swayed in the empty air.

"I didn't know you had it in ya," Auden said from behind me. I shook my head with exasperation.

"Do you ever shut up?" I glared at her. My kid sister still knew how to push my buttons.

"No...seriously," she said, her eyes glistening as she shook her head back and forth at a slow pace. "I've never been so impressed. You really love her."

"Yes...I do."

"So what are you doing out here with me? Get in there." She picked up the bear, dusted him off and placed him in my hands. I looked down at the little brown bear with tiny black hipster glasses. Giving him one more dusting, I walked back into the hospital room, the room that held everything that mattered to me.

CHAPTER TWENTY-FIVE

Hadley
Three weeks postpartum

Marty's wail pierced the air and sent the lights of the baby monitor into crazy manic flashes. I woke up with a start, rubbing the sleep from my eyes as I walked down the hall to his nursery. It was nearly daylight, just a hint of sunrise peeked through his navy blue curtains. He'd managed to wriggle himself out of his baby blanket in the few short hours he'd been in his crib. With a yawn, I carried my boy to the glider in the corner, placing my feet on the stool and opening up my nursing tank top.

"There you go, sweet boy," I said, stroking his head as he nursed greedily. It was amazing how much the baby ate; it was constant. Obviously, I wasn't completely naive. I knew that babies ate frequently. But for the last few days, it'd been every two hours and nursing him took about thirty minutes each time. I felt like a dairy cow. I was sore and exhausted, and deep bags sat beneath my eyes on a pretty consistent basis. The past three weeks had been the best, yet the most stressful, of my life.

I was constantly questioning myself. I called my mother more times in one day than I had for weeks at a time while away at college. She was gracious and patient. She gave advice, while also reminding me to follow the guidelines given by Marty's pediatrician.

"So many things have changed," she said again and again. It was hard to believe that anything of merit could've changed in the twenty-three years I'd been alive. But it was amazing how many guidelines had changed since my mom was raising me. Different car seats, sleeping positions, bottle usage, etc. I called her regardless. She was my safety net and my guru when it came to child rearing. But my rock... my rock was Jason.

He arrived every morning with coffee and breakfast. He spent most days writing at the dining room table while I nursed and changed Marty. He made me lunch, he watched the baby while I showered. He was amazing. It almost felt like we were a family. Almost.

At the end of the day, though, he went home to his place. We still hadn't kissed. In fact, he hadn't really touched me at all.

Tucker had called only once since I left the hospital. But he had left several hundred dollars underneath the door. *So classy.* Don't get me wrong—I wasn't going to be ungrateful for the help. But he knew money was not what I needed from him. My father's life insurance policy would support Marty and me until he started grammar school. I had plenty of time to decide when I would return to work. I could make the best decision for my child. Anything Tucker provided, at this point, was a bonus. I just wished he would make a choice. He either wanted his son or he didn't. I had nightmares, wondering how I would ever explain to Marty that his father didn't want me and therefore didn't want us. I hoped I'd never have to have that conversation with him. But it was impossible to know for sure.

When I dreamed about the future, though, I had to be honest with myself. Tucker wasn't there. It was Jason...always Jason. I envisioned the three of us playing at the local park. Marty as a toddler gliding down the large green slide, landing in Jason's arms. Jason twirling Marty in the air before placing him back at the top of the stairs. Repeating the slide again and again and again.

I saw us becoming a family. A *real* family. But I couldn't and wouldn't ever deny Tucker access to his son. As long as he wanted to be in his life, I'd allow it. But I refused to beg him...Marty would gain nothing from a forced parent in his life. He would see it—he would feel it and I could *never* do that to him.

As my thoughts continued to bounce around, I burped Marty and switched him to the other side to nurse. He drifted off to sleep as he drank. Gently, I rubbed his head to keep him from easing into a deep slumber. He startled briefly and went right back to nursing...but not quite as vigorously as he had before. Remembering my mother's tips, I broke his latch with my finger and carried him to the changing table. Diaper changes always woke my boy up.

His cry ripped through the apartment as I stripped him of his soiled diaper and quickly replaced it with a fresh one. After sanitizing my hands, we returned to the glider. My boy was now very much awake and ready to finish his breakfast.

I stared down at his precious little face. His slate blue eyes opened every so often as he nursed, a tiny dimple in his cheek as he drank. I loved his smell. I loved the little wrinkles in his wrists. I loved everything about this little boy I was lucky enough to bring into the world. Even when I was exhausted and even when I felt like a failure, at the end of each day, the love I felt for him kept me going.

An hour later, Marty was happily drifting to sleep in his swing. Jason arrived with the morning coffee as well as some bagels, lox and schmear from our local deli. My favorite.

"No capers for me, thanks," I said as Jason loaded my bagel up with goodies. He smiled and nodded as he built my breakfast.

"There you go, m'lady," he said with a fake British accent as he placed my bagel in front of me. Considering both of his parents were originally from England, it really was a pathetic excuse for an accent. I resisted the urge to tease him, though.

"Ahhh, it looks so delicious," I said, taking a big bite. With the saltiness of the lox combined with the creaminess of the schmear, I predicted I'd be in a food coma by the time the meal was through.

"Best deli in town." He smiled, biting into his open-faced sandwich.

"Nice t-shirt, by the way. It looks new," I said, gesturing as I wiped my mouth with a napkin.

"I thought Marty would like it." He laughed as he looked down at his emerald green shirt. It read: *Nobody puts baby in a corner.*

"It's perfect," I said, leaning in to nudge him on the arm. He gave me a lopsided grin before taking a sip of his coffee. "How's Madeline?"

"Good. Almost finished with Chapter Twenty-Seven. Now I just need an epilogue."

"Great. I can't wait to read it," I said with genuine enthusiasm.

"I'll let you read it later. Gotta get all the wrinkles out first."

"I love your books," I said, attempting to boost his confidence.

"I know, but... it's a matter of pride. I want the book to be awesome and I don't want you to read it before it's ready."

I shook my head. "Okay."

"There is something I've been meaning to ask you," he said with a cocky grin as he pushed his glasses up further on his nose. Usually a nerdy move, but Jason somehow made it sexy.

"What's that?" I asked, my pulse racing.

"Well, this might sound silly since I'm here... well, pretty much all the time. But Haddie, I'd like to know if you'd go on a date with me this Saturday night."

"Oh, wow..." I said with a smile, heat growing in my cheeks.

"Too soon?" He looked confused and a little nervous.

"No, no... I mean... maybe. For Marty, I mean. I'm not sure if I can be away from him yet."

"We could bring him with us," Jason suggested.

"No, no... I want us to have our own time. Maybe next weekend. He'll be a month old by then."

"Whatever works best." He nodded. "Whenever you're ready. Honestly."

"You're so awesome." I sighed. And suddenly, the idea of waiting another week was unacceptable. I pursed my lips with determination. "This Saturday."

Jason cocked an eyebrow. "Seriously, no pressure," he said, raising his arms up near his handsome face.

"It'll be wonderful," I said with sincerity. "I'll see if my mom can watch Marty."

"Perfect. And if not, mine will. You know how much she loves babies."

"I know," I replied with a smile. Mrs. Kelly had been fantastic. She had knitted everything under the sun for Marty: blankets, booties, sweaters and beanie hats. She was such an incredible woman. Every few days, Jason arrived with more gifts from his family. Poetry books from his father, knitted items from his mother and music from Maya. Auden had been showing up daily with gifts of her own. She already thought of Marty as her nephew and probably always would, no matter what happened between her brother and me. I loved that the Kelly family had embraced us both so completely.

There were moments, though, when I wondered if they'd ever see Marty as their own. Could they? Would they? And whenever I thought of the Kelly family, I inevitably thought of Tucker and his dysfunctional family. His mother and father had made no attempts to meet their grandson. The thought made me so angry at times I could barely see straight.

I stood and walked to the sink, placing my plate and half-eaten bagel on the counter top. Glancing down at the untouched container of capers, I was overcome with emotion. It took over my body completely and I had to grip the handle of the nearest drawer just to stay upright. Dad would not approve of untouched capers. He always did love those disgusting things. But he was gone... and no one was going to eat the capers.

"Try the capers, sweetheart."

"Ew, Dad, no." I shook my head vigorously. Those things looked like canned peas and smelled like sea salt. Yuck.

"You don't know what you're missing."

"I'll try one." Auden shrugged, popping one into her mouth. She chewed and made a face I'd seen anytime she tried something gross. She grabbed her can of Coke and downed most of it. "That was the most disgusting thing I've ever eaten."

My dad just shook his head and laughed. "You'll see. Your taste buds are always changing. When you're my age, you'll love them. Just wait."

"Whatever, Dad." I rolled my eyes like the dramatic twelve-year-old I had become. It was just another Sunday morning with my dad. Bagels, lox and schmear from the local deli. Mom didn't care for lox, so it was our thing. And when Auden slept over (which happened often) she was always happy to join us. Dad continued to pop them in his mouth just to gross us out. And each time, he shook his head and said something like, "Seriously, so good. Wanna try one?"

Around and around we'd go. Every single time.

God, I miss Sunday mornings.

"Haddie, what's going on?" The look of sheer horror on Jason's face dragged me back to reality. I was still holding the small plastic container, tears spilling down my cheeks.

"He always ate them. Always."

"Who? Your dad?"

I nodded in response, letting out an audible sob from my throat. I felt so caught up in the moment that I didn't even have time to notice just how crazy I must've seemed to Jason. All that mattered to me was the gaping hole in my heart.

"I miss him so goddamn much. And he'll never meet Marty. He'll never know his grandson."

"I know," he said, pulling me close, stroking my hair.

We stood in silence, Jason running his hands through my hair and letting his fingers glide across my shoulder blades. My sobs softened into soft whimpers in the comfort of his arms.

"I'll eat them," Jason said. I pulled away, my eyes stretched wide in shock.

"You hate them just as much as I do," I reminded him.

"So?"

"So, don't be stupid. It'll just gross you out... it won't bring him back."

Jason shrugged. "I'll be fine. It's nothing. Give them to me, please."

I narrowed my eyes at him, waiting for him to change his mind. But he tipped his head forward, raising his eyebrows expectantly, and reached out his hand to take the small container of capers.

"Do you want something to drink? You've got to wash those bad boys down, ya know."

"No, I'm okay," he said, popping three of the little mushy green capers into his mouth. He did his best not to grimace, but I knew he was disgusted. Without even realizing it, I laughed. And not just a small giggle. I let out a huge belly laugh as Jason popped more capers into his mouth, one after another after another. Soon we were both in hysterics, sitting in the middle of the kitchen floor. I couldn't remember the last time I'd laughed that much.

"Okay, okay, okay," I said, doing my best to pull myself out of my fits of laughter. "Give me one."

"No, you don't have to do that," Jason said, shaking his head. "I'm fine taking one for the team. Seriously."

"No, that's not it. My dad always said that when I was older, my taste buds would be more mature and that I'd like them. I want to test that theory."

A huge smile crossed my face and I felt almost giddy, picking up one caper from the small plastic dish. I stood up, plopping the caper on top of my open-faced sandwich. I took a deep breath and closed my eyes, bringing the bagel to my lips.

The saltiness overwhelmed my mouth at first, but the creaminess of the schmear and the crusty texture of the bagel all came together to make something even more delicious than I could have imagined. My eyes widened as I chewed. Tears formed again. Only this time, they were tears of amazement, tears of surprise, tears of absolute joy.

"He was right. It's so good. You have to try them on your bagel."

Jason and I returned to the kitchen table, piling our bagels with the rest of the capers, marveling at how all the tastes really did come together. Jason was the perfect breakfast companion. He encouraged me to talk about my dad instead of avoiding it. And so, over my dad's favorite breakfast, I shared all sorts of stories about the man who had had such a profound impact on my life. The man who cleaned up my skinned knees with Bactine and had tea parties with my stuffed Hello Kitty doll. The man who encouraged me to climb trees and to always believe in the goodness of others. It felt so good to discuss the wonder of the man who was Martin Foster. The man who had raised me. The man who had taught me to believe in myself. The man who had known his daughter would enjoy capers on her bagel when she was all grown up.

CHAPTER TWENTY-SIX

Hadley
Four weeks postpartum

My heart was racing all afternoon. My mom had just arrived to spend the evening with the baby and I was putting the finishing touches on my hair. Thick, loose waves, the way Jason seemed to like it best. He hadn't touched me much since the baby was born, but sometimes when we watched television, he ran his fingers through my hair. And I loved it. So there was no way I was going to put my hair up. I wanted him to have full access to my curls.

I finished my hair and joined my mother in the kitchen. I'd just nursed Marty, so he would be okay for a little while, but she needed to see the prepared bottles in the refrigerator. She listened intently, nodding at each instruction I gave. She understood how strange this was for me. I'd been with him constantly for the last month, never even leaving to grab a coffee or go to the store. I just hadn't had any desire to be away. But tonight was my very first date with Jason. A date I'd been waiting for since I was eight years old. It was the best motivation I could ever have to leave my baby with my mother for a few hours.

The bell rang and in an instant, the lovesick teenager in me returned, knowing Jason was on the other side of the door. And tonight, he wasn't there as a friend. He wasn't there as a helper. He was there as a man who desired me, a man who *wanted* me.

"Are you gonna get that?" My mom smirked. Since the doctors had altered her medication, bits and pieces of the Allison Foster I grew up with were shining through—her smirks, her sarcasm. Each little glimpse made me smile and lessened the ache in my heart.

She's coming back to me.

"Oh...right," I said. "Do I look okay?"

"Gorgeous." My mom smoothed my hair down with her hand, gliding it across my cheek. That was all the reassurance I needed.

Quickly, I opened the door and was taken aback by the man standing before me. His hair was cut, his stubble was gone and a brand new pair of glasses sat on his nose. They were slim and black. They complemented his features perfectly. As fancy as his face appeared, though, he was dressed as only Jason Kelly would be. He had a navy blue t-shirt on underneath a blue-and-white checkered button-down oxford. He was holding an elegant bouquet of calla lilies, wrapped with a simple satin ribbon.

He handed me the bouquet of gorgeous flowers. "You look beautiful."

As I held the flowers in my hands, I glanced back at my handsome date. Since the flowers were no longer blocking my view of his chest, I saw it peeking from behind the checked oxford. The Camp North Star t-shirt I had given him for his birthday all those years ago. The shirt I had assumed he'd forgotten about a long time ago. I couldn't believe my eyes.

"You remember this?" Jason asked, grasping his shirt between his fingers.

"How could I forget?" I asked. "I can't believe you still have it."

"Are you kidding? It's one of my most prized possessions. Always has been," Jason replied, his voice soft and gentle as he took my hand in his.

Wow, this is all happening. This is real. The man I've loved for fourteen years wants me in return.

Jason entered the apartment, giving me a quick peck on the cheek. My skin grew hot beneath his touch and I started to feel flustered.

"Hey, Mrs. Foster," Jason said with a large smile.

"Jason, you look nice," Mom said.

I stopped myself from rolling my eyes in embarrassment. I had never dreamed that when I was twenty-three years old, my mother would be present for a first date. Funny how things never turn out quite as planned. I was starting to realize that my plans had never been set in stone. They were ideas of how things should be. And it was okay to have new ideas, new plans, new dreams.

"Where are we going?" I asked Jason as he opened the passenger door to his Jeep Wrangler. I gladly climbed in as I waited for his answer. He just smiled and closed the door, trotted around the car, not saying a word. He climbed in next to me, still silent.

"You know you want to tell me," I flirted. But he didn't budge. He just shook his head, started the car, and tried his best to focus on the road.

Ten minutes later, I knew exactly where we were going. Once again, this man knew exactly what to do... exactly how to impress me, to bring the memories flooding back to my lovesick brain.

"I can't believe you remembered."

"I've already told you, Haddie. When it comes to you, to *us*... I remember everything."

"You're going to love this pizza," Auden said. It was a regular Saturday night and we were having a sleepover at her house.

"You've never been to Bill's Pub, honey?" Mrs. Kelly looked at me as if I was an alien from a distant planet. Everyone in our town went to Bill's on a somewhat regular basis. But my family didn't. My dad was highly allergic to peanuts. When my parents had moved to the town after they got married, they had visited the infamous neighborhood pizza parlor, only to discover that every table was given a bowl of peanuts to eat. My dad couldn't be near peanuts or the surfaces where peanuts had been. Needless to say, my parents had left Bill's Pub as quickly as they'd entered it. And never returned.

"Her dad's allergic to peanuts," Auden replied. "You knew this, Mom." She rolled her eyes and twirled her hair as we pulled into the parking lot.

"Are you allergic?" Jason asked from the other side of the minivan. He looked concerned.

"No, not at all."

"Have you ever had them?" Mr. Kelly asked, looking concerned as well.

"Yes, at my grandpa's house. And my mom gets me peanut butter cups sometimes," I said. Both men in the family looked like their fears had been calmed.

We walked into the restaurant, and as we were led to our table, I heard the sound of crunching under our feet.

"That's the shells," Jason said with a grin. "You can throw them wherever you want."

"Within reason," Mrs. Kelly corrected him.

We sat down and Auden's parents began to read the menu. Luckily Maya was sleeping at a friend's house, so no one would be forced to share an anchovy pizza with her. She was the only person I knew who actually liked to eat them. The thought of them made me gag. Mr. Kelly usually appeased her and shared the revolting dish, while the rest of us crinkled our lips in disgust.

"Are you gonna get Cinderella cheese?" Jason asked as we popped peanuts in our mouths. I glared at Auden. She'd told him about my stupid habit as a little kid. I called mozzarella cheese Cinderella cheese up until I was seven years old. And as a fourteen-year-old who was hopelessly smitten with my friend's older brother, it wasn't something I wanted to be reminded of.

"You never said 'vault.'" Auden shrugged, her words defensive and a little bratty. Sometimes my best friend drove me crazy, but I loved her just the same.

"True," I said, rolling my eyes.

For the rest of the meal, it was hard for me to make eye contact with Jason. I couldn't figure out why he teased me. It wasn't usually his style. Sure, he made fun of Auden every so often, but with me he was always kind and sweet. I hated to think that something had changed.

I was quiet for a long time before excusing myself to go to the washroom. When I walked out of the ladies' room, I was startled to see Jason leaning against the wall, looking my way. I looked behind me, unsure of why he was standing there.

"Auden's not with me."

"I know. She's still at the table," Jason said casually.

"Oh."

"I needed to say something... to you."

"Um... okay," I said, pressing my clammy hands into my pockets as he closed the gap between us. My heart thumped rapidly in my teenage chest as my one and only crush got closer and closer to me.

"I'm sorry about the cheese thing. I didn't mean to hurt your feelings."

"Oh... no, I'm fine," I said, looking away.

"No, I can tell. You got upset."

"Yeah," I said, shrugging my shoulders. "You were different."

"I'm sorry," he said, looking me in the eyes. His green eyes sparkled in the track lighting above our heads. My cheeks reddened as his lips grew closer and closer to mine. Gently, his soft lips pressed gently to mine and my breath caught in my throat. I couldn't believe it. My very first kiss... and it was with Jason. My head was swimming. I knew it wasn't his first kiss. After all, he was seventeen and had had lots of dates. But that didn't matter. In this very special moment, the boy I adored was kissing me. On the lips! And it exceeded any expectation I'd ever had.

Just as quickly as it had started, Jason pulled his lips from mine. He gave me a warm smile, running the pad of his thumb down my cheek before turning to walk back to the table. I stood next to the bathroom door, completely stunned. Several women walked past me, each saying, "Excuse me." Finally, I was able to make my way back to the dinner table, even though my brain was still locked in that moment with Jason. It was my first kiss and he'd made it unforgettable.

"Did you honestly think I'd forget our first kiss?" Jason asked as he pulled into the nearest parking spot.

"I guess I did." I shrugged. "I mean, it was special for *me*, but..."

"And me," he insisted, killing the engine and taking my hand in his.

There was a reason I thought he'd forgotten, but maybe he'd forgotten that, too. Forgotten how he had completely broken my heart just days after that kiss.

"This is mortifying," I said, shaking my head, not making eye contact, and wanting desperately to change the subject.

"Going back to the place we first kissed?" He looks confused.

"That was my first kiss...like, ever."

"That was your *first* kiss?"

"You couldn't tell?" My eyes widened in utter surprise.

"You seemed nervous, yeah. But I had no idea," he said with a laugh. "Is it a total guy move if I think that's pretty awesome?"

"That you were my first kiss? Why?" I smiled, the tension lessening with each laugh that came from his beautiful mouth. He squeezed my hand in his.

"Because I'm planning to be your last."

I was stunned, frozen.

I can't believe he just said that.

I was elated, surprised, and (if I was being honest myself) a little turned on. Jason was unfazed. He didn't look the least bit embarrassed or exposed. He wanted his intentions to be clear.

He quickly hopped out of the Jeep, walking around to open my door for me. He took my hand in his and helped me out. We walked, hand in hand, into Bill's Pizza, the place where we had first kissed. I hadn't been there in years. I had accompanied the Kellys there on many occasions. I loved the pizza so much and had wished I could come here with my own family.

Jason put his name in at the hostess station before raising an eyebrow and dragging me toward the washroom. A nervous giggle escaped my lips as we stood in the exact same spot as we had nine years ago. The corners of Jason's mouth rose as he looked into my eyes, running his fingers through my hair. I took a deep breath in, waiting to feel his lips on mine.

Just as he leaned in, the door opened and hit me square in the back.

"Ouch," I yelped.

"Oh no! Are you all right?" Jason asked after the woman had apologized and walked past us, looking confused.

"Yeah, sure.... I guess that wasn't how you pictured, was it?" I asked with a laugh.

"Just because things aren't as you pictured them, doesn't mean they're any less perfect," Jason said, moving me back to the wood paneling. Swallowing hard, I backed into the wall, leaning my hands against the knotty pine.

Jason kissed my neck, his lips barely tracing a soft line up to my chin. My breath grew heavy as I tried to tune out the noises of the restaurant. By the time his lips reached mine, I was aching for him, completely ready for my second kiss with Jason Kelly.

His lips brushed mine gently at first, just like they had all those years ago. But this time, I knew what I was doing and I wanted more. So much more. His fingers threaded through my hair as I opened my mouth, allowing him to deepen the kiss. His tongue swept into my mouth and I felt as if I'd come apart right there in the hallway of a family restaurant.

After several moments, Jason gently took my bottom lip into his mouth, grazing it with his teeth. It was the most sensual feeling I'd ever had. Part of me wanted to tell him to forget about dinner and take me home to his place. But would that be cheap of me? This was only our first date...although we'd had over a decade of foreplay.

I resisted the urge to pull Jason back to his car and followed him to our table. We sat in the clunky wooden booth and smiled as a bowl of peanuts was placed between us. Jason ordered a Diet Coke for me and a beer for himself.

"Would it be awful if I sent my mom a text? I want to make sure the baby's okay."

"I'm surprised you waited this long," Jason teased. I arched an eyebrow and he smiled. "I'm kidding. Check on the baby."

Quickly, I sent a text to my mom: **Everything okay?**

Placing the phone on the table, I gave him a sheepish smile. It chimed within seconds.

I glanced at the screen: **Everything's perfect. Enjoy your date!**

∽

The rest of the night went by easily with playful banter and revisited memories. When I brought up his old tree house, Jason became quiet. And I knew I *had* to pester him about it. Maybe, just maybe I'd stumbled upon his "Cinderella cheese" topic.

"I want to know why you never let us go up there," I pressed.

"You know why," he said, fidgeting with the peanut bowl.

"You're blushing," I flirted, kicking him lightly under the table.

His eyes grew serious as he looked into mine.

"I know you went up there, Haddie."

"What?" I was stunned once again. Auden and I had gone up into his tree house just once...and never went again. We were snooping, big time. All of a sudden, it made sense. I realized why Jason had gotten shy.

"You dropped your lip gloss. I found it behind the trunk," he said.

"Oops," I said, looking embarrassed. "How did you know it was mine?"

He blushes. "It was strawberry. You always smelled like strawberries. Auden smelled like...Auden," he said, grimacing at the thought of his sister's scent.

"It was only once, I promise."

"It's okay. They weren't all mine, though." He shifted in his seat, looking awfully uncomfortable.

"I don't know what you're talking about." I snickered as I stirred my Diet Coke flirtatiously with my straw. But I knew *exactly* what he was talking about.

"Jason said we weren't allowed up here!" I yelled up to Auden as she climbed up the wooden stairs attached to the large oak tree in the Kellys' backyard. We'd been scheming to sneak up into Jason's tree house for weeks, but I never intended to go through with it. He'd warned us that if we went up there, Auden would get her butt kicked. Hard. But I guess she wasn't very scared.

Jason was thirteen and I had just turned ten. I knew by then that I had a crush on him. I had gotten used to blushing in his presence. He and his buddies spent a lot of their time up in his old tree house. We'd hear them laughing up there for hours and we got curious. That day, Jason had gone to his friend Lucas's house, so Auden felt it was safe.

"I'm the one he's going to beat up, not you! Stop being such a baby!" Auden said, just as I reached the top. I looked into the small wooden space. A simple desk sat in one corner of the small square, and a trunk with a very large combination lock sat in another.

"Wow," I said, looking around the tiny space, "this doesn't look too impressive."

"Not yet," Auden said with a Cheshire Cat grin as she walked toward the simple black trunk, covered with all sorts of stickers from the European countries their family had visited over the years.

"It's locked, dumbass."

"This is my dad's old gym lock. I know the combination." Quickly, she fiddled with the lock, but it didn't budge, despite her pulls and yanks.

"It must be a different lock," I said with a shrug. "Come on, let's go."

"No, this is it. It's neon green with pink numbers... straight outta the '80s. That's why Jason likes it so much. Just gimme a second to figure it out." She spun the lock this way and that until we heard a tiny pop right as the lock sprang open.

"You did it!" I squeal, walking to her side.

"Ew! My brother's a pig!"

Inside the trunk were dirty magazines... and lots of them. So many Playboy magazines stacked one on top of another. Next to the magazines were candy bars, Twizzlers and all sorts of snacks. Taking my hands out of my pockets, I quickly grabbed a piece of evidence from the pile.

"So, wait... he comes out here to look at naked ladies?" My voice came out like a whine. I could never compare to the women in the pages of those magazines. They were perfect. Huge boobs, rounded hips and smooth skin. My body was getting awkward, and I swear I was getting my first pimple. I had the flattest chest in my class and no hips to speak of. To say I was intimidated by the images in my hands would be a giant understatement.

"Looks like it," Auden said, placing the magazines carefully in the trunk. "At least the pages aren't sticking together."

"Eww, you're gross, Auden!" I said, pushing her on the arm. She laughed.

"If you had a brother, you'd understand," she said, rolling her eyes. "C'mon, let's get outta here."

As quickly as possible, we locked the trunk up and ran back to the house. Jason was still at Lucas's house. We were in the clear. Thank God.

"Ahem," he cleared his throat. "The things you found up there, they *weren't* all mine."

"How do you know we found something?" I teased as I felt Jason's foot rubbing against my calf. Tiny goose bumps stood on my arms.

"Because all the magazines were out of order. That plus the lip gloss... I kinda figured it out."

"So, whose were they?"

"Did you look at the address label?"

"No, we weren't exactly taking our time. We didn't want to get caught," I said with a laugh.

"Ahhh, well, they were Lucas's. When his dad took off, he left all his Playboys. Lucas didn't have anywhere to hide them."

"So, you took one for the team, eh?" I teased. He gave me a wink and took my hand in his.

"I do what I can." He tried to say it with a straight face, but laughter erupted from both of us.

"I had no idea I dropped my lip gloss. Auden would kill me if she found out."

"It was like twelve years ago!" Jason scoffed.

"With your sister, that's a minor detail. She'd kick my ass if she knew I blew our cover."

"You're hilarious." He shook his head, his eyes gazing into mine.

"Thanks." I smiled, tucking my hair behind my ear. Tucker never thought I was funny.

Why on earth did I waste so much of my time with someone who barely noticed me?

"You're also gorgeous."

"Tell me more," I said, suddenly feeling bold. I drew shapes on his hand with my fingernail. Just enough to tickle and entice.

"Your heart... it's what I love the most."

"Why?" I pushed, my voice hushed.

"Because it's so full. No matter what life places ahead of you, you come out stronger. And you continue to love. When I see you with Marty, it kills me."

"Kills you?"

"In a good way," Jason said, slightly defensive. "C'mon, you know what I'm saying."

"I do." My voice was low and soft. He swallowed hard, looking into my eyes. Suddenly his emerald eyes looked dark and more intense than I'd ever seen them.

"I've wanted you for years."

"And I you." I smiled, drawing zigzags repeatedly on his palm. My heart was racing and I felt more turned on than

I had in years. I wanted him so badly I could feel it all the way to my toes.

"You wanna get outta here?" Jason asked, narrowing his eyes at me.

"Yes," I said with a nod.

Within seconds, we were walking out of Bill's Pub and climbing into Jason's Jeep.

"Where to?" he asked, glancing at me before focusing on the road.

"The tree house," I said brazenly.

"Are you serious?" Jason asked.

"Completely serious."

"My parents are there, ya know...."

"I know." I was not backing down. I wanted him in the tree house. And I didn't want to wait a second longer.

Thunder struck as we drove to his parents' place. They lived in one of those subdivisions where the houses are far away from one another. Jason parked the car a few houses down, walked around and helped me out of the Jeep. A nervous laugh escaped me as we walked hastily toward his parents' home.

Drops of water landed on my arms. I looked up to see drop after drop pouring from the sky. Jason pulled my arm a little tighter and we ran to the backyard, laughing as we brushed the rain from our hair. Luckily the tree provided plenty of shelter from the impending storm. Water pounded around our feet as we stood beneath the tree, panting for breath. Our laughter subsided as Jason placed one hand on my cheek and the other against the tree. He eased me back, pressing me against the oak. I swallowed hard as he looked into my eyes, my hand pressed against his chest. The rapid beat of his heart was hypnotic.

"You're the sexiest woman I've ever laid eyes on," he said, stroking my cheek with his thumb. He looked down at my lips and then up to my eyes again. I nodded furiously, knowing I needed him to kiss me hard.

He crushed his lips to mine, pushing me back into the tree. His tongue twisted with mine and I felt myself coming apart at the seams. He was all I'd ever imagined he would be.

His strong hands raised my arms above me and pressed them against the brittle bark. My hands extended and felt strong branches on each side of me. I grasped the branches and pulled myself up, wrapping my legs around Jason's waist. He pulled away briefly and gave me a naughty smile before kissing me again with so much fervor I could barely contain myself. My heels dug into the small of his back as he placed both hands on my ass, gently kneading with his fingertips, making me moan into his mouth.

He pulled away and placed his forehead on mine. His breathing was harsh, his chest heaving up and down.

"I should take you home," he said softly.

"What? Now?" I asked, tilting my head to the side. I needed to see him, to see the expression in his eyes. I couldn't imagine that he didn't want this just as much as I did.

His glasses were fogging up and I had to laugh since I could barely see his irises peeking through the white mist on the glass.

"We can't do this, Haddie. Not yet."

"Are you sure?"

"No." He laughed, putting his head on my shoulder. I wrapped my arms around his neck and slowly eased my feet to the ground. I stroked his hair with my hands.

"I want you...so bad."

"Me too... But not like this. You deserve *so* much more."

"What, like flowers and candles and all of that?"

"Why not? You deserve it. Absolutely all of it."

"Thanks." I smiled, feeling modest. "I guess I should get home to the baby."

He took my hand in his and we walked slowly in the pouring rain, back to his Jeep. As he helped me into my seat, he gave me a wicked grin.

"Ya know, the fact that you wanted to do that with my parents just a few yards away was risky."

"Yeah?" I said, raising an eyebrow.

"And a total turn-on. I didn't know you were such a rule breaker."

"Well, you know now," I flirted.

"Yes, I do."

Jason drove back to my apartment building. The rain had stopped and we were able to say a proper goodbye outside my door. Jason kissed my forehead, the tip of my nose, each of my cheeks and finally my lips. It was the most exquisite kiss of my life.

"Goodnight, my sweet," he said, lifting my hand and kissing it softly. My skin tingled from his touch as he turned to walk back to his car. I watched as he drove away. With a deep breath, I unlocked my door and prepared to return to my role as Mommy, knowing Marty would be awake (and hungry) in just a few short hours.

CHAPTER TWENTY-SEVEN

Jason
Eight weeks after Marty's birth

"This is nice," Haddie said as we walked through Target, sipping our coffee. Marty slept in his carrier; the motion of the cart kept him in dreamland. Haddie's cheeks were pink and I swear she still had a glow to her skin, just like she did during pregnancy.

"Motherhood suits you," I observed, running my finger across her cheek. Haddie leaned into my hand, nuzzling against it.

I'm not sure I've ever been as happy as I am right this minute.

"You think so?" she asked, gazing into my eyes in the middle of the diaper aisle.

"Absolutely."

I leaned in for a quick peck on the lips before Haddie placed a box of Pampers under the cart. I pushed the cart into the main aisle and just as we made our way to the grocery department, Haddie gasped next to me. Her feet were suddenly glued to the floor.

"What is it?"

"Mrs. Montgomery," she said, her face ghostly white.

I was still confused. That last name escaped me.

"Marty's grandmother."

"Oh," I said, doing my best not to show how much that word stung. I wasn't a moron. I knew my parents weren't Marty's grandparents. But Tucker had basically been nonexistent since his birth, so I usually thought of them that way. I tended to see us as a family. Maybe I was kidding myself. Maybe Tucker and his family and his fucked-up ties to this little boy would never go away. Maybe it was time I got used to it.

"Let's say hi," I urged her, rubbing her back gently. Before Haddie had a chance to answer, the woman approached. She looked like someone you'd see at fancy cocktail parties and charity banquets. Wearing pearls in the middle of Target, hair in a bun and at least two layers of makeup caked on her wrinkled face. She could be a fantastic villain in my next book.

"Hello, Hadley," she said as she approached. Her skin paled when she noticed the baby carrier inside the cart. She immediately glared at me with daggers in her eyes.

She had no idea this was her grandson. She thought he was mine and that Haddie had deceived her son. Her Mama Bear claws were about to come out. How could I protect Haddie?

"Hello, Lydia," Haddie said, her voice cracking. Her hands were shaking as she placed them on the handle of the cart. I quickly reached for her left hand and held it in mine. Standing tall, I was ready to defend her if necessary.

"Who is this?" Lydia Montgomery said in a fake perky tone as she gestured towards the baby. Haddie looked shocked, completely taken aback.

"This is Martin," Haddie said. She hesitated, waiting for recognition from the woman standing before her. But nothing. Nothing at all. Haddie's breathing picked up, her chest rising and falling with each breath she took.

"Your grandson," Haddie said. Her voice strong and assertive...and completely calm.

Lydia stopped dead in her tracks, looking at Haddie as if she'd just been poisoned.

"I don't understand."

"Tucker didn't tell you? This is his son."

We stood in silence for what felt like several minutes. Haddie looked angry and disappointed. Lydia still looked shocked....But not the good kind at all. She looked furious...and skeptical. I felt anger rising in my chest.

"No," Lydia said, "you two broke up months ago."

"After he found out I was pregnant," Haddie asserted.

"He wouldn't do that."

"No, he backed me into a corner and made *me* do it."

"I don't believe you."

"Honestly, Lydia, I'm not sure I *care*. This is your grandson. Tucker obviously didn't want you to know."

"He wouldn't lie to me...not about this."

"He did."

"And who are you?" she asked, glaring in my direction.

"I'm her boyfriend."

"That's convenient," she scoffed.

"And what is that supposed to mean?" Haddie asked defensively.

"How do I know you're not trying to trick my son? You *know* how much money our family has."

Haddie stopped, shook her head and resumed pushing the cart.

"I'm not listening to this. Go talk to your son. Until then, you don't deserve to be anywhere near *my* baby." With hands still shaking, Haddie pushed the cart away from Lydia. Lydia's eyes followed us as we turned the corner, walking to a different department of the store. I put my arm around Haddie, comforting her as best I could. As my hand squeezed her shoulder, she closed her eyes and took a few deep breaths.

"I'm so proud of you," I said, kissing her on the cheek.

"Thank you. But I've never been more ashamed in all my life."

"Why? Because Tucker's an idiot?"

"Because he kept my pregnancy a secret. I obviously meant nothing to him. So many years wasted on a selfish prick who can't even take responsibility for being a father."

"That's not about you. He's an asshole. And so is his mother."

"I haven't heard from him at all. He doesn't call. He doesn't check on Marty. Every so often there's a check in the mailbox. That's it."

"He has no idea what he's missing," I said, stroking Marty's tiny foot with my finger.

"I wasn't worth it to him. I wasn't worth anything to him."

"That's his loss. You're everything... everything."

Wrapping her in my arms in the middle of Target, Haddie sighed into my shoulder. No tears, but I could feel her body shaking as I held her. It took everything in me not to drop her off at her place and continue on to Tucker's apartment. My love for Haddie and her son was the only thing that would keep me from wiping the floor with that dipshit. He was lucky... for now. But the deeper I fell in love with this woman, the stronger the desire became to pummel him until he couldn't see straight.

He's put her through so much... so goddamn much. Karma's a bitch, though, and that bitch had better get to work.

CHAPTER TWENTY-EIGHT

Hadley
One hour later

"You've gotta be kidding me."
"What is it?" Jason asked, unloading the groceries as I stared down at the angry text from Tucker.
"'**WTF did you say to my mom**?'" I recited, reading the message on my phone.
"Is he serious? He lies to his parents, denies the existence of his own kid and he's coming after *you* because you bumped into her?" Jason said, fists clenched, his cheeks getting redder by the second.
I texted back: **Grow up, Tucker.**
His response: **Whatever. I was going to tell them.**
And mine: **Your son is 8 weeks old. Shit or get off the pot.**
There were no more text messages from Tucker. He knew he was in the wrong, even if he denied it. But I'd had enough. If he didn't want to be involved in raising Marty, that was fine. I wouldn't force him. But to pretend he didn't even exist? That was completely unacceptable and I wouldn't tolerate it any longer.
"Should I go talk to him?" Jason asked, his feet planted to the floor, his muscles tense. I hated that Tucker had so much power over us. We had a brand-new relationship

and yet he was able to completely ruin a perfectly pleasant Sunday afternoon.

"No, no. Don't let him ruin our day. Marty will be waking up soon. Let's just finish up here and watch a movie or something."

"Okay." He smiled reluctantly and kissed me softly on the cheek. I knew he was fuming. I knew he wanted to beat the living hell out of Tucker. But I also knew his feelings for me were stronger than his rage. And I was immensely grateful for that.

About thirty minutes into *Better off Dead*, Marty stirred in his carrier. He was hungry. I loved that I was learning his cries. I knew when he was tired or when he was wet. Each cry was slightly different. Just knowing I'd figured that out was building my confidence. Maybe I could handle being a mom. I was learning to understand my son. He was communicating with me and I loved it.

After nursing Marty and changing his diaper, I brought him back into the living room. Jason immediately extended his hands with a giant smile on his face.

"Come 'ere, big guy," he said as I placed Marty in his arms. He gave him a small kiss on the top of his head and carried him to the couch. Just then, there was a knock at the door. I knew immediately who it was.

I opened the door cautiously. Tucker was fuming on the other side of the wooden door. I stood, blocking the entrance.

"Aren't you going to invite me in?"

"I don't think that's a good idea."

"You said to shit or get off the pot. So, I'm here."

"Oh... how *big* of you," I said, shaking my head. I resisted the urge to roll my eyes.

"He's my kid. Let me see him."

"Did you tell your mom he's yours?"

"No," he said, crossing his arms in front of his chest.

"Then no."

"What the fuck?" His eyes darkened as he stared at me.

"You will not deny the existence of your son, your flesh and blood, and then expect to spend time with him."

"It's not her business."

"He's her *grandson!*" I said, raising my voice.

"She doesn't *want* a grandson, Hadley!" He stopped, looking up at the ceiling. Something he always did when he lost his temper and said something he didn't mean to say.

"She thinks I'm after your money."

"Yeah."

"And so do you," I said, raising a suspicious eyebrow.

"I don't know. Maybe," he said with a shrug, avoiding eye contact.

"Get out," I said, anger growing deep inside my belly. I never imagined Tucker or his family would so blatantly question my integrity.

"Had, c'mon. Let me see him."

"Why? You want to study his hair color? See if he looks like you? He's your spitting image, asshole. And don't think that's easy for me, because it's not. But he's mine and I love him."

Just then, Jason walked up behind me, placing his hand on my shoulder.

"Oh, for fuck's sake," Tucker grunted, his hands on his hips.

"Is there a problem?" Jason said. He crossed his arms against his chest, standing tall and glowering at Tucker.

"I want to see my kid," he grumbled, gritting his teeth.

"That's not up to you," Jason said.

"Listen, you two can play house all you want. Looks like she roped you in pretty good."

"What in the hell does that mean?" I practically screeched, seething.

"You know exactly what it means. You've conned this poor bastard into taking care of my kid." Tucker sneered.

"I haven't conned anyone into *anything*," I said in disbelief. I couldn't believe what I was hearing.

"I think you'd better go," Jason said, gently urging me to step back into the apartment.

"Fine. Whatever."

"I'm so tired of your goddamn whatevers, Tucker. Make a decision for god's sake. Either be there for Marty, or go the hell away. Sign away your rights and he won't be yours anymore."

I didn't even think about the words. I just wanted him to go. I knew I was acting hateful, but I couldn't stop the venom from seeping through my veins.

"I may just do that," Tucker said quietly, piercing my eyes with his.

He walked away and I slammed the door. Marty wailed and I felt like the worst mother in the world. I was screaming at my kid's father with my baby in the room.

What kind of person have I become?

"I've got him. Go lie down for a few minutes, Haddie."

"No, I'm fine...really."

"It's all good. Little man and I are gonna hang out and watch some football. Go rest. Put your feet up, read a book. Get lost in a story. And when you feel better, come and join us."

"Okay," I said, still feeling pins and needles all over my skin. I was edgy, angry and confused. Would Jason think I was using him? Would he think I just wanted him around so he'd help me with Marty? As I turned to walk away, he took my hand in his as he cradled the baby.

"You know I don't believe a word he said, right?"

I gave him a weak smile and replied, "You always know just what to say."

And even though I adored Jason for trying to make me feel better, Tucker's words were sticking with me...and I despised him for it.

CHAPTER TWENTY-NINE

Hadley
Three months after Marty's birth

This morning, as I stepped outside to get the morning paper, I found a gift basket by the door... inside was the final first draft of his latest book as well as several wildflowers and a candle.

What is he up to?

A small envelope was attached to the pages of his manuscript. I opened it to find a simple card.

H-

Tonight is ours.
My parents will be coming to sit for Marty.
They will arrive at 6:00 and I will arrive soon after them.
Dress comfortably.
I can't wait to see your gorgeous face.

You amaze me,
J

The rest of the unseasonably warm December day dragged on and on as the anticipation grew. I did what I could to keep busy. I cleaned the apartment, took Marty on a couple of walks in his stroller, and read Jason's newest masterpiece as the baby slept. Before I knew it, it was 5:00 and time to get ready. Luckily I had some time before the baby would be up, so I showered and got ready for my date with Jason.

My heart was pounding with the very best kind of anxiety. We'd shared several passionate kisses since the night against the tree in his parents' backyard. But nothing more than that. Maybe tonight would be the night. God, I hoped so. I felt an unbearable amount of tension building between us. It grew heavier and heavier in the air the more time we spent together. If we waited any longer, I swore I would fall apart.

Jason's parents were right on time, eager to see the baby. When I asked them if they had any idea what their son was up to, Mrs. Kelly gave me a wink and looked away, focusing back on the baby. I scrunched my nose, knowing he was up to something. And knowing Jason, it was something fantastic.

When Jason arrived a few minutes later, he was carrying a large bouquet of wildflowers, similar to the ones he'd left in the basket. His eyes widened as he looked at me from head to toe. I'd kept it simple with a black sweater and lovely green jewelry that matched his eyes. My hair was swept up in a loose bun and my ballet flats were comfortable on my feet...just as I had been instructed.

"You...you're...wow," he said, lightly tracing his fingers down my cheek. I closed my eyes briefly, again feeling the heaviness of our tension and chemistry. What this man did to me... he had no idea. When I opened my eyes, he was smiling so wide, obviously proud of the effect he had on me.

Giving the last few instructions to his parents, I kissed my baby on the head and followed my date to his Jeep. Just before he started the engine, he pulled out a bandanna.

"Um... are you going to tie me up or something?" I asked, my heart racing. It wasn't something I'd ever imagined I would do. But I was so ready for Jason to make love to me that I was open to just about anything.

Jason snickered as he rolled the bandanna and placed it over my eyes, carefully tying it in the back.

"I'll take this off when we get there," he said reassuringly. His voice was soft and gentle, but deep and husky. He felt everything I felt. He was just as ready as I was.

No matter how much I begged he refused to tell me where we were going. I did my best to focus on the songs coming out of the speakers. Almost all of them were from the '80s. God, this man knew me so well.

Jason parked the car and killed the engine. He stepped out of the Jeep and, in a matter of seconds, opened my door and helped me down. Surprisingly, I felt grass beneath my feet rather than the cement of a parking lot.

Where are we?

"I'll take that off in just a minute. Be patient," he said, kissing the top of my hand as we walked. I must've looked like the biggest idiot, holding my arms out in front of me, as if they would guide me or keep me safe. I already knew Jason would do both of those things.

We stopped walking and Jason kissed my hand once again before placing my palm up against a rough and brittle surface.

Tree bark.

We were back at the tree house. A smile crossed my lips as I tore off the blindfold.

Jason tilted his head in disbelief. "I was supposed to do that."

"Oh...sorry." I wrinkled my nose at him. He shook his head and smiled.

"Well," he said, his eyes bright, "we're here."

"I see that," I said with a smile.

"You said you've always wanted to come up here."

"Yeah, well, aside from that one time." I snickered.

"Yeah." He blushed as he gestured for me to begin climbing the cracking wooden steps hammered into the bark of the tree. He guided my legs as I climbed and followed me into the tree house. When I reached the top, my breath caught and my heart leapt into my throat.

"Oh my god," I said, looking around the transformed tree house. Tea light candles were spread throughout the room. A fleece blanket covered the floor of the small space. A basket sat in the middle of the blanket. Wildflowers were spread across the floor, lots and lots of wildflowers. "I can't believe you did this."

"Ever since we came here weeks ago, I could think of nothing else. Come, sit."

He turned on his iPod speakers and soft music surrounded us as we sat on the warm blanket. He opened up the basket to reveal some of my favorites...crackers and Brie cheese, dates stuffed with goat cheese and veggies with hummus. Damn, this man paid attention.

"I don't know what to say." I shook my head in disbelief.

"Don't say anything," he said, taking my hand in his. "Come on, let's eat."

∼

When our bellies were full and we'd polished off a bottle of chardonnay, Jason cleaned up the picnic basket, placing it off to the side. He retrieved a few extra blankets from the top of his trunk. There was a slight chill in the air and it wasn't safe to use a space heater. So I was glad I dressed warmly.

Everything Jason said was setting my skin on fire. He turned me on with every laugh and every cocky grin. And he knew it. I was giggly and turned on; not the best combination, but one I was enjoying. I was dying for him to touch me....

"What are you thinking about?" Jason asked as his fingertips lightly stroked my inner thigh. The hair on my arms stood at attention at his soft, arousing touch.

"You," I whispered.

"Really?" He smirked. "What about me?"

"How sexy you are." He cocked an eyebrow and moved closer to me, planting soft kisses along my jawline, making his way down to my neck as I breathed in deeply.

"Tell me more," he said, continuing his hypnotic kisses. But words were failing me. My entire body was tingling... the combination of Jason and wine was completely intoxicating. He pulled away when I stumbled on my words. He pushed my bangs from my eyes before releasing my hair from its bun. My curls spilled down over my shoulders.

"God, you take my breath away," he said, looking at my features as if he was drinking in every inch of me.

Brazenly, I reached for the buttons of his oxford shirt and begin to unbutton them. First one, then the next. This time, Jason was the one whose breath caught in his lungs. I felt how much my touch affected him and it turned me on like nothing else.

Stripping the oxford from him, I laughed as I read the t-shirt underneath.

"That's the most beautiful thing I've ever read," I said.

The red t-shirt simply said, "Once in a while, in the middle of an ordinary life...love gives us a fairy tale."

"It's how I feel," he said, swallowing hard. "I think I've been in love with you since I was fifteen years old."

I didn't know what to say, I stared at him in shock and total elation. Jason was able to read me so well. He knew I wasn't rejecting him. He crushed his lips to mine with an urgency I hadn't felt since our last time at this tree house. Every part of me was ready for him.

Straddling his lap, I yanked his t-shirt off. My eyes bulged out of my head as I took in the sight of him. His body was gorgeous. He was toned and muscular, something he hid behind his t-shirts. But that wasn't the only thing he was hiding. He leaned back on his elbows and looked at me with a devilish grin.

"Tattoos?" I asked, surprised and excited by this side of him.

"Yeah," he nodded, swallowing hard once again, "is that a problem?"

"God, no...not at all." I'd always thought of Jason as the sweet guy behind the hipster glasses. But now I could see there was so much more. My fingers traced over the first tattoo, on the left side of his chest, a quote that I was familiar with: *The art of art, the glory of expression and the sunshine of the light of letters, is simplicity.* I traced it once again with my fingers, kissing the tight skin of his chest gently as I finished.

"That's beautiful."

"Walt Whitman," he said with a grin. It seemed fitting that he would have a quote from his namesake somewhere on his body...especially one that reflected his attitude about writing.

My eyes searched his skin for more body art. He chuckled as I stumbled upon another quote along his bicep. He flexed slightly as I gazed at the words. This one said: *All my life I've looked at words as though I were seeing them for the first time.* I traced this one with my fingers as I read it aloud. A genuine, heartfelt smile crossed his lips.

"Hemingway. He fascinates me," he said, running his fingers through his hair. Beneath me, I felt Jason getting hard. The touch of my fingertips along these words of script was turning him on just as much as it was turning me on.

"There are two more quotes." He pointed to his opposite shoulder: *To be alive at all is to have scars.*

Jason opened his mouth to explain, but I already knew. "John Steinbeck," I said, tracing this one slowly with my finger. Something must have hurt him...something big.

"Someone hurt you," I said.

"She didn't mean to. She didn't even know," he said, looking guilty. And I knew. I was that person.

"When did you get this?"

He swallowed, narrowing his eyes as he paused.

"Tell me," I insisted.

"Almost seven years ago."

I searched his eyes and I had my answer. That's when I had started dating Tucker. My eyes searched his, asking for confirmation as we stared at each other in silence. He just nodded, and I closed my eyes tightly to keep the tears at bay. I wouldn't spoil this night.

"You said there's one more?" I asked with hope.

He nodded. "Yes. This one's new. I got it after our date a few weeks ago."

I raised my eyebrows, searching frantically for this new quote, for the hope that it was something about renewal, something about beginnings, something about *us*.

He pointed down to his side, just below his ribs. I sat back on my knees and gazed down at the quote. Instantly, I knew it was a love letter to me, to us: *There is always some madness in love. But there is also always some reason in madness. —Nietzsche*

"I know ours is not the typical boy-meets-girl story. But I love you. And I have for most of my life."

"Shh," I replied, dragging my fingers seductively over his lips. "Don't say anything more. Show me."

Jason's eyes widened as he flipped me gently onto my back, kissing me hard. He deepened the kiss immediately, his tongue gliding gracefully into my mouth. His hands roamed underneath my sweater and camisole until I felt his fingers tickling the lace of my bra. I moaned softly into his mouth before I rolled him onto his back and straddled him again.

Slowly and methodically, I unzipped his jeans. His breathing was ragged as he watched me. As I pulled down his pants and boxer shorts, I discovered another tattoo: a simple, large ampersand, low on his hip. It had been hidden all this time.

"You were holding out on me." I let out a wicked laugh before tracing this final tattoo with my fingers.

"I forgot about that one." He laughed. "That's just for me. For my love of the written word."

"It's beautiful," I said, leaning down, tracing the symbol once again, only this time with my tongue. Slowly, ever so slowly, I traced that symbol. Jason's breath hitched. With each stroke of my tongue, I felt him getting more and more aroused beneath me.

"Aw, hell," Jason said, breathing in deeply.

"You like that?" I asked, not holding back any longer. I wanted him. Now.

"Oh yeah," he said. "Get up here."

I crawled slowly up to him, gently removing his glasses from his face, kissing the tip of his nose. He pulled me down to him and bit my bottom lip. That slight amount of pressure sent me into a frenzy. I ran my fingers through his sandy hair again and again as he kissed me deeply, his lips full and strong. He sat up, taking me with him and gliding my jeans past my hips. I kicked them off eagerly as Jason removed a condom from his pocket.

"Can't forget this." He chuckled.

"Oh, thank God," I sighed, "I was hoping you had one."

"I, uh... have a few." He chuckled again as he gazed into my eyes. He was worried about embarrassing me. But I wasn't ashamed to want him. I'd wanted him for most of my life.

"Good," I said, matter-of-factly, tipping my chin. Jason's smile widened as he ripped the package open. I took it from his hands. "Let me."

I slid the condom onto him as slowly as I could. Jason breathed in deeply through his clenched teeth. I was still straddling his lap, and he eased me onto him. I gripped his shoulders as he entered me. It'd been so long since I'd been intimate with a man. And it would be the first time since giving birth to Marty. It stung at first, but my body adjusted quickly.

Jason placed his hands on my ass and gently guided me up and down as he nibbled and sucked on my neck, craftily releasing my breasts from my bra. His hands caressed my skin, tickling my nipples gently as I moved. Delicious pressure was building inside of me.

Jason moaned as he took a nipple into his mouth, gently grazing the tip with his teeth. I shuddered and quickened my pace, throwing my head back as Jason pressed his hips into me again and again. I cried out as I climaxed, gripping his shoulders tightly. He continued thrusting until he found his release, and groaned into my shoulder.

For several minutes, we stay glued to each other, not moving at all, except to grasp each other tightly.

"I love you," Jason whispered into my ear, kissing me on my neck.

"And I love you...so much." I sighed into his shoulder, my arms wrapped around him, clutching him for dear life. His fingers ran up and down my spine, his fingertips tickling my hot skin.

He was mine. And I was his. It had taken us way too long to get there through all the madness we had both created. But we were there. And I refused to go back to a life without him. It had all been worth it. All of it.

CHAPTER THIRTY

Hadley
Four months after Marty's birth

"The pizza will be here in ten," Jason called from the kitchen. I finished burping Marty and laid him down for the evening. He was sleeping through the night and it was incredible. I was also sleeping through the night, so I felt like a new person. I had forgotten how much I missed getting several hours of sleep *in a row*.

Soft music played in the living room. Giving Jason a quick peck on the lips, I noticed he'd taken his glasses off and was rubbing the bridge of his nose.

"You okay?" I asked, pulling on the neck of my wool sweater. Jason took my hand away from the fabric, shook his head and smiled. He knew my nervous habits. And he hated to see me worry.

"Sometimes these things hurt. No big thing," he said, picking up his glasses and swinging them slightly in his hand.

"Ever thought about contacts?" I asked.

Jason placed his tortoiseshell glasses back on his nose, crossed his arms and tilted his head. "What are you trying to say? Aren't I sexy in these?"

He was only teasing, but I still felt a little guilty. He placed his fingers through the loops of my jeans and pulled me into his chest. A smart-ass look upon his face, he leaned in close, so close I could smell the peppermint on his breath and the fresh scent of soap on his skin.

"What are you worried about?" he asked, narrowing his eyes.

"You."

"I'm just fine. Never better."

"That's what you do when you're upset. You grasp the bridge of your nose."

A look of surprise crossed Jason's face. As if he had no idea I could read him as well as he read me. That surprise turned to satisfaction, though, and he nuzzled his nose into the sensitive spot behind my ear.

"I love that you know me. Like, really know me," he whispered.

"I do. I hope I do, anyway." I laughed as he hit my ticklish spot, right next to my earlobe.

"Is he down?" Jason asked, his voice still soft, but menacing.

"Yes," I breathed out, "But the pizza…"

"Shit." He laughed, pulling his head back.

"Plus, my mom is stopping by."

"Oh?" he asked, curious.

"Yeah, she said she had something to show me. Probably something for the baby."

Jason kissed my cheeks, my forehead and chin before responding, "Later then."

"Definitely." I nodded. Just as I pulled away and started to walk back into the living room, Jason pulled me back by my belt loop, twirling me into his arms. A surprised yelp escaped my lips. Jason threw his head back, laughing at me.

"Did I scare you?" he asked, placing his hands on my ass and hoisting me into his arms. Quickly, I wrapped my legs around him as he backed me into the counter, placing me on the granite and moving his hands up to my waist.

"Never," I responded with a simple shake of my head.

"That's good." He smoothed down the hair in front of my face, placing it behind my ears, and never breaking eye contact. His stare gave me goose bumps.

Lightly, he pressed his lips to mine, teasing my top lip with his tongue. Every part of me stood at attention with that tiny movement. I opened my mouth, inviting him in, but he took his time. Tempting me with tiny licks of his soft tongue. My bottom lip, my top, and back to my bottom. Each time I tried to lean in to deepen the kiss, he pulled back, torturing me further. There was nothing sexier than Jason Kelly pressing me into the kitchen counter as he teased me with his tongue. Nothing.

Finally, when I couldn't take it any longer, I grabbed the back of his head with both hands, pressing him to me. My legs worked in tandem, pulling him closer. He chuckled as he allowed me to deepen the kiss, running his fingers through my hair as his tongue swept through my mouth. Pulling away again, he moved to my neck, sucking and licking as I sighed, completely wrapped up in the moment. Just as his fingers lifted the bottom of my sweater, the bell rang.

"Nooooo," he said, digging his fingers into the granite and sighing into my shoulder. I had to laugh. I felt Jason's arousal through his jeans. I knew he was no longer in the mood for pizza. Quickly he walked to the door, paid the delivery man and with flushed cheeks placed the pizza on the kitchen table.

I hopped down from the counter and opened the cabinet, reaching up for the plates. As I reached, I felt Jason's fingers tracing the skin on the small of my back. A delicious shiver ran up my spine and goose bumps returned to my arms.

"What are you doing?" he asked with a sexy, troublemaking tone.

"It's time to eat."

"I wasn't done with you yet," he whispered. And now instead of his fingers, I felt his lips on the skin just above my jeans. Leaning forward in surprise, I clutched the counter, not exactly sure where this was headed.

Quickly, I reached for the phone and dialed my mother's cell.

"Seriously?" Jason asked with a groan, kissing the freckles on my back. "You're making phone calls?"

"I need to know if she's on her way."

Mom answered on the second ring. "Honey, I'm here. Just parking the car."

"Okay," I responded with a sigh. Jason groaned as I hung up the phone.

"She's here, isn't she?"

"She won't stay long. She never does," I attempted to assure him as I turned his way. Still on his knees, he pressed his forehead into my belly button. Running my fingers through his hair, I did my best to calm down, knowing Allison Foster would be walking through the door in less than a minute.

She knocked briefly before walking in, just as Jason jumped to his feet. When her eyes meet his, Mom looked embarrassed, knowing she'd interrupted us. But I couldn't focus on that because my eyes were glued to her hair.

Her thick hair, normally just tied back in a simple bun, had been cut, colored and styled. She now had an angled bob that sat just below her chin. She looked stunning...and somewhat like her old self.

"Mom, your hair!" Walking quickly to her, I inspected her new locks. She turned around so I was able to see the entire cut, smiling as she spun.

"Too much?" she asked, suddenly looking sheepish.

"No. Gorgeous," I insisted, taking her hand.

"It was time." She shrugged as she removed her coat and scarf. Jason placed her things in the closet, gave her a kiss on the cheek and echoed the compliments that I showered on her about her new look.

Mom joined us for pizza, smiling as she enjoyed each bite, as if she was tasting it for the first time. When I raised an eyebrow at her, she quickly wiped her mouth with a laugh.

"Sorry, it tastes different. My old meds...they kinda made everything dull. This is great, though."

I loved that she didn't hesitate discussing her issues in front of Jason. She'd accepted him as the man in my life. And, I suspected, had also accepted him as part of our tiny family.

"That's awesome, Mom." Wiping my mouth and taking a sip of my drink, I caught Jason's smile. It was genuine and warm. I loved his compassion and care for my mother. Even though I knew he'd like nothing more than to ask her to leave so he could take me down the hall to the bedroom.

After the meal, I fully expected Mom to leave. However, instead of grabbing her coat from the closet, she simply took a seat on the couch and thumbed through my photo album of Marty's first days. Scrunching my nose, I looked to Jason, who was watching her almost painfully, as she made herself comfortable on the green sofa. Briefly, he joined me in the kitchen, kissing me behind my ear.

"I want you...now." Another shiver ran up my back.

"Sorry," I whispered. "Soon, I promise."

Such conflict brewed inside of me. My desire for Jason was battling the longing I had to bond with my mom. It was taking some time, but she was becoming herself again. Haircuts, new makeup, a few new outfits this winter...the small things had become the big things. The woman who had spent three years as a ghost of herself was having a rebirth. My heart was bursting with contentment as I watched her ooh and ahh over the pictures she'd already seen several times. This was the mom I remembered.

I was seven years old and had finished my very first ballet recital. Blotches formed in my line of sight after the show from being photographed by my parents over and over and over. My dad had purchased his first digital camera. I didn't really know what that meant at the time. A camera was a camera, wasn't it? Regardless, he was so excited about it and had taken over a hundred photos of me and the other girls in our pink tutus and leotards.

After the show, they took me to our favorite restaurant, Trudy's. It was an eclectic place where all the waitresses wore 1950s glasses and cardigan sweaters as they served incredible burgers and sweet potato fries. My favorite. We feasted on burgers with all sorts of toppings. And my parents surprised me with Trudy's famous Oreo brownie sundae. I felt like I might burst after that meal. But my cheeks were glowing. I knew I had made them proud. I felt it in my bones.

Later that evening, I was playing Monopoly with my dad when Mom rushed through the door with a huge batch of photos she'd just developed at the drug store. She insisted we stop the game and look through the photos.

"Oh, Martin," she said. "Look at our beautiful girl. Look at her form. She's a natural."

"I agree," he'd said as he passed me each picture.

She made all sorts of faces while looking at the different photos, as if she herself hadn't just seen me dancing a few hours before. She oohed and ahhed over and over again, occasionally stopping to wipe a tear as it rolled down her cheek. Her tears made me nervous. I was too young to really understand why people cried at happy times. I cried when I fell off my bike and when my friend Tommy had moved away to Iowa. But my mom wasn't sad. She was happy, and the more she spoke about my performance that day, the more I understood. She was proud of me.

Mom was still thumbing through the album as I joined her on the couch. Wrapping my arm around her waist, I rested my chin on her shoulder, pulling her into me. Her hand clutched mine as she shut her eyes tight, a simple tear running down her cheek.

"I'm so proud of you, my sweetheart. You're such a good mom."

Her words stunned me. I couldn't remember the last time she had voiced her pride in me. And I had no idea how much I had missed hearing it until this moment. And so I sat with Allison Foster and paged through all of the pictures of my son's first weeks at home. We oohed and ahhed together looking at my gorgeous boy. The boy who gave my life meaning. The boy who had brought us back together. The boy who had inspired Allison Foster to return to herself, to the woman she used to be.

∼

Two hours later, Mom left for home. As I closed the door behind her, I leaned back, glancing at my watch. Jason looked curious as I stared at him in awe.

"I haven't spent that much time with her in a long time...a very long time."

"You look so at peace," Jason said as he approached.

"I think I am. So many things make sense now."

"Tell me," he said, tucking my hair behind my ears and looking deeply into my eyes. The warmth of those eyes radiated through me, and I knew that talking about Allison Foster was no longer on the agenda.

"Later," I purred, tugging on the collar of his button-down shirt. My fingernails pressed gently into the soft skin of his neck. He breathed deeply and his eyes grew darker as he drank me in.

Jason leaned in, repeating the ritual of earlier...teasing me with his lips, his teeth, and his minty breath. He could have had his way with me right then and there, against the cold door of my apartment. But instead, he pulled away, gave me a devilish grin and pulled playfully on my hand. I followed his lead, and we laughed and shushed each other as we ran to my bedroom.

Jason lay me down on top of the covers, stroking my hair and neck as his tongue dipped into my mouth seductively. Suddenly, his muscles tensed and he pulled back.

"Be right back," he said, as he jogged out of the room. I was confused. I knew I'd locked the door. The baby was fast asleep. What on earth was going on?

Jason jogged back into the room holding the baby monitor.

"Seriously?" I screeched. "His room is ten feet away."

He shrugged and placed it on my nightstand. "Force of habit, sorry."

"No, it's sexy," I replied, pulling him back down to me.

"Remind me to carry that thing around all the time," he said with a laugh.

"Not the monitor... the fact that you *thought of* the monitor. Here, now. That's huge."

"Oh, I wasn't looking for brownie points, but I'll take 'em."

He smirked as he pulled my sweater off and tossed it to the floor. He was wasting no time and I couldn't blame him. Our entire dinner had been filled with stolen glances and unspoken sexual tension. We had had hours of foreplay, being so close to each other without being able to act on our feelings. But now we were alone and we didn't have to wait a second longer.

Popping the buttons on his shirt, quickly, I pulled it from his body, revealing the t-shirt underneath. I laughed as I saw the shirt for the first time.

"Six out of Seven Dwarves are not Happy?" I asked with a laugh. He cocked his head to the side.

"It's so sad, isn't it?" he teased, knowing full well that I got the joke. Snow White was my favorite princess movie. I had watched it constantly when I was young.

"Those poor dwarves." Doing my best to go along with the joke, I shook my head, looking disappointed. But being the terrible actress that I was, I broke out into laughter.

"No poker face... at all." He shook his head before tearing the t-shirt off, revealing all of the tattoos that I'd grown familiar with over the last month. Tracing the ink on his chest, I could feel his heart pounding beneath his firm skin as he gazed down at me.

"Is that a problem?" I asked, narrowing my eyes.

"Not at all. I love your honesty. Your face tells me everything I need to know."

"So does yours."

"We're a lot alike, aren't we?"

"Sometimes," I whispered, tracing my finger down to the button of his jeans, popping it free. He sighed as he crushed my mouth to his. His tongue swept into my mouth, tangling with mine, hypnotizing me with each stroke. Pushing his jeans and boxers down, I grasped his ass in my hands and he moaned into my mouth. Knowing I excited him like that was such a turn-on. I kneaded his skin again and again, thrusting my hips into him over and over. He yanked his jeans off before pulling mine past my toes and throwing all of our clothes into one giant heap on the carpet below.

Pulling a small packet from the drawer of the nightstand, he tore it open with his teeth and handed it to me. I was more than happy to slide the condom onto him. He was hard and completely ready to lose himself in me.

I lay down and he hovered above me, pushing my legs open with his own. Throwing my head back as he entered me, I gripped his shoulders, my fingernails digging in slightly. Jason released another moan as he found his pace. His elbows rested on the bed as he tangled his hands in my hair, kissing me all over my face and neck. Jason continued thrusting, again and again, the muscles of his ass tightening beneath my hands.

Pointing my toes towards the ceiling, I felt him going deeper with each thrust. And the pressure was building inside of me. His brow was furrowed as he continued to move, sweat building on his forehead and behind his neck.

Just as I was about to come, he took a nipple into his mouth and it sent me over the edge. I called out his name as my orgasm consumed my entire body.

Jason smiled in satisfaction as he twisted his hips. I matched his thrusts with my own, determined to have him join me in my state of euphoria. Jason pressed his face to my neck as he found his release. He groaned deeply and bit into my skin as he came.

We stayed connected for several minutes, Jason planting feathery kisses along my neck and chest. He knew how much I loved the sensations on my skin...it deepened the euphoria and made me feel like I was floating in mid-air. After several minutes, he lay next to me, stroking my back with the pads of his fingertips. It tickled in the best possible way. My eyelids grew heavy as I basked in the sensation of his touch. Before I knew it, I was fast asleep.

~

Marty's cry pierced the bedroom and I sat up with a start. Jason was startled, too. I looked at him in panic. He'd never spent the night before. It felt irresponsible, somehow. Jason had always gone home at the end of the night, but he must've drifted off to sleep just like I had.

"I'm so sorry. I know you don't want me to spend the night." Jason put his glasses on and looked at me with concern.

"Don't *want* you to? Is *that* what you think?" I asked, perplexed. Of course I wanted him to spend the night. If it were up to me, he'd be here every night of the week. It just didn't seem like the right thing to do...like a slippery slope that could lead to disaster and confusion for the baby. Things with Tucker were still confusing and unsettled. I hadn't seen him since he'd shown up after my run-in with his mother. He knew nothing about Marty's growth or development. But he was still his father... and he complicated things with Jason.

"Well, yeah. I mean—I get it. I really do."

"But you think I don't want this?" I asked, gesturing toward the space between us.

"Get the baby. He's hungry," Jason said, kissing me gently on the tip of my nose. His smile was genuine and forgiving. But as I walked out of the room, I turned to see him grabbing the bridge of his nose. I scrunched mine, knowing this conversation had only just begun.

An hour later, as we lounged in the living room, I knew we needed to talk about it. Marty was playing in his soft play gym, swatting at cloth elephants and monkeys as he kicked his legs and giggled. Jason was reading on his Kindle, his feet up on the ottoman. He looked deep in thought. Part of me wanted to leave him be, but the other needed to face this head on. I hated that I made him feel this way.

I crouched on the cushion next to him, leaning on his shoulder. He looked over his glasses at me, his mouth slowly turning up into a hesitant smile.

"For the record," I said, running my fingers across his chin, "I love waking up with you."

"Oh, really?" he asked, putting his Kindle on the end table.

"Absolutely." I nodded, looking him dead in the eye. There was no room for doubt. He had to know that my conflict had nothing to do with him.

"I know ours isn't exactly the most traditional of scenarios," Jason said, leaning his elbow on the back of the couch and staring me in the eyes, "but I'm ready when you are. And if you aren't ready, then we'll be more careful next time. I don't want to confuse him."

"Me neither," I said, looking over at my boy, just as he smacked an elephant upside the head. Jason took my hand in his and kissed the back of it.

"I'll follow your lead."

CHAPTER THIRTY-ONE

Jason
Six months after Marty's birth

"Hey, little guy. You're a droolin' mess." Marty's bib was soaked completely through. Spit poured from his little mouth. Poor guy. Quickly, I grabbed a fresh bib from the kitchen and placed Marty in my lap. He'd been doing this for over a month. His pediatrician said that he was teething, but there was no sign of teeth. He'd been so miserable the past few weeks—crying uncontrollably and waking up during the night when he used to sleep for ten hours straight.

A year or so ago, the thought of having a baby drool on my arm would've grossed me out. I'm not gonna lie. But now, as I felt Marty's drool spilling off the side of my wrist, I had to laugh. I'd changed enough diapers in the last few months that a little bit of spit didn't scare me away.

Marty smiled wide as I snapped the new bib around his neck. That grin got me every time. It was impossible not to return a smile from a baby...especially one as cute as *this* baby. *This* baby made me laugh so hard sometimes I snorted. Which was really embarrassing when I did it in front of Haddie. But I couldn't help it. He was hilarious and he had the biggest smile on the planet.

"Wait, hold up," I said, looking back into Marty's mouth as he smiled. A tiny hint of white was poking out from his gums. "Haddie, c'mere. I think he has a tooth!"

"Seriously?" Haddie called from the washroom where she was applying her makeup. She jogged into the room and looked at her smiling boy. He giggled when his mommy smiled at him, revealing the little tooth making its way through his bright pink gums.

"Did you see it?" I asked in excitement.

"I did," Haddie said, taking Marty in her arms and placing a kiss on his forehead. "You have your first tooth, sweet pea."

Taking in the sight of Haddie, I felt like a teenager all over again. She was stunning, wearing a new sweater dress and leggings. Her hair cascaded past her shoulders in loose waves. Her lips were deep ruby red and her eyes were smoky gray. I'd never seen her look like this. She didn't look like a young mother. She looked like a seductress...and I couldn't stop staring. We were going out tonight while Auden watched the baby.

"What?" she asked when she saw that my eyes hadn't left her since she'd taken Marty from my arms.

"You look...gorgeous," I responded, gesturing to her. The apples of her cheeks turned pink as she saw just how taken with her I was. She smoothed down the wool of her dress with one hand as she swayed back and forth with Marty. He reached back for me. Haddie pretended to be irritated.

"You fickle little boy," she said with a *tsk*. "I have to finish my makeup anyway. Auden will be here any minute." She kissed him on the forehead as she walked back to the bathroom.

Marty and I headed back to the carpet to practice stacking his plastic pots and pans. He was getting pretty good at it. Such a smart kid. Just a few weeks ago, he could barely sit up on his own. But this week, he was sitting up all the time and stacking toys. Soon, Haddie said, he would be crawling. Something about the way he rocked back and forth and pushed up with his arms while playing on his stomach.

Each time he stacked the pans, they sang to him and he cracked up. It was hilarious. Just as he placed the top on the pans, Auden let herself in.

"Sorry I'm late. Forgot I needed to pick up dinner." She rolled her eyes as she placed a fast food bag on the counter.

"No worries. Haddie's still getting ready."

"Where are you crazy love birds off to?" Auden teased as she shoveled several fries into her mouth.

"We're meeting a couple of my friends for dinner and drinks."

"The photographer and her husband?" Auden asked between bites of her hamburger.

"Kate and Evan." I nodded.

"Sounds exciting." Auden winked as she sipped her drink. For some reason, Auden had always assumed my friends were boring, even back in school. I'd never been as much of a free spirit as she was, I guess. But I thought it was funny that she assumed her big brother was dull as hell... even when I was dating her best friend. Whatever.

Haddie joined us, looking even more beautiful than she had a few minutes ago. I had no idea what she'd done, but my mouth was agape as she walked past me to hug my sister and fill her in on Marty's schedule for the night. Auden listened attentively as she continued to shovel her dinner into her mouth. I spent my last couple minutes stacking pans with the little guy as the two women talked and laughed.

"Ready, Jase?" Haddie asked as she knelt down to hug and kiss her boy.

"Yep. See ya, kiddo." After a quick kiss on top of his head, I followed Haddie out the door, saying goodbye to Auden as she joined Marty on the carpet.

"She's amazing," Haddie said as she zipped up her jacket.

"Yeah, sometimes." I couldn't help smirking when my sister was mentioned. She'd always been a royal pain in my ass. Sometimes, even though I saw Haddie as a grown-up woman, it was hard for me to see Auden in the same way. Our dynamic hadn't changed too much since we were kids. And I wondered if it ever would.

∽

An hour's drive into downtown Chicago and we arrived at Greek Islands, one of the places Kate had been pressuring us to try. I'd never been a huge fan of Greek food, but Haddie loved it, so I was more than prepared to take one for the team.

"Maxwell, party of four," I said to the lovely woman in her late sixties who stood behind the hostess counter.

"Oh yes," she said, glancing down at her reservation booklet. "The rest of your party just arrived. Follow me, please."

I had to hand it to the owner of the restaurant. The ambiance of the place was awesome. Rustic and European wall coverings, authentic wooden chairs that looked like they were taken directly from a restaurant my family had once visited in Mykonos. I hadn't been there since I was twelve, but I honestly felt like I'd been transported as we walked to our table.

Evan and Kate greeted us with smiles and hugs as we arrived at the table. Everyone settled in and Evan ordered a bottle of red wine as we inspected the menu. Immediately, Kate asked if we had pictures of the baby. Giddily, Haddie dug into her purse and retrieved her latest order from the one-hour photo place.

Kate smiled wide as she flipped through the pictures of Marty sleeping, playing, eating and, of course, drooling like crazy.

"He...uh, has a lot of, um..." Kate said as she stared down at a picture of Marty and his soaked bib.

"Drool?" I laughed. She nodded, wide-eyed, scrunching her lips.

"I know absolutely nothing about babies." Kate smiled behind clenched teeth, embarrassed. But there was something more to her expression. Something I was unable to put my finger on.

"He's teething," Haddie said.

"That sounds like fun," Evan joked as he shifted in his seat.

"It's brutal, man. The poor guy is always in pain. And let me tell you, that goo that's supposed to numb the gums only works for about three minutes."

"And you know this because?" Evan pressed me.

"He tried it," Haddie said, looking at me with pride.

"I wanted to see if it helped him." I shrugged. "No better way than to try it myself."

"And?" Kate asked, all smiles.

"And, it wore off...way too fast. Those commercials are a lie."

"I knew you'd be a natural," Kate said softly, almost to herself. But I heard her and that compliment was one of the best I'd ever received. I had always known I wanted to be a father and I'd always liked kids. I just never *really* thought about it until Haddie and I fell in love. And by then, I was all in. It was still nice to hear.

The table was quiet as Evan poured wine for Haddie, himself and me. Kate sipped her ice water with lemon and Haddie and I exchanged a suspicious smile. She was hiding something, and I was pretty sure I knew what it was...which would explain the sudden questions about babies. She'd always been sweet with Haddie when it came to Marty and motherhood. But she'd never seemed as genuinely curious as she did tonight.

Once our food arrived, Evan and Kate exchanged a glance. Evan nodded his head with a lopsided grin. He took her hand and Kate's cheeks turned crimson as she wiped her mouth and cleared her throat.

"We have something to share."

"Oh?" Haddie said, placing her fork down, listening intently.

"We're going to have a baby," Kate said, smiling as she squeezed Evan's hand in her own.

"Congratulations," Haddie and I said in unison. And then she asked question after question like a giddy firing squad.

"How far along are you?"

"Fourteen weeks."

"When's your due date?"

"September twenty-eighth."

"Will you find out what you're having?"

"Absolutely. I don't like surprises," Kate said with a laugh. "Neither does Evan."

"You must be so thrilled," Haddie said, looking starry-eyed as she stared at our friends. They were married; they were settled. And we both knew they would love being parents.

"We were a *little* freaked out at first," Kate admitted, as she glanced at Evan. "We weren't exactly trying to get pregnant. It just sorta happened."

"But it's awesome," Evan said, kissing Kate's hand.

"You'll be great, you guys. Seriously, if *we* can do this, so can you," Haddie said, looking self-conscious after saying the word "we." Our co-parenting of Marty was something we didn't really discuss. And every time I thought she knew just how happy I was in that role, she hesitated like this. Reaching my hand under the table, I gave her knee a reassuring squeeze and instantly felt her muscles relax.

"I'm sure we'll be asking a lot of questions over the next few months."

"Please do," I said with a smile. "We'll be honest... the good, the bad and the disgusting."

"Lovely," Kate said, her words laced with sarcasm, before she turned to Haddie.

"Jason told me all about your job. Do you think you'll go back?"

"I really want to," she said, her head tilted slightly to the side as if she were lost in memories. "Just not sure if I can make it work with the baby."

"That makes sense," Evan said.

"I worry about that, too," Kate said. "I love what I do; it's like it's a part of me."

"I know what you mean," Haddie said. Her face fell and I knew she was missing her clients. They were so important to her. Hell, I missed joking around with Bryce every week; how could she not miss them all?

As our dinner continued, Evan and I joked around as Haddie told Kate all about her pregnancy, birth and first weeks home with the baby. At times, Kate stiffened up as she listened, but overall she seemed excited. And even though she was trying to resist it, I could see a change taking over in my friend, a softening of Mrs. Maxwell. She had always had a tough exterior with softness under the surface, but I knew that tough exterior would crack and fall away, revealing the gentle heart of a woman who'd never been happier. And that made *me* happier than I could ever say. My friends deserved all the happiness headed their way in the months to come.

CHAPTER THIRTY-TWO

Hadley
Seven months after Marty's birth

"Babababababababa," Marty said, squirming beneath my arms as I changed his diaper.

"That's right, little stinker tush." I laughed, grinning at my boy. "After this, Mommy's going to give you a bottle."

The babbling was awesome. I never thought I'd enjoy listening to a baby rattle off sounds as much as I enjoyed everything my boy said. It was an unexpected joy of motherhood. The simple things that just seemed like a part of life... teeth, appetite, babbling, crawling... it was all so incredible. Soon he'd be saying real words, walking around like a little boy. The time was going by way too fast. I wanted to bottle up this feeling and keep it forever.

Just as I finished preparing his bottle, the doorbell rang. Jason was meeting with his agent today, and my mom was working. Perhaps it was a solicitor. We'd had so many of those lately. It was more than frustrating when the baby was taking a nap. *Maybe I should get one of those little stickers for the door.* I never thought I'd be one of those people to put "No Soliciting" on my door, but if Marty was woken up one more time, I would not be a happy woman.

Placing Marty on the Boppy pillow with his favorite blankie, I gave him his bottle before walking to the door. I gasped as the face on the other side of the peephole came into focus. *What on earth is she doing here? We haven't even taken the DNA test yet. Do I open the door? Should I pretend we're not here?*

"Hadley?" she said with a sharp tone to her voice. She must've heard me coming. *Here we go.*

"Lydia," I said, doing my best not to clench my teeth as I opened the door.

A plastic and rehearsed smile sat upon her clearly unhappy face. "Hadley, dear. How are you?"

"How...how did you know where I live?" I asked, my forehead creasing in confusion.

"Phone book," she said dismissively. "This morning, I thought, 'Where are my manners? I haven't given Hadley's son a gift.'"

"Oh," I replied. Conveniently, she had neglected to mention he was *her grandson*.

"May I come in?" she asked. Her eyebrows were raised, but her forehead didn't budge. Not a wrinkle in sight. No doubt, she had just had her latest Botox injection.

"I'm not sure that's a good idea."

The makeup on her face was thick and I could smell her perfume. The same scent she'd worn for ages. Tucker used to joke that her perfume was called Old Money. That memory repulsed me as I studied her for the very first time in the seven years I'd known her. Her chocolate brown hair spilled down her shoulders. Her dark eyes were embellished with fake eyelashes and way too much eye shadow for 11 in the morning on a weekday.

She let out a sigh before handing me the metallic blue wrapped box. She then reached into her Dolce & Gabbana handbag. "Well, if we need to have this discussion here, so be it."

"Discussion? What is there to discuss? I already told Tucker we'd take the test." As much as I hated the idea of subjecting Marty to a DNA test, I had absolutely nothing to hide.

"That's just it. I've had some time to think it over. I'd like to ask you to reconsider."

"I don't understand. You planted the idea in Tucker's head."

"Yes, I know, but..." she stopped and looked down at my feet. Two little hazel eyes peeked out from behind my feet. Marty had abandoned his empty bottle and crawled to the door. Lydia turned pale, staring down at her grandson, really looking at him for the very first time. She had to know, even if she had no desire to be a grandmother. But then again, maybe she'd had a change of heart? Maybe we could all move forward... have peace.

"He's so big," she said, tilting her head to the side and giving him a small smile. He sat back on his bottom and kicked his feet, a large smile plastered on his face and drool dripping from his chin.

"Seven months now," I said, relaxing my posture. Just as I relaxed, however, Lydia tensed right back up. She looked me dead in the eye, her eyes cold and distant. A complete 180-degree shift.

"Yes, well..." she cleared her throat before handing me a set of documents. I looked down at them in pure confusion.

"I—what is it you want?" I asked, looking up from the papers.

"You and Tucker have no future. Am I right?"

"You're right." My voice cracked with apprehension.

"I'd like to give you an opportunity, Hadley. If you'll sign these documents and have Tucker's name removed from the birth certificate, his father and I will place a very large trust fund in your son's name. College, car, you name it. We'll take care of it."

"Wait," I gasped. "You want me to lie?"

"For lack of a better word? Yes."

"Lydia, I don't understand. Tucker and I dated for six years... *you know me*. Why are you acting like this?"

"You don't understand. Tucker has a bright future ahead of him. He's not ready for a child. And a quality woman will never consider marrying him if he's a single father."

"Are you kidding? A *quality* woman?" My nose flared in shock. What decade were we living in? I knew his parents were part of the elite social group in Wilmette, but this was ridiculous.

"You and Tucker dated when you were children. You were never a good match. If you sign this, you can each have a fresh start. You can marry someone else. They can raise your son as their own. You can do *whatever you want*. And your son will want for *nothing*."

"But you'll force me to lie to him. For his entire life. *My* son... I'm not going to lie to him, Lydia. And I don't want your goddamn money."

"Just think it over."

"I don't need to," I said, ripping the papers in half and handing them back to her. "Now, get the hell out of my house. You don't deserve to be anywhere near your grandson."

Slamming the door, I leaned back into the cold wood. My son's grandmother had just tried to buy me off. How did I not see this family for what they were when I was dating Tucker? I kept a brave face for Marty until naptime; we played on the floor with his pots and pans. The blue wrapped gift stared at me from the kitchen table. *Don't open it. Don't open it. Don't open it.*

I had never been the best with willpower, but at least I came by it honestly. I stood up, crossed the room to the box and brought it back to the floor. There was no card, but the wrapping was elegant. Foil wrapping paper with a large grosgrain ribbon tied at the top. Pulling the ribbon off the box, I quickly tied it in several knots so that it wouldn't be dangerous for Marty.

With slight hesitation, I peeled back the paper on the box, revealing clothes...lots and lots of clothes. Tommy Hilfiger, Ralph Lauren and several other labels. Sweater vests, hats, jeans and chambray shirts. As I held up each item, though, it was obvious that Marty would never fit into anything in this box. Everything was size 3 months. Hundreds of dollars worth of clothing that we couldn't use. *How could she think he was this small?* This woman never ceased to amaze me. Scooping up the clothes, I placed them back in the box. Our local Goodwill would be thrilled to receive brand new clothes in their donation box. And I'd be happy to never have to dress Marty in something that woman had purchased. Ever.

CHAPTER THIRTY-THREE

Hadley
Eight months after Marty's birth

The rich scent of coffee surrounded me as I pushed the clunky stroller through the door of Beans. A smile crossed my lips when I heard my name called from a large table near the back of the shop.

"Hey there, lady. We've missed ya," Warren said, planting a kiss on my cheek. His smile was wide and his bright eyes shined as he beamed at me. God, I'd missed that face. I'd missed his greetings each morning when he stepped off that bus. I took his hand briefly, giving it a squeeze before greeting the rest of the smiling faces at the table.

Violet was hopping up and down as she looked down at the baby. "He's so pretty."

"Thanks," I said, pulling her in for a hug. Lucy dove in for a group hug and I held her tight. When the girls pulled away, Bryce tore out his earbuds and practically pounced on me, hugging me with his strong arms.

"I miss you," he said softly into my ear. The pain in his voice killed me.

"I miss you, too, Bryce. I really do," I said, tapping him gently on the back as he clutched me. I tried to step back, but his grip on me didn't let up.

"What music does he listen to?" He pointed to Marty with a look of suspicion covering his normally chipper face.

"His favorite is Jack Johnson."

"No, no, no. I don't know him."

"He sings the 'Upside Down' song from the Curious George movie. His voice settles the baby."

"I don't like it." Bryce glowered down at Marty. "He should be listening to Tears for Fears. Or Flock of Seagulls."

"Well, those aren't really appropriate for a ba—" My eyes widened as I interrupted myself, "Bryce, are you listening to '80s music?"

"Maybe," Bryce said, staring at the floor, before pulling me in for another strong hug. I guess he missed me more than I realized.

"Okay, buddy," Nick said, stepping in and pulling Bryce gently from me. Bryce looked annoyed with Nick but took a seat next to me.

Nick opened up his arms and gave me a warm smile. I didn't realize just how much I'd missed him until this very moment. Ellie had come by many times to visit the baby and me, but I hadn't seen Nick since before the baby was born. Funny, easy-going, would-do-anything-for-our-clients Nick. He was a gem. It was so good to see him.

Nick pulled me in for a hug. "Missed ya, kid."

"Same here."

"So tell us about the man, the myth, the legend...Marty," he said, crouching down to get a better look at the baby. He was wide awake and playing with his squishy book with bright colored pictures of animals. He glanced up briefly at Nick, offering him a toothy grin with his two front teeth before cramming his fist into his mouth with a laugh.

Pulling up a chair, I told Nick all about Marty. How he was crawling, sitting, getting teeth and eating solid foods. After a few minutes, I realized everyone else was feeling left out of the conversation. It was time to focus on what they'd been doing since I left.

"So, how's Sunnyside?"

"It's awful," Lucy said, pouting, pulling at her curls.

"No, it's not!" Violet argued with her. "It's fii-iiine."

"They miss you," Nick said matter-of-factly. Clearly, he didn't want me to feel guilty.

"When are you coming back?" Warren asked, his eyes wide.

"I'm not sure, buddy."

The truth is, I really wasn't. I would have loved to go back and work for Sunnyside again. But having this time with my son was priceless and it was time I'd never get back. The idea of working full time gave me knots in my stomach.

"Why not?"

"Well... Marty needs me."

"So do we," Lucy said, her lips forming a full-on pout. My heart ached.

"Listen, guys. Right now, Hadley is where she needs to be. Let's enjoy our time today instead of making her feel bad," Nick said in his best authoritative voice.

"I'll visit more often. I'm sorry it's taken me so long. Motherhood takes time to get used to, I guess."

"Is it hard?" Violet asked.

"Sometimes."

"Does he poop a lot?" Bryce asked with a laugh.

"All the time," I responded with a chuckle.

"Babies like milk," Warren said.

"Yes, they do. He also likes bananas and pears."

"I like pears!" Lucy sat up straight in her seat with a new appreciation for the baby. She'd found common ground with him. Sometimes that's all we needed. All of us.

"Me too," Violet added. "I have one in my lunch today."

"That's awesome," I replied, remembering just how much these wonderful people made me smile and laugh. I'd really missed them. A lot.

"They still haven't filled your position," Nick said, pursing his lips with hesitation. As if he couldn't decide whether or not to tell me.

"Seriously? Why not?"

"Everyone's kinda filling in with the classes. And Ellie and I are taking over the show."

"But why? I don't understand."

"I guess Pamela is hoping you'll come back."

My stomach flipped. I didn't want anyone to wait around for me. But I was flattered.

"Why didn't you tell me about the show? You know I'd help out. Jason and I both."

"We didn't want to pressure you. That's all."

"Pressure me." I nodded assertively.

"Fine," he said, raising his hands up near his head in surrender. "Still bossy, I see."

"You'd better believe it. Sounds like I need to have a conversation with Pamela, huh?"

"That's up to you," Nick said. "You have to put your family first."

Taking Bryce's and Violet's hands in my own, I said, "This is my family, too. I need all of you. I'll figure something out."

CHAPTER THIRTY-FOUR

Jason
Nine months after Marty's birth

When I arrived at Haddie's place today, I noticed the mailbox was full. I scooped several envelopes out of the simple metal box and carried all of it to her apartment.

She greeted me with a kiss and thanked me, asking me to put everything on the counter. As I joined Marty on the floor to play with Grover and friends, Haddie sorted through the mail.

"Oh...." she said quietly to herself.

"What is it?"

"The results. They're here."

"I thought Tucker wanted them sent directly to his family."

She scoffed. "Or his parents' lawyer."

"I can drop them off, Haddie," I offered. She looked relieved as soon as I said the words.

"Are you sure?" she asked, scrunching her nose and clenching her teeth. God, she was adorable.

"Absolutely."

There was something I wanted to discuss with Tucker anyway. The coward hadn't been back to see his son since he'd freaked out over Haddie revealing his secret. And since then, I had some things I wanted to discuss. Important things.

Haddie excused herself to use the bathroom. Her cell was on the counter. Quickly I sent a text to Tucker from her phone. Probably not the smartest move on the planet, but I was eager to see him. Face to face.

I have results for you. Would like to deliver them.

After a few minutes without a reply, I was starting to get nervous. Haddie had returned from the bathroom and had scooped Marty up for a diaper change. Just as I heard him cooing through the monitor, her cell phone chirped.

I'm home.

A man of very few words, I thought to myself as I deleted the messages and placed the phone back on the counter. My heart was pounding in my chest. I'd never lied to Haddie before. I'd never used her phone or checked her email. But I had to do this. For all of us. When Haddie and Marty returned, Marty was cuddling his favorite turtle toy.

"Listen, I'm gonna deliver these," I said, clutching the envelope. Haddie looked perplexed.

"But you just got here. Tucker can wait."

"I know, but..." I hesitated. My nerves were getting the best of me. "I just want to get it over with."

"Oh my god," she gasped, "you want to see the results."

"Don't be silly," I said, panicking. She was totally misreading my intentions. *Shit.*

"I can't believe this. I thought you trusted me!" she said, placing Marty in his playpen before turning back to me, hands on hips and chest heaving.

I walked towards her, placing my hands on her shoulders. "I don't need to look in this envelope to know who his biological father is. I just have some things I need to say to him. All right? Don't turn this into something it's not."

I smoothed down her hair with both hands before kissing her softly on the lips. She closed her eyes and kept them tight. The *last* thing I wanted was to make her doubt my trust in her. I trusted her implicitly.

"I'll be back soon. I'll pick up dinner on the way." I planted one last kiss on her forehead and then walked to Marty and kissed him there as well. "See you in a bit, little guy."

Haddie put on a brave face as I left her apartment. It was killing me to leave them, but it was more than necessary. This conversation needed to happen. I couldn't wait any longer.

∼

The lights of Tucker's luxury townhome were on and luckily it seemed like he was home alone. His curtains were open and he was sitting on the couch, watching the Cubs game as he drank a beer. I took a deep breath before ringing the bell. *Let's do this.*

He opened the door apprehensively. When he noticed the envelope in my hand, his muscles tensed and he lifted his chin in defiance. He was ready for a fight. Well, maybe he'd get one.

"Hey, man. I thought Hadley was bringing those," he said, opening the door, gesturing for me to come in.

"Change of plans," I said as I entered his home. "Nice place." I looked around at the rustic leather furniture and large flat-screen TV mounted to the wall. His place was the epitome of bachelor pad. This was not a child-friendly place. Even if he *wanted* to have Marty here for the day or, God forbid, overnight, it wouldn't be safe at all. Marty was almost walking and he'd been crawling for months. Glass coffee table, a bookshelf made of wrought iron, two antique guitars propped up with metal stands. This place would be a disaster waiting to happen for the baby.

"You have the results?" he asked, pointing to the envelope in my hand.

"Yep." I passed him the large envelope. He looked down at his hands, knowing he held all the answers he needed in regards to his son's paternity. He couldn't avoid this any longer. Tucker took a deep breath and walked to the fridge.

"Beer?" he asked.

"Sure."

He popped the top of a Stella Artois, handed it to me and we walked to the living room. He nodded for me to sit. I took a sip of my beer and settled in on a leather chair. I couldn't stop staring at his hands. He still hadn't opened the envelope. *Because he already knows the results. He knows Marty's his son.*

"You don't even need to open it, do you?" I said, glaring at him through hooded eyes.

"No," he said, tapping the envelope on his knee.

"Well, you might as well," I said, trying to stay casual. I didn't want him to know how much I was seething between each swig of my beer. I hoped the amber liquid would calm my nerves, but it didn't. I was there to protect my family.

Tucker swallowed hard as he opened the envelope and revealed the smaller white envelope containing the results. He opened it, nodded, closed the paper and tossed it to his coffee table. No surprise. But the look on his face killed me.

It was as if he was *hoping* he wasn't the father. He had no idea how lucky he was... how much he was missing.

"I don't get you, man," I said, leaning on my elbows.

"What?" he snapped, crossing his arms and glowering at me. Classic defensive stance.

"You don't have any idea how cool that little guy is. No idea at all."

"I don't want a kid. You know this."

"It's not that easy."

"You don't get it," he huffed, looking away.

"Then tell me."

"We were done, over. I didn't want to be with her any more. I was trying to break up with her... and then this... I'm twenty-three, for fuck's sake. I don't want a kid... and neither does my family."

"Yeah, that was obvious."

"What are you talking about?"

"The ridiculous offer your mother made. Did you honestly think Haddie could be *bought?*"

"My mom? What the fuck are you talking about?" He looked taken aback.

"Whatever, dude. I'm not getting into this with you. You want the test, and then you don't want the test. Don't you think you've put her through enough?"

"What the fuck? I never changed my mind about the test."

"Well, your mom sure as hell did."

"No, she didn't. She's been asking me for days when we'll see the results."

"She went to Haddie's place a few weeks ago. Tried to convince her not to have the test done at all."

"You're full of shit," he said, slamming his beer so hard on the glass I flinched, waiting for the table to shatter. Luckily, it remained intact. He stood up and paced.

"No, I'm not. But your family sure as hell is."

"Watch it, man."

Adrenaline pumped furiously through my veins. Gripping the side of the armchair, I felt my pulse racing. *Don't knock his ass out. Be the better man. Haddie deserves more.*

"You don't know, do you?" I asked, in shock. I thought he'd sent his mother to Haddie's place to humiliate her. To protect his reputation among the single ladies in his wealthy circle.

"Know *what?*"

"Your mom showed up and offered to pay Haddie off. If she dropped the DNA test, Marty would be set for life. College, trust fund, everything. She even had a contract drawn up. As long as your name wasn't on the birth certificate, she'd never have to work another day in her life."

"You gotta be fucking with me." Tucker tilted his head back, searching my eyes for some sign of a joke or a prank.

"No, man. . . . I'm not." I insisted.

"I can't believe her. . . ." His words trailed off as he continued to pace his living room, grabbing his beer from the table. "Hadley must've been pissed."

"Obviously." I nodded.

"I can't believe my mother. Anything to protect our family's fucking reputation." He took another sip of beer, shaking his head as he stared off into space.

"So, now you know everything. You know he's yours. You know what your mother did. Now, make a choice."

"What?" He glowered at me with dark eyes. The same eyes as Marty.

"Haddie told you months ago...you need to shit or get off the pot, dude," I said, crossing the room to stand in front of Tucker. He stopped pacing and ran his fingers through his hair, puffing out his chest.

"*Don't* tell me what to do. He's *my* kid."

"You don't even know him. Not at all," I said, shaking my head.

"He's a baby. What is there to know? He sleeps, he cries, he shits." He threw his hands in the air, placing his empty bottle on the bookshelf.

"You don't have a clue, dude. He drools like crazy because he's always teething. He got his first one at six months and is getting another. He hates peas but loves carrots...but only if you put a spoonful of applesauce in too. He can't sleep without his blankie. And this shirt," I said, gesturing to my Super Grover t-shirt, "always makes him laugh."

"Huh...." Tucker said and his eyes softened slightly. He knew I wasn't the enemy. Maybe he even realized how much I loved *his* son. And how much he didn't.

"There's something else in the envelope. Look it over and get back to me."

He raised his eyebrows in confusion, crossed to the table and looked inside the large manila envelope. Pulling out the documents, he read quietly to himself.

"If this is what you wanted, why didn't you two just take the money? It would've been a hell of a lot easier."

"Because Marty deserves the truth. And Haddie can't be bought."

I walked out of his place feeling proud of myself, but also at Tucker's mercy. I hated that his decisions affected us. But that was the reality of all of this. I had to get used to it.

As I opened the door to my Jeep, I heard a door slam.

"Jason, wait up," Tucker yelled to me, jogging to where I stood.

He stopped, swallowed hard and handed the manila envelope back to me. He looked embarrassed...but to me, he was just pathetic.

"Here."

I nodded and got in the car, leaving him standing on his driveway staring as I drove away, surrounded by nothing but his own guilt and shortcomings.

I left Tucker standing in front of his perfect bachelor pad. He may have needed to be surrounded by pristine collectors' items, high-tech television and stainless steel appliances. He could keep all that shit. I was headed back to the messy toy-laden apartment of my girlfriend and her amazing kid.

The best things in life aren't things. Maybe one day Tucker would get a clue. Until then, I was reaping the benefits of his selfishness and stupidity. And I was going home to *my* family.

CHAPTER THIRTY-FIVE

Jason
Ten months after Marty's birth

It was a lazy Saturday afternoon and we were doing what we did best. Hanging out with the little guy. He was doing so many new things. It was incredible. Walking and babbling, placing his turtle toy in his shopping cart and taking him for a stroll—he was becoming an actual toddler. When did that happen? It felt like we were just in that hospital room a few weeks ago.

I'd been planning something for a long time now, and hanging with my little guy was the best inspiration. And Haddie, of course. Even wearing sweat pants, a hooded sweatshirt and a ponytail, my girl was stunning. I couldn't keep my eyes off of her. She was the best inspiration a guy like me could ask for.

"What should we do today?" she asked from the kitchen as she poured a bottle for Marty.

"This." I smiled, crossing my hands behind my head and spreading out on the couch.

Haddie pretended to roll her eyes and joined us on the floor. Marty handed her toys from the shopping cart and she gladly took them. One minute later, he was taking them back and placing them in the cart. I swear this boy never stopped. He was awesome to watch.

"My mom can watch Marty next week if you want to take me out on a *real* date," she teased. We'd spent plenty of time alone, but as excited as I was to spend time alone with Haddie, I got just as happy to see Marty when we returned. Was that weird?

Last night, my older sister Maya had called me. She was the only one in my family who wasn't very excited about Haddie's and my relationship. She was just beginning the process of a divorce. She and her husband couldn't make it work and they were going through a horrible custody battle, neither of them willing to give up seeing their child every day. *Jaded* would be a great word to describe her when it came to all of this. But last night, her words had stuck with me. I was unable to shake them, even though I wanted to. Desperately.

"He's not yours, Jase. He never will be. You have to remember that."

"Nice attitude," I said in revulsion. "His DNA doesn't matter to me. I love that kid."

"That's the problem."

Maya had always been protective of me. Ever since I was Marty's age, she'd been looking out for me, guiding me like a mommy-in-training. But this time, she'd struck a nerve. As much as I loved and cared for Marty, he would never really be mine. Haddie and I could pretend, but Tucker would always be his real father. And that frustrated the shit out of me.

"Mama, Gogo," Marty said, handing Grover to Haddie. She lit up. He'd just started labeling things and it was incredible how simple words could make us giddy. The first time he called her Mama, I was at my place. She called me sobbing, so ecstatic she could hardly see straight. Thank goodness, she had waited for his nap before breaking down that day.

Haddie took Grover in her arms, gave him a hug and kiss and handed the blue stuffed animal back to Marty. He grabbed Gogo with a grin before running to the kitchen, taking a lap around the island and heading back to the room. Haddie shook her head as she stared at him with pride and admiration. I stared at her the same way. She was such a good mom.

"Dada, Gogo," the little voice startled me. Marty's deep hazel eyes were looking into mine as he handed Grover to me. I opened my mouth to speak, but nothing came out. Recovering as quickly as I was able, I cleared my throat and smiled. *He just called me Dada. Holy shit, he thinks I'm his Dad. Is this good? Is this bad?* I had no idea what to think and it was written all over my uncomfortable face.

"Thanks, buddy," I said, rubbing the top of his head as he walked back to Haddie, climbing into her arms. Our eyes locked. She looked just as stunned as I felt. But instead of looking confused, her eyes looked disappointed. There was no coming back from that reaction. I'd hurt her and I was pissed at myself for letting my insecurities take over. Of course I wanted him to think of me as Dada. *Of course I did.*

Marty sucked his thumb as he rested his head on Haddie's shoulder. It was time for his afternoon nap. Without making eye contact with me, she grabbed his turtle and blanket and carried him to his room. She didn't emerge for quite a while.

By the time she walked out of the nursery, my pulse was racing. Leaning my elbows on my knees, I tapped my foot restlessly on the carpet. I hoped I hadn't hurt her. Silently, she sat down across from me in the armchair. Her hands were in her lap and she looked calm. But her eyes told another story. They were red and puffy and I knew I'd caused this.

"Haddie, look, I—"

She held up her hand, urging me to stop. Her eyes were closed as she waited to see if I'd let her speak. "You don't have to say anything. Your face said it all."

"No, that's not true." I shook my head emphatically, but she looked up at the ceiling, avoiding eye contact...as if looking at me would make her lose her resolve.

"I knew this would come up sooner or later."

"It doesn't change anything," I said, practically pleading.

"Yes, it does. We can't ignore this anymore," she said, gesturing to the space between us.

"This?" I asked in confusion.

"Tucker was right. We're just playing house. This isn't real."

"Tucker? Why are you letting that arrogant shit have anything to do with us?"

"I—I'm not, I just have to do the right thing. For *my* son," she said, finally looking me directly in the eye. But her eyes were cold. She didn't look away...not even for a second.

Her words had bite...especially the word "my." How foolish was I to think of him as ours? She was building up a wall...with each word that escaped her lips, another brick was placed on it. I wanted to kick it down, tear it apart, but she wouldn't let me near her. She just stacked the bricks, shutting me out, pushing me away.

"I love you," I said.

"I know..." Her words trailed off as she looked to her side, avoiding my eyes completely.

"Don't do this. I was just surprised. That's all."

"No...." She shook her head. "Please, stop...I just need some time, that's all."

I crossed over and crouched before her, placing my hands in her lap. Her eyes closed tightly as she pulled her hands away from mine. Resting my head on her knee, I realized begging was my last resort. I wasn't too proud to do it, not if it meant I had the slightest chance of changing her mind, of making things right again.

"Please, please don't."

"I'm sorry," she whispered. "It's not fair to Marty. He needs someone who loves him as much as I do."

"And you think I don't?" I looked up at her in shock. "You know I'm crazy about him."

"I don't know much anymore. Please...just go."

"Haddie, c'mon. This is *me*."

She said nothing. Her eyes were distant, as if she were peering at me from behind the fully built wall. I searched her eyes for an answer, but she was gone. Maya was right. He wasn't mine. And now it seemed like Haddie didn't even *want* him to be. I was trapped in a nightmare. My very own nightmare that I couldn't seem to escape. I had to go. I had to get out of there before I became trapped under the weight of that wall.

∽

Hadley

Jason stood, wiped his tears from his cheeks and reached for his keys. He took his copy of my key off his key ring and placed it on the coffee table. He looked at me one last time, pausing, but I was unable to speak. I was too terrified to let him stay. He'd broken my heart years before. And I couldn't let him break my son's heart, too. I just couldn't.

It had been two weeks since Jason kissed me at Bill's Pub. Since that night, I'd been walking on clouds, imagining us together—him giving me a corsage at the Prom, taking me to movies on the weekends, calling me his girlfriend. I was so excited. I didn't have a lot of experience with boys, so it didn't bother me when he didn't call me. In fact, I thought nothing of it.

When I arrived at the Kellys' house that Saturday afternoon, my heart was trembling inside my adolescent chest. I couldn't wait to see him, talk to him, and hopefully kiss him again. Would he kiss me in the hallway? Or maybe pull me into the walk-in pantry and kiss me there? Would he sneak me away to talk? Would he be as excited to see me as I was to see him?

I was ecstatic when he answered the door. But he looked different. He looked concerned and a little annoyed. His brow furrowed as he opened the door for me.

"Hey," I said with a large smile, hoping my enthusiasm would be contagious.

"Hey," he said, looking away from me. "Auden's in her room."

"Oh," I replied with a weak voice crossing the threshold. Like a moron, I stood there staring at him for a minute, simply trying to process what on earth was happening. But he never looked my way. He just closed the front door and walked away from me.

That was that. He'd kissed me and dropped me. He didn't want me. I wasn't good enough for him. No explanation, no apology. Everything I had spent years dreaming about had been in the palm of my hand and he'd ripped it away. Instead of walking to Auden's room, I let myself out of the Kellys' house and didn't return for a very long time... not until Jason left for college.

The moment Marty said "Dada" Jason made that face... the exact same face he'd made that Saturday afternoon. The day he split my heart in pieces and walked away like I was nothing to him. And in that moment, the protective Mama Bear came out in me. I never wanted my boy to feel that way. He deserved so much more than that.

To be abandoned by someone like Tucker was one thing. He had never really been involved and had seen his son only a couple of times. But Jason had been with us almost every day since Marty was born... and if, after a year together, he was able to make a face like that, then I needed to protect myself... and my son.

Being abandoned by Jason Kelly was the worst pain I could possibly imagine. Worse than that awkward Saturday afternoon at his front door. Worse than Tucker being a deadbeat dad who didn't believe Marty was really his own. *Worse than anything else I could possibly think of.*

So I had to push him away and make a clean break. I didn't want him to wake up one day and feel trapped... like I'd tricked him into becoming a father. Jason had to do things in his own time. That face told me he was *not* ready. I'd been so selfish... practically forcing him to go through the motions of being a family. I needed to protect us. All of us.

CHAPTER THIRTY-SIX

Hadley
Eleven months after Marty's birth

"Seriously?" Auden asked from the other side of the door. I snarled at her as she entered the apartment. In her arms, though, was something unexpected...and my heart skipped a beat the moment I saw it. A basket. Only one person in my life left baskets in front of my door.

"Where'd you get that?" I asked, pointing at the simple basket.

"It was outside. I know who it's from, though."

"I do, too."

"When was the last time you showered?" she asked, looking disgusted. Granted, it had been a couple of days. I hadn't exactly been motivated since I'd pushed Jason out of our lives.

"Just give it to me, brat," I said, reaching for the basket. She pulled it away, out of my reach.

"No....I'm pissed at you."

"Why? What the hell did I do to *you*?"

"What do you think? Jase is miserable...and you did that to him."

"We did it to each other."

"No," she said, shaking her head. "You're punishing him for shit he hasn't done." She held her hand in front of her mouth, looking around the room for Marty after dropping a curse word.

"Marty's napping, but watch your mouth. He's starting to babble a lot lately."

"Yeah, I *heard*." Her words stung. Jason must have told her about "Dada." My heart was breaking all over again.

"For God's sake, Auden, give me a break!" I lashed out, glowering at her.

"Fine, take it," she said, rolling her eyes, passing me the basket. "But if you don't know my brother is completely in love with you, with *both* of you... then maybe you don't know him at all. And maybe you don't deserve him."

"You don't understand. He made a face. The same face he made a long time ago...."

"What face?"

"Okay, so I never told you this, but years ago at Bill's, Jason kissed me by the bathroom."

Expecting a look of shock and awe from my dramatic friend, I saw nothing but a blank stare.

"Did you know already?"

"I saw you." Her blank stare turned to an expression of uncertainty. She looked guilty.

"Why didn't you say anything?"

"I did... only not to you." She bit her lip, looking nervous.

"What do you mean?" I tipped my head to her, raising both eyebrows in irritation.

"Shit.... Had, I'm sorry. I was angry. So... I yelled at Jason when you went home the next day. I told him to back off."

"What? Why did you do that? You knew how I felt about him!"

"We were fourteen! I didn't want to share you. And seriously, if you two had dated, that's what would've happened. Three's a crowd."

"Wow."

"I know it was selfish. But I mean, we were kids. And when I saw you two, I panicked. I couldn't stand to break your heart, but I *couldn't* lose you."

"Oh my god. That's why you pushed me to date Tucker."

She nodded, scrunching her nose, knitting her brow.

"I wanted you to be happy...just not with him. He blew you off because of me."

"So when I saw him a few days later and he made the face, it was a look of uncertainty?"

She shook her head. "I don't know. I wasn't there."

"I *need* to know."

"No...you don't. It's my fault. He promised me he'd back off. He didn't want to. And honestly, I think he still holds a grudge about it. Things with us have been strained since that day. And now, you're pushing him away and it's like I've hurt you both all over again."

"You didn't do this. I did."

We stared at each other for several moments before I broke eye contact to study the items in the basket. A large hardcover children's book called "Marty My Smarty" was the largest item in the basket. I stared at the cover in disbelief. When I looked for the author's name, it said Whitman J. Kelly.

"He wrote a children's book?" My eyes widened as I ran my fingers over the cartoonish picture of my little boy, sitting on the cover, holding his blankie and favorite turtle toy.

"He's been working on it for a while. He wanted to surprise you. And then you broke up with him before he had a chance."

"Oh my God," I said, sitting down in the nearest chair, nearly speechless. I opened the book as quickly as possible. The dedication started my tears flowing: *For my sweet little guy. I treasure you. Every. Single. Day.*

Tears clouded my eyes and I furiously wiped them away with the back of my sleeve as I turned the pages. The illustrations were hand drawn; my sweet little brown-haired boy looked up at me from the pages. He was playing with his Grover doll, playing on his keyboard, and laughing his little head off as his Mommy kissed him. When I got to the last page, I couldn't believe my eyes.

Marty My Smarty
So quick to say each new word
When you called me Dada
Marty My Smarty,
It was the most beautiful thing I'd ever heard

The final illustration was a hand-drawn depiction of Jason. I laughed as I studied him. Sandy brown hair, a few freckles, green eyes behind his tortoiseshell glasses. He was wearing Marty's favorite Super Grover t-shirt. Jason and Marty were holding hands as they walked, Marty looking up at him with a sweet smile of admiration. My heart was soaring and breaking all at once. *What have I done?*

"I have to fix this," I said, panicked.

"Yeah, you do," Auden replied, putting her legs up on the ottoman and leaning back on Jason's favorite armchair. His reading chair.

"Tell me how," I said, walking over to her, sitting on the couch, hands in my lap, eyes completely on Auden.

"You were just punishing him for the Montgomerys and all of the shit they put you through. We all lash out at the ones we love the most. Just apologize. He'll forgive you."

"It can't be that simple," I replied, shaking my head in disbelief.

"It is." Auden shrugged. "He left this for you; he wanted you to see it. What else is in the basket?"

I hadn't even noticed—I had been so busy reading the book. I looked back inside the wicker basket and found three packs of Marty's favorite Gerber snacks and Sesame Street sippy cups.

"He remembered we needed more sippies," I whispered. "I was complaining a couple of weeks before we broke up. I needed to get the next stage of cups now that Marty's such a big boy...." My words trailed off as I stared at a basket full of thoughtfulness and love.

I'm so lucky. And Jason needs to know that.

"He's a good guy," Auden said, giving me a weak smile.

"He's amazing. Seriously, help me win him back."

"Okay...so, I don't think he wanted me to tell you this since you two split. But he's having a book signing this Saturday at Em Pea's Bookstore over on Fifth Avenue."

"I've seen that place. It's adorable."

"It starts at one o'clock. I can babysit Marty if you want to see him."

"I'm going.... But I'll bring the baby with me. He needs to see his Dada."

~

An hour later, Marty was pushing his shopping cart around the living room as Auden and I talked. I finally had the gall to ask her what I'd been dying to ask for months. And now that she'd confessed her involvement in Jason's and my being apart all those years ago, I wasn't holding back. It was time to find out what was going on with my best friend.

"Don't get pissed, but we need to talk."

"Uh oh. I have a feeling this isn't about Jason anymore."

"You're right. It's about you. And it has nothing to do with Jason or me."

"All right..." She looked nervous. She picked at her cuticles, something she only did when uncomfortable. Auden was such a free spirit, such a cheery person—it wasn't something she did very often. But when it happened... something was definitely up.

"You're not happy. It's obvious."

"I know," she paused, biting her bottom lip before looking up at me. "Vault?"

I breathed a sigh of relief before responding, "Vault."

"I'm moving."

"What? Where? Did you get a new job?"

"Yes. But I don't think my family will be too happy about it."

"I'm confused," I said, raising an eyebrow. "Just tell me."

"I got a job with a tour company in Europe. Jordan Tours. Remember we saw their buses all the time while we were there?"

"Yeah, I remember.... But what about pharmaceutical sales? You said your sales have been awesome."

"They have...it's just," she paused, "It sucks." She groaned. And we both laughed.

"It's boring as hell. I need adventure. I need excitement. And I miss Europe like crazy."

I nodded, knowing that she had really been the best version of herself while we were there. I knew she had visited many countries there since she was a child. Maybe that's where she really felt at home.

"So...have you told anyone?"

"Besides you?" She shook her head. "No, not yet."

"When do you leave?"

"January nineteenth."

"Wow, that's only a few months away."

"I need to get lots of training out of the way before Spring Break comes. That's when I'll start doing tours on my own."

"So, you're going to live...where, exactly?"

"They have housing for their tour guides in London. But I'll have to live out of a suitcase once I start working my own tours."

My nose wrinkled inadvertently. I could never live that way...like a vagabond or something. It didn't suit me, but Auden was another story. Auden would shine. I was certain of it.

"I miss you already," I said, tipping my head, pursing my lips.

"I know, but I have to do this. It's time."

"I get it...and I'm excited for you...really, I am. When are you going to tell your parents?"

"This weekend at Sunday dinner."

Puzzled, I looked at her. "So, why the vault? That's just a few days away."

She rolled her eyes. "In case I lose the nerve."

"You won't. This is too important."

"You're right. What would I do without you?" she said, rubbing Marty's back as he walked by her with his cart.

"I feel exactly the same way. Don't ever doubt that. Not ever."

CHAPTER THIRTY-SEVEN

Hadley

"You're gonna be late," Auden yelled. Pulling my cell phone away from my ear, I grimaced, knowing she was right. Ever since I'd become a mom, I was late. Always. Marty usually napped in the morning, but today he wouldn't go down until noon. I told myself that I could just wait to make it to the signing at the tail end of the event. I justified that it would be easier that way: not as many people, less chance to make a spectacle of myself. But now, as I sat in traffic, listening to Auden yell at me, I knew I'd made the wrong choice.

Two extremely shitty things had happened before we could even leave the apartment. Literally. The peas Marty had eaten this morning hadn't sat well, and he'd soiled two diapers before we could even get out the door. Poor boy. I'd kept glancing at my watch as I changed him and his clothes, hoping we'd still have time.

When I'd got him in his car seat, I'd realized his stroller wasn't in the trunk. I had taken him for a walk yesterday and had left it upstairs. So, up we went to grab the stroller and set off on our way to the bookstore.

And finally, I sat at red light after red light after red light, kicking myself for not leaving the apartment an hour earlier. But this was my life as a mom. I was unable to control everything. I couldn't do everything perfectly. I just wished that today (of all days!) I could've had better forethought to handle all of this.

"Look, I'll be there in a few minutes. Traffic is horrible." I groaned into the phone.

"Fine. Call me later."

Quickly, I hung up and focused on the road, trying my very best not to be frantic. Marty babbled in the back seat talking to his Gogo—at least I hadn't forgotten his favorite Muppet. Finally, we arrived at the small bookstore. Parking spots were few and far between, but luckily I was able to find one about a block away from the front door of the shop.

The stroller resisted my foot's pressure as I attempted over and over to snap it into place. Finally, it complied and I heard the pop of the plastic fitting in. Breathing a quick sigh of relief, I placed Marty into the seat and jogged towards the store.

Em Pea's Bookstore was unique and modern, unlike any other children's bookshop I'd ever seen. A chevron-patterned mural lined the wall behind the registers. Cartoonish pea pods, the symbol for the store, were spread throughout the signage in the entire place. Whimsical mobiles hung from the ceiling, each with a different book theme—princesses, wizards and magic school buses. You got the feeling that you were in the house of a friend who just adored books, rather than an actual bookstore. Marty and I would be spending a lot of time there.

An employee was taking down a large sign that had been placed at the entrance to the small children's department.

"Book Signing: Whitman J. Kelly debuting his self-published children's picture book, 'Marty My Smarty.' 1–3 p.m."

"Did we miss it?" I asked, panting. He nodded with a sympathetic eye as he dismantled the sign.

It was 3:15. *Shit.* It was over. But maybe he was still there. Taking a deep, cleansing breath, I pushed the stroller back into the children's area. A Harry Potter–themed mural, complete with a magenta and indigo harlequin diamond pattern, greeted me. It was like the cover of a book had come to life.

Placing my hands on the stroller, I pondered what to do next.

A very sweet pregnant woman with short blond hair approached me. "Are you here for the signing?"

"Yes," I replied with a frustrated sigh.

"You just missed the author. He left about five minutes ago."

"This may sound weird...and I promise I'm not a stalker, but...do you know where he was going?" As soon as I said the words, I knew it was the wrong thing to ask. She raised an eyebrow but glanced down at my son.

"Is this...Marty? He looks just like the boy in the book." Her eyes softened as she gazed down at my grinning boy.

Relief. Sweet relief filled my body.

"Yes." I nodded.

She crouched down in front of the stroller.

"Well, someone is crazy about you, little man."

"I know. We're crazy about him, too," I said, glancing at my watch again. "I'm sorry to leave so abruptly, but we need to find Jason. It's kind of important."

"Of course. Come back and see us again," she said, waving goodbye to Marty, who blew kisses back to her. "I hope you find him."

"Me too."

∼

Fifteen minutes later, I pulled my car into Jason's parking lot. My heart raced to my throat as I saw him unpacking his trunk. Stopping the car in front of his, not even bothering to pull into a parking spot, I killed the engine and took the baby from his car seat. I jogged to Jason who looked completely shocked to see us. He looked at me with earnest eyes.

"What are you doing here?" he asked, looking excited, yet apprehensive. He was trying hard not to get too optimistic. And I hated that I did that to him. That I made him feel so uncertain about my feelings for him. Maybe Auden was right. Maybe I didn't deserve him.

"We were late to the signing. Traffic, poop, nap troubles...story of my life. I'm sorry."

"You got the book?" he asked, eyes wide. I nodded emphatically.

"It was beautiful, Jase."

"I'm glad you liked it. I'd been working on it for a while."

"You had?"

"Of course. It was going to be his birthday present. But then when everything happened...I figured now was the right time."

"It was perfect."

"I was stuck on the ending... until Marty wrote it for me." Jason looked proud. I ran my fingers through his hair and he closed his eyes and relaxed into my touch.

"There's one problem," I replied. Jason's eyes opened immediately and concern traveled across his face. I gave him a smile before continuing. "That was Marty's copy. I need one, too."

Jason sighed, shaking his head and looking at the blacktop. He rubbed his neck, before locking eyes with me. His emerald eyes were watering. He was fighting back tears with every ounce of strength he had.

I took his hands in mine. "You didn't deserve the things I said. None of them."

He pursed his lips and nodded, raising both eyebrows, urging me to continue. I guessed I needed to grovel a little more.

"I just got scared... for me, for the baby, for you. I don't want to trap you. And, you didn't sign up for this. I know that."

"What are you talking about?" he scoffed. "I signed up for this a *long* time ago. I want you. I want Marty. I want *us*."

I nodded, looking up at the sky, unable to look into his gorgeous, pained eyes.

"We're a family, Haddie. Don't you see that?"

"I do now." I nodded, tears spilling from the corners of my eyes as I gripped his hands with all that I had.

Jason let out a sigh of relief before pulling Marty and me into his arms.

"I'm sorry," I whispered into his ear. "I'm so, so sorry."

He sighed again into my hair as he gripped my back with his strong hands. I never wanted to leave his arms.

"Dada," Marty said, pulling away from me and practically diving into Jason's arms. Jason smiled the widest smile I'd ever seen before pulling Marty in for a hug.

"That's right, buddy," Jason said, rubbing his back. "Dada's here."

EPILOGUE

Hadley
Twelve months after Marty's birth

"Happy Birthday to you...," everyone sang as Marty clapped his hands and giggled. The number 1 candle sat atop his little Grover smash cake. He clutched Gogo in his arms and looked at me like I was crazy when I showed him how to blow out the tiny orange flame. When the candle went out, everyone cheered. His giggle fit started all over again.

Jason made sure Marty's bib was fastened, removed the candle from his smash cake, and pushed it closer to Marty on the tray of his high chair. Marty carefully touched the blue frosting with his fingertips, hesitant to eat the bright blue depiction of his favorite friend from Sesame Street.

"It's nom nom, sweet pea." Gently, I scraped a small amount of frosting from the cake with my finger and licked the sugary buttercream. Marty smiled and mirrored my actions as best he could. His eyes widened as he tasted the sweetness of the frosting. Within seconds, he was digging in with both hands, clutching fistfuls of yellow cake and blue frosting.

Our friends and family watched as he covered himself completely in blue. His cheeks, his forehead, even his hair.

I would've groaned, but laughter kept escaping my throat. A very pregnant Kate snapped picture after picture after picture of our messy boy while Jason laughed with Evan. Maya chased her toddler around the apartment as Mr. and Mrs. Kelly smiled at the little boy they adored.

Auden stood next to Marty, stroking his hair as she watched him cover his body with frosting. She gave him a quick peck on the head before winking at me. She would be leaving after the holidays, so we were trying to savor as much time together as possible. Only a few months left of seeing each other whenever we wished. Unofficial or not, she was Marty's aunt and I was determined to have him remember her. We'd Skype, show him pictures of Auntie Auden holding him, whatever it took to keep her present in his life.

Once everyone had been served a piece of cake, I sat and chatted with my mom. She was as cheerful as I'd seen her in years, basking in the enjoyment of watching her grandson demolish his first birthday cake.

"He's starting to look like you, sweetheart," she said, staring at my boy.

"You're such a liar." I chuckled, shaking my head. Marty was still the spitting image of his father. And although he wasn't in attendance or participating, in any way, in his son's life, I'd always be grateful to Tucker for giving me this incredible little boy. Tucker's choices regarding his son frustrated the hell out of me all the time, and there were days that I dreaded ever having to discuss him with Marty. But I had to take each day as it came. And Jason... well, *Jason* was his Dada. And an amazing one at that.

"So... how's Steven?" I asked my mom, curiosity all over my face.

Mom's cheeks turned pink. "You mean *Steven-from-work-Steven?*" She swallowed hard as she pushed frosting around her plate.

"You could've brought him, Mom."

"No, no. That would've been inappropriate." She shook her head as her lips formed a firm line.

"I'm just saying...I'd like to meet him."

"We're just...getting to know each other."

"Okay. When you're ready." I placed my hand on top of hers; she closed her eyes tight and smiled a relieved smile.

Steven had been pursuing Mom cautiously for several months. It turned out he was part of the reason she had started paying better attention to her appearance. She was still struggling with the guilt of moving on without my dad. But I knew he'd want her to be happy. He'd want her to move on.

Her doctor had her on a much lower dose of medication and she seemed to be handling it fine, for the most part. Although occasionally, if I stopped over unannounced, I'd find her still in her pajamas at noon on a Sunday. Or a new picture of my dad would pop up on the bookshelf, usually one from their first days as a couple. And then I'd know she was having a rough time. But Steven had been a good distraction for her. He gave me hope that one day she might be happy again.

"Are you excited to start back at Sunnyside?"

"Yes, very. It'll be weird, though."

"Marty will be just fine." She reassured me, tapping me lightly on the hand.

"Thanks again for doing this."

"It's my pleasure. I'm excited to spend two days a week with him. We'll have fun." Her smile was genuine, her enthusiasm obvious. It warmed my heart. All the concerns I had were diminishing when it came to my mom. She loved her grandson and she was able to show it. And I was comfortable with her having an active role in his life. It was good to feel that way. Good to let go of the worry, the shame and the concern that had weighed on me for years.

∽

When our guests had gone and Marty was down for the night, Jason and I cleaned up the sea of blue wrapping paper that covered the living room. Ironically, Marty's favorite gift was the empty box from his new tool bench set. He had climbed in and out, in and out of that box as the guests shook their heads, each thinking about the real toy they brought that was being ignored for an empty cardboard container.

"Looks like we missed one," Jason said, pulling a small shirt-sized box from the coffee table. It was wrapped in simple navy blue wrapping paper. He handed the box to me with a look in his eye that I couldn't quite put my finger on.

"No card," I said, flipping the box over and over, looking for some sign of who the gift was from.

"Just open it," Jason said with a soft smile as he wiped his forehead with the back of his hand. He was nervous.

What is he up to?

Quickly, I tore off the wrapping paper and opened the box. Two thick stacks of paper sat inside the box. Inspecting the first stack, I turned each page, looking for an answer. All I could see were pages and pages and pages of legal jargon. And on several pages, there was a signature. *Tucker Montgomery*. In the second stack, there were several more pages full of jargon, only I kept seeing Jason's signature next to another blank box, presumably for my own.

"I know this was presumptuous of me," Jason said.

"Oh my god, Jase. What are these?"

"Tucker...he's giving up his legal rights to Marty. But only if that's what you want."

"You got him to do that?" I couldn't believe what I was hearing. Tucker had been completely uninvolved with his son, but for some reason, he'd always wanted to hang on to the option of coming back into our lives. I couldn't contain the relief in my heart. It poured out in the form of tears.

"Yes. I spoke my piece...and he got it." Jason adjusted his glasses, still looking unsure of himself.

"I'm in shock." I couldn't stop shaking my head from side to side in disbelief. I was stunned, I was shocked and I was *so* relieved.

"There's more. The second set of documents is from me. I want us to be a family. Officially."

"You want to...adopt Marty?"

"Yes, I do. But if it's not what you want, we can tear the papers up right now. I don't want to pressure you. And if you still want Tucker in Marty's life—"

"No, no." I held my hand up in front of me, begging Jason to stop questioning himself. "*Of course* this is what I want," I said, choking on the words, wiping my soaked cheeks with my hand.

"Then I need to ask you something." When I glanced up to look him in the eye, he was no longer sitting next to me. Instead, he was kneeling down, holding a ring box in his shaking hands. His plaid shirt was unbuttoned, revealing a navy blue t-shirt that read, "Marry Me, Haddie."

"Jase." I laughed and cried as I read his shirt over and over. Savoring it. Loving it. And understanding what it meant for me, for him, for us. I breathed in deeply before holding my breath, my teeth digging into my top lip as I awaited the question I've always dreamed of.

"My love," he said, clearing his throat, "will you do me the honor of becoming my wife? And will you give me the greatest honor of allowing Martin to be my son?"

"Yes, yes, a thousand times, yes," I said, rising to my feet, jumping up and down.

He placed the ring on my finger and my heart beat rapidly in my chest.

He stood, pulling me into him. I rested my head on his chest, knowing this was the happiest moment of my life.

"We're going to be a family," Jason said into my ear.

I pulled back and peered into Jason's misty green eyes. Gently, I grasped his chin and looked him dead in the eye.

"We're *already* a family. You know that."

He heaved a sigh of relief, running his fingers through my hair.

"Yes," he smiled, "yes, I do."

ACKNOWLEDGMENTS

I'm really lucky. I'm surrounded by some of the most incredibly supportive people out there. Family and friends who are happy to give their input, brainstorm ideas and offer encouragement when I hit a stumbling block in the road. That is not lost on me. Not at all. I'm going to do my best to remember every single person who supported me throughout the writing, editing and marketing of this book, and I really hope I remember everyone. Because every single one of you deserves to be acknowledged.

Maggi Myers and **Janna Mashburn,** thank you both so much for helping me to sort through this story when it was just a couple of ideas. All of our conversations before I'd written anything at all helped me to make the story. You are both responsible for the light bulb above my head that said, "Those two things could make one good story!" Thank you also for countless conversations of brainstorming, plot elements and characters. I appreciate you both so much.

Deb Bresloff, you had some absolutely fantastic ideas that helped to shape a very important aspect of the story, and I can't thank you enough! I loved our chats and your "What about this?" questions that pushed me to take the plot further!

Thank you to Lori Sabin for editing the original version and to Jennifer McIntyre for your edits for the Montlake edition. I appreciate you both so much. And thank you to my beta readers, **Melissa Perea, Shelly Pratt, Kate Mathias, Erin Roth, Lindsay Sparkes, Lisa Rutledge, Nina Gomez** and **Amy Burt.**

Calia Read, my critique partner. Thank you for pushing me to challenge myself. And thank you so much for gifting me formatting by the awesome **Angela** at **Fictional Formats!** You do such beautiful work and it was so fun to pick out cute fonts and symbols! Thank you, **Angela!**

Thank you so much, **Natasha Tomic,** from **Natasha is a Book Junkie,** for organizing my blog tour. I am so lucky to have you in my corner. You amaze me at every turn! And thank you to all of the fabulous blogs who are participating! **Angie's Dreamy Reads, Flirty and Dirty Book Blog, The Indie Bookshelf, Beauty, Brains and Books, Morning After a Good Book Shh Mom's Reading, TalkSupe, First Class Books, Bridger Bitches Book Blog, The Book Avenue, Reading Books Like a Boss, Always A Book Lover, Mommy's Reads and Treats, My Secret Romance, All Aboard the Book Blog, Three Chicks and Their Books, Becca the Bibliophile, Sugar and Spice Book Reviews, A Love Affair With Books, The Little Black Book Blog, Book Bitches Blog, Into the Night Book Reviews, The Autumn Review, Devoured Words** and **ToBeThode.** I am so grateful to all of you for taking the time to read, share, review, etc. on your blogs!

Pamela Carrion, your enthusiasm, support and creativity mean the world to me. Thank you for running Brownie's Book Buddies as well as the Release Day Party. You are such an amazing person whom I am so lucky to call friend. I will forever be grateful for every bit of time that you have devoted to my books and to me! And thank you to **Sharon Cooper** for all of your fantastic posts about the books, your help with the release day party and all of your enthusiasm about my writing. **Denise Tung** and **Lisa Kowalski,** thank you for all of your help with the Release Party, as well. It would not have been the same without you ladies!

Leslie Fear, thank you for creating the title of this book. It's such a great fit and I'm so grateful to you for thinking of it for me!

Thank you to my indie "co-workers" who were always there for encouragement, brainstorming, and feedback. You are all so awesome! I would attempt to name everyone, but then I know my brain would leave people out. Just know that I appreciate every single one of you!

Thank you to the readers. I'm so lucky to have readers who "get me"—who get my style, my voice and my optimism. It means so much to me. Thank you to everyone who took a chance and pushed the "one click" button on this book as well as the first two. I am so, so, thankful for each of you!

And finally, thank you to the clients of Countryside Association in Palatine, Illinois. You taught me so much more than I could ever have taught you. You will always have a very special place in my heart. And I treasure the time I spent being a part of your day-to-day lives. Thank you so very much.

ABOUT THE AUTHOR

Melissa Brown is a hopeless romantic living in the Chicagoland area with her husband, Chris, and their two children. She loves baking, travel, and '80s pop culture. She speaks fluent movie quotes and loves to laugh. She has an addiction to Facebook and a slight obsession with Henry Cavill.

Connect with Melissa:
Blog:
http://melissabrownauthor.blogspot.com/
Facebook page:
https://www.facebook.com/MelissaBrownAuthor
Goodreads page:
http://www.goodreads.com/author/show/6457549.Melissa_Brown
Twitter:
LissaLou77